LIFE IS
BUT A
SCREAM

LIFE IS BUT A SCREAM

A
MERMAID BAY
CHRISTMAS
SHOPPE
MYSTERY

HEATHER WEIDNER

To Stan, Thanks for coming along with me on this writing journey!

Praise for the Mermaid Bay Christmas Shoppe Mysteries

"Selected as one of the best Cozy Debut Novels of 2023."—**The Book Decoder**

Sticks and Stones and A Bag of Bones

"Another fun and interesting installment in an already popular cozy mystery series. Mystery and scandal rule this charmer. With main characters you feel like you know, twists and turns keep you reading."—**Heather Douglass**, NetGalley Reviewer

"Heather Weidner has everything I like in a cozy mystery. Good characters, charming town, and a bag of bones washing up on shore. Plus, a local murder. Jade Hicks the owner of a Christmas shop, and Christmas shops are always popular in beach towns, looks into the crime and hopes to save the town's Christmas in July festival. This is a terrific start to the Mermaid Bay Christmas Shoppe Mystery series."—**Jackie Layton**, Author of the Low Country Dog Walker Mysteries

"I enjoyed this light and fresh whodunit that kept me on my game. The author did a great job in presenting this well-written and fast-paced drama where mischief and mayhem was afoot where scattered notes and bits of voodoo seemed to plague the residents of Mermaid Bay. Who wanted the bookstore owner dead? There's a town full of potential suspects and I had a great time following along with Jade as each clue gathered took us closer to the killer's identity. What drove this tale was the visually descriptive narrative, the engaging dialogue, the small-neighborly atmosphere and the likeable cast of characters that includes Jade, Nick and Chloe. Overall, this was a great read and I look forward for more exciting times in Mermaid Bay with Jade and her friends."—**DruAnn Love**, Dru's Book Musing

"*Sticks and Stones and a Bag of Bones* by Heather Weidner is the first book in the Mermaid Bay Christmas Shoppe Mystery series. This is a good beginning to what looks to be a fun series. I really like amateur sleuth Jade Hicks, who owns the Christmas Shoppe, "Tis the Season in Mermaid Bay. She is very personable and intelligent. The secondary characters are quite likable too. I especially like Sheriff Nick Driscoll and Jade's new friend Amy. This was a fun read and I look forward to the next book in the series."—**Margey Hager**, NetGalley Reviewer

"Very entertaining cozy mystery with a bunch of fun characters. I knew I would like it from the title and cover, and the story was a smooth read start to finish. The motive was obvious to me almost from the start, so I was surprised that the investigation did not move along more logically and quickly. The spark between Jade and Nick is sweet, and the two seem well suited to each other. Nick may be the cop, but Jade is a bonafide sleuth in her own right. And the recipes at the end are quite a bonus!! Fun read!"—**Autumn Danner**, Goodreads Reviewer

"What a pleasant surprise. This is a new to me author. I came across this book on a New Release page and added it to my TBR list. Because of the series name and cover, I was just going to add it to my Christmas TBR list (because I never read the synopsis). Then, this showed up in the Recently Added list at my library, so I figured what the heck. I'm so glad I borrowed it.

This book starts off like a traditional Cozy Mystery but it really doesn't follow the typical footprint, which was fun.

No spoilers; however, the murder happens early but it's almost an afterthought throughout the rest of the book. Yes, it's mentioned but there are other mysteries to be solved that may or may not be connected (you'll have to find out for yourself).

I really enjoyed the cast of characters and beachside small town they live in. I'm really looking forward to more books in this series."—**Debra Jo Burnette**, Room of Required Reading Bookstagrammer

"On a cold and dreary January weekend I took a virtual vacation to sunny, summer-y Mermaid Bay, thanks to the wonderful writing of Heather Weidner. *Sticks and Stones and a Bag of Bones* celebrates Christmas in July in a fictional beach town, which not only brought a favorite holiday into play, but was accompanied by peaceful and relaxing strolls on the beach. Oh, and did I mention murder? Yes, the main character Jade Hicks is in a perfect position to help solve the untimely death of a local store owner, along with the unfunny pranks that plague this small town. From the get-go when a suitcase of bones washes up on the beach, until the exciting ending when the mysteries (plural) are solved, well, what's not love about this well written, character-drive, fast-paced cozy mystery? Only downfall is that it will be a YEAR before I can make another visit to Mermaid Bay!"—**Jayne Ormerod**, Author of *Goin' Coastal*

"Good start to a new cozy series! I was approved for this one after it was already released and I listened to the audiobook. The narrator was delightful-entertaining, different voices for each character and emotions thought out. I loved getting to know these easy to like characters and look forward to reading the next one in their series!"—**Anne Edester**, NetGalley Reviewer

"This was a really good start to a new series! The characters were so much fun and I can't wait for more of them in the future books! The mystery itself was also entertaining and interesting and kept me reading. Definitely a quick read too!"—**Tiffany Newton**, NetGalley Reviewer

"I loved the range of characters, some quirky, others annoying, and some

I'd like as friends. The relationships between the friends were warm, and I wondered if or when the sheriff would move into the love interest column."—**Cynthia Smith**, NetGalley Reviewer

"This is a really good mystery very well written with great characters I highly recommend for all mystery lovers."—**Shelly Meyer**, NetGalley Reviewer

"First in a new series. I found it highly enjoyable. Mermaid Bay sounds like a fun town. With Christmas in July comes a bunch of trouble ensues ending up in murder. Jade, the owner of the Christmas shop sets out to find the murderer. A good solid mystery with characters that are wonderful."—**Renee Winter**, NetGalley Reviewer

"The first book in the Mermaid Bay Christmas Shoppe Mystery series is *Sticks and Stones and a Bag of Bones* by Heather Weidner. This is a strong start to what appears to be an entertaining series. I liked the small-town seaside location, the Christmas store, and the cat and dog's role in the narrative."—**Jody Joy**, NetGalley Reviewer

"If you love starting cozy mystery series with book one, read this! *Sticks and Stones and a Bag of Bones* has so many of the elements that make a cozy mystery enjoyable: a diverse batch of characters, an adorable small town, a dog and a cat, and a perplexing mystery. I highly recommend that you read this charming cozy mystery!"—Christy's Cozy Corners, Book Blogger

"If small-town mysteries are what you enjoy, *Sticks and Stones and a Bag of Bones* won't disappoint."—**Lori Van Buren**, Novels Alive

"This is a "feel good " story, great for a beach visit or travel. Don't expect page-turning action. Do expect likable characters in an adorable village by the sea. I would definitely visit Mermaid Bay myself."—**Beth Youngblood**, NetGalley Reviewer

"I am not new to Heather Weidner's writing so I will say this: I knew this was going to be a brilliant series debut. I enjoyed reading every bit of this book. There were plenty of red herrings, an interesting set of characters and side stories, a couple of furry babies—a dog and cats, and, not to forget, a dash of romance.

The mystery kept me guessing till the end. I loved the characters and their side stories. Apart from Jade, the one other character that I liked the most is that of Amy. She's so energetic, enthusiastic, and full of ideas—I would love to see a cozy series featuring Amy as main character.

If you are looking for a new cozy series, love year-round Christmas shoppes and furry babies, and excellent storytelling, you might want to give *Sticks and Stones and a Bag of Bones* by Heather Weidner a try."—**Rekha Rao**, NetGalley Reviewer

"She pens an intriguing tale of the lengths a shady character might go to. It is engrossing."—**Amary Chapman**, NetGalley Reviewer

"*Sticks and Stones and a Bag of Bones* combines Christmas and beach living in an enjoyable start to a new series."—**Cozy up with Kathy**, Book Blogger

"Great book by Heather Weidner. I'm really liking this series, and its characters. This was a fun cozy. I liked trying to figure out who done what. I'll definitely be reading more from this author."—**Valerie Blankenship**, NetGalley Reviewer

"I enjoyed this first in the series book. Lovely characters, fun to read and a great mystery. I can't wait for the next book."—**Stacey Bradley**, NetGallley Reviewer

"An entertaining and compelling cozy mystery I thoroughly enjoyed. Well plotted, likeable and fleshed out characters, a lovely setting. The mystery is solid and kept me guessing. It's the first I read in this series and won't surely be the last. Highly recommended."—**Anna Maria Giacomasso**, NetGalley

Reviewer

"Quick, easy, entertaining and a year-round Christmas shop. What's not to like about that?

A good cozy mystery that takes you one a ride, entertains you and as it isn't too long you can read it quickly and easily. I love a book like that. Great characters, a bit of fun and of course a good old bag of bones!

I enjoyed this one and recommend as a fun, easy reading book."—**Donna Robinson**, NetGalley Reviewer

"I enjoyed the characters and the realistic problems of any town dependent on tourist dollars and the ever present problem in beach town areas of development vs. keeping a smaller town feel. There were plenty of twists and turns in this mystery to keep you guessing until the end. Of course, I loved the furry friends and the touch of romance. A good read when you are looking for a light cozy or longing for a beach getaway."—**Juliane Silver**, NetGalley Reviewer

"I enjoy my visits to Mermaid Bay. I like the characters and enjoy the dialog between Jade and Nick."—**Dawn Tarrant**, NetGalley Reviewer

"The quiet beachside community was thrown into disbelief by the murder of one of their own. Jade couldn't help being curious about the strangeness happening in their community, so she put on her sleuthing cap and began searching for answers. She was a businesswoman with a penchant for investigating crimes. This cozy was an intriguing and entertaining one."—**Cherry-Ann London**, NetGalley Reviewer

"Fine start to a brand-new cozy mystery series! Mermaid Bay is a tourist town in coastal Virginia and has a bunch of small shops with Christmas themes. The first sign of trouble is a suitcase found on the beach with a collection of bones in it. Then there are the threatening notes, voodoo dolls, and finally a murdered (unpleasant) bookseller. Jade does her part to help solve the crime even though no all of her efforts are appreciated by her good friend Sheriff Nick."—**Jan Tangen**, NetGalley Reviewer

"This was a fun start to a new cozy mystery series, and I would definitely pick up the second! I enjoyed the cast of characters and the beach town setting. The story is as much about the relationships of the town residents as the mystery, making it a very enjoyable read."—**Amanda Waggoner**, NetGalley Reviewer

"I recently discovered Heather Weidner and was really intrigued to read this book, the first in the series. I might be a little biased as I live in Virginia, but I enjoyed this book and hope to see more in the series. There's never a dull moment in this town…a suitcase of washed up bones, voo doo dolls, threatening letters and smashed windows…oh my!"—**Kim Schade**, NetGalley Reviewer

"I really loved this book in a new to my series and author. I can't wait to read the next one. The characters and location really add to the plot. This book keeps you guessing until the end."—**Lori Ruth**, NetGalley Reviewer

"This was a light, fun cozy with some great characters. I love Chloe."—**Lisa Garrett**, NetGalley Reviewer

"Well written and super cute."—**Jenn Ross**, NetGalley Reviewer

Twinkle Twinkle Au Revoir

"This was such a wonderful and enjoyable read!!!! I loved this book and highly recommend it to anyone who enjoys this genre."—**Sophie L.**, NetGalley Reviewer

"Cute cozy mystery."—**Kaye Temanson**, NetGalley Reviewer

"*Twinkle Twinkle Au Revoir* by Heather Weidner is a candy-cane sweet and totally engrossing mystery. Highly recommended!"—**Rekha Rao**, The Book Decoder

"Just loved this cozy mystery. Loved the plot and characters. Couldn't stop reading. Love the fact that the recipes for the cookies mentioned in the book is given at the back of the book. Will definitely try making them."—**Jacqueline Van Der Merwe**, NetGalley Reviewer

"This is a fun, entertaining, cozy read. The various characters are quirky, entertaining, intriguing and fun. I found the amateur sleuth Jade relatable, and I enjoyed spending my time with her."—**Laura Lagace**, NetGalley Reviewer

"A nice and solid cozy mystery that kept me guessing. Well plotted and fast paced, well rounded and likeable characters."—**Anna Maria Giacomasso**, Librarian

"The perfect who done it! The story is easy to get into and I would recommend this book. I will be looking out for this author in the future."—**The Little Book Corner**

"The mystery, while light in keeping with typical cozy style, was well plotted, and made you wonder if the incidents were related to one another."—**Melanie Steward**, NetGalley Reviewer

"*Twinkle Twinkle Au Revoir* by Heather Weidner is the second book in the charming Mermaid Bay Christmas Shoppe Mystery series."—**Christy's Cozy Corners**

"*Twinkle Twinkle Au Revoir* is a lighthearted breezy mystery that combines Christmas decor and Valentine's Day dreams showing that there's no business quite like show business."—**Cozy up with Kathy**, Book Reviewer

"This was a very enjoyable story where Hollywood comes to Mermaid Bay. It had great characters and a plot that kept you trying to figure out who dunnit. I would recommend it to everyone!"—**Helen Scaglione**, NetGalley Reviewer

"Loved reading this book. I missed the 1st book in the series. But I will definitely be reading it. I couldn't put this 1 down. I highly recommend this series!"—**Chris Gerst**, NetGalley Reviewer

"I love holiday themed movies and cozies,so this one was marriage made in Heaven. the characters are great and I love how they all made this even better with quirks and all. I will definitely keep this author on my reading list for further books."—**Cindi Austin**, NetGalley Reviewer

"I highly recommend the highly entertaining cozy mystery, *Twinkle Twinkle Au Revoir* for its charming setting, true to life characters, and captivating mystery!"—**Christy Maurer**, NetGalley Reviewer

"*Twinkle Twinkle Au Revoir* is book two in Heather Weidner's cozy mystery series Mermaid Bay Christmas Shoppe, and is equally as charming as book one, *Sticks and Stones and a Bag of Bones*. This reads easily as a standalone if readers are new to the series."—**Sarah Erwin**, *Kings River Life Magazine*

"It was supposed to be all love and roses. Everyone is a target when the Love Channel takes over Mermaid Bay to film their next holiday movie and Christmas shop owner Jade Hicks unwittingly finds herself drawn into all of the drama be it by helping out with the bad press her B&B owner pal is garnering or making a timely rescue when one of the cast is poisoned. The author has weaved an intriguing and incredibly enjoyable Hallmark worthy whodunnit. Kudos!"—**Valleri Sullivan**, NetGalley Reviewer

"Heather Weidner's *Twinkle Twinkle Au Revoir* is a delightful and enchanting novel that beautifully blends romance and mystery. Weidner's engaging writing style and vivid storytelling create a captivating narrative filled with charm and intrigue.—**Hannah**, NetGalley Reviewer

A Tisket A Tasket Not Another Casket

"Thanks for the good read!"—**E. B. Davis**, Mystery and Paranormal Author

"I highly recommend *A Tisket, A Tasket Not Another Casket* for its well-plotted mystery, the town's cozy vibe, the quirky characters, and the Christmas shop! 5 stars!"—**Christy's Cozy Corners**, Book Blogger

"I loved this story! Jade, Chloe, and the rest of the crew really kept me guessing throughout the story."—**Lisa Currier**, NetGalley Reviewer

"This book brings plenty of fireworks as firework companies compete in Mermaid Bay. All the while, a "mermaid" is running around spilling the tea."—**Melanie Stewart**, NetGalley Reviewer

"I love Christmastime cozies. Mermaid Bay was definitely giving off cozy small-town vibes. I would for sure check out other books by this author!"—**Shaina Burris**, NetGalley Reviewer

"I have spent several years in the Williamsburg area and this series makes me feel like I'm visiting again. There are so many quaint towns in the area That it makes me want to find one and move back. Add in a solid murder mystery, the cutest puppy, and some quirky, fun, and lovable characters and you have yourself one heck of a murder mystery."—**Cindi Austin**, NetGalley Reviewer

"I would recommend this book and series."—**Christine Elsaieh**, NetGalley Reviewer

Chapter One

Juggling an iced mocha, her take-out breakfast bag, and Chloe's leash, Jade Hicks stepped out on the Busy Bean's deck and soaked in the warm spring sunshine before she started her day. Her white butterball of a French bulldog paused and sniffed the air. The briny smell of Mermaid Bay tickled Jade's nose and reminded her that the tiny beach community nestled on the Virginia shore was home. It always would be.

A high-pitched squeal echoed off the water and fractured the peacefulness. Jade and Chloe looked around for the source of the noise. Next door to the coffee shop, Amy Pemberton, owner of Mermaid Books, wrestled with one end of a banner on the store's large porch. Vivian Turner, president of the town's business council, supervised from the bottom step. The large neon yellow banner announcing the Mermaid Festival's Book Events slumped on the other end and fluttered in the breeze.

"Dern. I can't get this right. I knew I should have had Todd hang this for me when he was over here yesterday, before he took off for that skimboarding contest in Virginia Beach." The diminutive bookseller rolled her eyes and started to climb down the ladder that made a screechy sound as she dragged it to the opposite side of the doorway.

"I've got this end," Jade said, handing her bag and Chloe's leash to Vivian, who continued to gawk from the bottom step.

"How is Todd doing?" Vivian asked, shading her eyes with her free hand. "I see he still has that hearse. For the life of me, I can't figure out how that fits in with his marketing plan for the hot dog stand or his image for that matter." She wrinkled her nose like she smelled rotten sushi.

Amy turned and looked down at the persnickety librarian. "He uses it to haul his surfboarding equipment around. It's nice and roomy, and I borrow it from time to time for events like the paranormal excursion this week. By the way, Jade, I saved you and Nick a spot for the tour. I am so excited. The East Coast Paranormal Investigators are coming." She let out another squeal. "Not only are we having famous cryptozoologists and treasure hunters at the Con, we're getting ghost hunters, too. It is going to be epic." Amy tugged on her end of the banner, and Jade stretched and pulled her end taut. "Hey, Vivian," Jade said. "Does that look straight?"

"Hmm." The business council president and head librarian moved to the center of the sidewalk in front of the porch and then took a couple of steps backward. "Jade, maybe up about an inch on your end. Amy, now your side is crooked. Move it down about two inches." She paused and squinted at the banner with silhouettes of Bigfoot, Nessie, Mothman, and mermaids across the bottom. "I'm not sure what all those other creatures have to do with our mermaid festival. The banner's level, and one can read it from the road. So I guess it looks okay." Vivian's mouth formed a straight line.

"Thanks." Amy tied a knot in the cord on her side. She hopped down to check the bindings on Jade's side. "I think it looks wonderful. I'm so excited that CreatureCon is here. I haven't been to a ComiCon in years. This will be so much fun, and it will dovetail nicely with all our Mermaid fun." She dusted her hands on her jeans and hurried down the stairs to check the view of her banner from the parking lot. "I'm loving it," Amy added. "I've made displays with all the creature, horror, and cryptid books in the store, and we have tons of signings this week. And thanks, Jade, for all of your help with the cross-promotions. I'm doing anything I can to get the word out." She jogged up the steps as Vivian handed Jade her things.

"I'm glad you've expanded the bookstore's offerings and activities. We all treasured your Aunt Emory, but we know that she wasn't interested in changing anything in her store or this town. She had her vision of how a bookstore should be run, and she never deviated from it. I'm sure she'd... Well, may she rest in peace," Vivian said. "It's nice to see all the events you host here. Ladies, it's time for me to get back to the library to make sure we're on target for all our planned festivities. See you soon." She did a little hand wave and bustled down the sidewalk toward the government center. The name of the facility sounded bigger than the actual complex that housed the town's library, administrative building, and sheriff's office. Mermaid Bay, a tiny beach town in a sea of tourist spots, prided itself on preserving its traditions and historical architecture.

"So, can you and Nick join us for the tour? I mean, if he's not involved in any heavy-duty sheriff work." Amy said, scanning the beach where two men were roping off a large portion of the sand. "What are they doing down there to our beach? Did I miss one of the many updates from Vivian?"

Jade and Chloe turned to see the action near Suggs Pier. A man in a reflective vest hammered stakes in the soft sand while his partner tied a neon rope around each one to mark off giant rectangles. "That's for the sandcastle contest. The artists do some amazing sculptures. It should draw a big crowd for the festival. Hey, that would be something cool for the socials. You know, like before and after shots for people who have never seen the ginormity of some of these creations. They aren't the sandcastles that we used to make with a pail and shovel."

"You are so good at coming up with creative ideas. I'm trying to build my online following. It's constant work. I feel like I spend as much time online as I do on my business." Amy shook her head like she was trying to erase an Etch-a-Sketch and made a crazy face. "Enough of that. Back to the fun stuff. Let me know if you all can go on the tour. The paranormal guys are so cool to talk to. They'll set up their equipment at the old Hankins farm. Do you remember Presidents' Park?" Jade nodded, and Amy continued before Jade could get a word in. "It was before my time in Mermaid Bay, but I read about it online. Who thought it would be a way to attract tourists by creating a park where people walk around and look at giant busts of the presidents? I know all about this area's love of history, you know, with Williamsburg, Jamestown, and Yorktown nearby. But the idea of a park full of giant heads is kinda weird. The pictures of people dwarfed by the giant statues looked odd, but what do I know?" She opened her eyes wide. "I don't get it, but maybe it's somebody's thing. Well, maybe not everyone's cup of tea because the park wasn't a hit, even with all the history-loving tourists who visit the area. Anyway, when the park closed, the owner moved the giant heads to a farm in Crozet. It's not open to the public, but you can schedule special showings." She paused and pointed at herself with both index fingers. "And I snagged one for our paranormal tour. It should be a scream. The big heads got damaged in the move, so they look even more creepy now. It'll be the perfect place for East Coast Paranormal's ghostly demo. Do I know how to set a mood or what?"

A slight smile crossed Jade's face. "I never visited the park, though I did see them trucking in some of the giant heads when they first arrived. It was like an impromptu parade when word got out that they were moving them. The busts were like twenty-foot tall, and they were supposedly inspired by Mt. Rushmore."

Amy shrugged. "This whole let's build a park around a bunch of giant heads…I can see why they weren't a big draw. Sorry. I'm not seeing the thrill. But I'm hoping the paranormal night will be spine-tingling. I am so stoked about it, and of course, we're transporting everyone in Todd's hearse. That should add to the ghostly vibes." She offered an exaggerated wink. "And if I play my cards right, it may turn into a ghost-tour side gig. I am so ordering T-shirts."

"It'll be an adventure," Jade said. "I'll check with Nick to see what his schedule is."

"Perfect. Can't wait. Oh, I know what I wanted to ask you. Can you do another article for my newsletter? I'd love to feature all those cute little monster ornaments you added for the festival. I saw the trees in your lobby when I stopped in the other day. Perfect for all the cryptid-lovers who're going to flock this way. Everybody needs a Kraken or Nessie on their holiday tree."

"Sure. I'm all over any opportunity to share info on 'Tis the Season. I'll send you some photos and a blurb on my not-so-traditional holiday ornaments. Patti helped me order the fun ornaments for CreatureCon and Mermaid Day. I'm hoping they'll be a hit. We've sold quite a few online already."

"And someone's giant hearse will be all decked out for the big parade."

What a hoot. Though you-know-who won't like it, but Vivian doesn't like many things that aren't her idea." Amy's dark head bobbed up and down as she checked out her display windows. "I'll pop by later this week to get some photos with you standing in front of the trees. You can Vanna White the ornaments. Thanks for helping me. Call me if you get a break this week for lunch. We haven't had a girls' day in a while. We're long overdue." Amy wrestled the step ladder inside, and the glass door closed behind her. Her Persian cat, Mr. Darcy, looked up from his snoozing spot in the front window on a pile of Bigfoot and sea monster books.

Jade took the last swig of her iced mocha and caught her balance as Chloe decided to dart down the porch stairs after a butterfly. "Okay. You've been good. We'll take the long way back to the store, and I'll get some photos of the beach before the sand sculptures go up."

The pair walked along the sand and checked out the morning's activity that included joggers and a couple of folks doing beach yoga. Jade snapped photos of where the sandcastles would later dominate the beach. Chloe was more interested in digging in the soft sand near the water. Jade nudged the roly-poly dog toward the path home. They trekked down the cut-through next to the small cottage she inherited from her grandmother. When she spotted Mrs. Swenson watching from her front window across the street, Jade waved. Her ever-vigilant neighbor ducked out of view. Jade let out a little laugh. *At least I know someone has an eye out for what's going on.*

Jade checked her mailbox and coaxed Chloe in the direction of 'Tis the Season, the town's year-round Christmas shop that Jade had also inherited from her grandmother. The chubby dog paused to sniff the curb. "Let's go see what's shakin' down the block."

When they finally arrived at the store, Jade stared at her shop's front porch with its welcoming spring decorations and mermaid pillows on the wooden rockers. *Maybe I should have ordered a banner too. Something to think about if we do it again.* She nudged Chloe up the wooden steps. The dog waited patiently for Jade to unlock the door. "Time to start a new day, Chloe. It'll be all things mermaid and fantastical creatures for the next couple of weekends."

The pudgy Frenchie looked around and sniffed the air, sure that there were still more outdoor adventures to be had. She reluctantly waddled closer to the door.

Jade let out a long sigh. She loved her life in Mermaid Bay, but sometimes the store made her feel nostalgic, and she missed her grandmother. She closed her eyes for several beats. Her move back to Mermaid Bay had led her to this amazing job, lots of new friends, and Nick. She smiled when she thought of her history with the town's sheriff. She had been friends with Nick Driscoll since middle school and that horrible car accident that killed her parents. They became fast friends who eventually drifted apart when they went away to different colleges. Jade's trajectory back to Mermaid Bay after her grandmother's death was perfectly timed with Nick's election win to replace the retiring sheriff. Jade glanced around at all the twinkling lights and bright colors. *Life's not as crazy here as it was for me in Washington, D. C., but I've had my share of adventures in this sleepy little town. I don't miss my old job. I think the quiet life and the sea air suit me.*

Jade stirred from her memories as a stream of loud horn blasts echoed down the street and caused Chloe to strain on her leash to see what all the hubbub was all about. Forgetting about breakfast and work for a moment, Jade and Chloe hustled down the steps across the empty lot next door toward the building that Mermaid Books shared with the Busy Bean Café.

More horn sounds drew a small crowd to Amy's parking lot like ants on an abandoned popsicle. A large white ambulance decorated to look like the Ecto-mobile from the *Ghostbusters* movies took up three parking spaces. It didn't take long for people to surround the vehicle for photos and videos. The honking of horns crescendoed, and more people ambled out of nearby shops and climbed the dune from the beach to check out the vintage car.

Amy bounded out of the store as Vivian rushed around the corner with a to-go cup from the Busy Bean. "What is going on here?" Vivian sputtered. A gray minivan and an SUV pulled in behind the crowd.

"Isn't it fabulous?" Amy said with her arms wide open. The doors of the ambulance popped open, and several twenty-somethings climbed out. A willowy female with chestnut hair rummaged through her olive-colored messenger bag and pulled out a pair of sunglasses.

"Hello, everyone!" Amy welcomed the visitors. Two more guys joined them. "Mermaid Bay, these are the East Coast Paranormal investigators, and I'm so thrilled to have them here for our festivities. They're doing a book signing and a demo for us, and we'll have a tour of some of our local haunted sites. We're so fortunate to have them visit. I am so excited to learn about spirits and the nether regions." One of the guys in the crowd snickered.

The hulking guy with shaggy hair said, "Hi, I'm Elliot Kellogg, and these are my colleagues." He did a round robin of pointing to the gang standing behind him. "That's Drew Nelson, Cliffy Johnson, Norm Wendt, Suz Brewster, and Noah Jenkins, our fantastic videographer. And we're here to see who we can contact from the spirit world."

"And we're jazzed to be in Mermaid Bay. There is so much history around here. Battlefields, feuds, murders, and pirates," Norm added.

Suz nodded and looked up from her phone screen. "And death…all those battles and mysterious tales of what went on around here that make this area ripe for paranormal activity. Lots and lots of mysterious deaths throughout the years."

"We should make some good contacts here," Eliot said. "We wanted to stop by and introduce ourselves before we find our hotel. Can't wait to see those giant presidential heads. That'll be a great subject for our podcast. We'll post videos and photos on our website. Everyone likes to see photos of abandoned places."

"Oooh, before you guys head out, I'd like to show you a couple of things and get you to review some paperwork," Amy said, waving Eliot toward the store.

Some of the ghost-busters gang wandered over to check out the beach while the others piled back in the vehicles. The loud ooga horn sounded again, and groups of passersby flocked to the decorated ambulance.

Vivian slammed one fist on her hip and made a harrumphing sound. "Not quite what I imagined when we planned the Mermaid Festival. Ghosts and creatures of the night. Not all that beachy or pleasant." She huffed again and stormed off toward the pier.

Jade took some photos and managed to get a couple of her and Chloe in front of the replica of the Ecto-mobile. *You never know what's going to show up on our charming little beach.*

Chapter Two

The bells on the store's front door jangled, followed by a loud "Whoooo hoooo!" Chloe yipped and darted out of the office area into the lobby before Jade could stop her.

"Good morning, Patti." Better known by her nickname, Peppermint Patti, one of Jade's part-timers waltzed in wearing a hot pink and teal mermaid sweater.

"I'm so excited about all the festivities around here." Patti set a large bubblegum pink purse on the counter and whipped out her phone. "Guess who I met over at the Busy Bean?"

Before Jade could answer, Patti waved her phone in front of her. "None other than Angel Cruz and his entourage." When Jade didn't reply, she said, "THE Angel Cruz from *Treasure Hunter of the High Seas*. Amy and the young gal at the coffee shop literally swooned when he greeted them. And of course, we had to take selfies. He is so tall and handsome. I love his show. He finds so many cool things on his dives. He's a modern-day explorer and treasure hunter. A hunky swashbuckler. And I got sidetracked. I didn't even get my coffee."

"He looks like The Rock," Jade said.

"Yes, so tall, dark, and handsome. Ooooh, don't tell Simon. He'll be jealous," she giggled, scrolling through something on her phone. "So, what's shakin' around here?" she asked, continuing before Jade could comment. "It's kinda quiet. I hope it picks up with all the festival goers. I saw that they're starting to build the sandcastles. That'll be fun. Oh, our monster trees turned out nicely with all the cryptids. Have a Merry Cryptid and Creature Christmas," she sang. "I was planning on updating your inventory spreadsheet. Have you checked the overnight online orders yet?"

Jade shook her head. "I'll print out the report while you get settled."

"I still love going on hunts in the showroom and packaging all the ornaments. But it's not the same without Simon's daily visits." She reached down and scooped up Chloe. "Come on. I bet it's been ages since you had a treat. And I need my caffeine this morning."

Jade smiled to herself. *Somehow, I doubt both of those statements. Patti is Mermaid Bay's own Energizer Bunny.* "And you like our new delivery driver."

"Still not the same," Patti yelled from the back. "But since Simon and I are exclusively a couple now, I'm over the moon. No worries here."

When the printer spat out the last sheet of the overnight orders, Jade handed half to Patti. "I've got this. You do boss things, and I'll be back in two shakes of a lamb's tail. Ooooh. Look at all of these orders from all over the country. You are rocking the ornament world." Patti grabbed her coffee mug and pushed the cart toward the showrooms to gather the requests. "Are you going to the CreatureCon?" Patti yelled from the toy room.

"It'll be a new experience for me. I've never been to one," Jade replied.

"Me either. And I can't wait to soak it all in." She popped her head in the office door. "I am so excited. Simon and I are going on the night they have all the actors and famous people signing autographs. And after seeing Angel in person, I'd like to attend one of his presentations. I bet it's as thrilling as his show. Bernie told me Angel's team hired the guys at Suggs Pier to take them on some charter boat tours of our very own bay. I heard he was interested in looking at old wreck sites. Oooo, maybe they'll come back and film here. It would be too cool if he found pirate loot off our fair shores. How exciting. There are so many legends of pirate booty around here. It's about time someone found some. Our little town could be featured on TV again."

Jade smiled at the thought of her part-time Santa, Bernie Nash, and his band of retired friends helping to discover shipwrecks and hidden treasure. Bernie and his bunch were mostly known around town for drinking coffee and hanging out at the pier gossiping. *Speaking of gossip.* "Hey, the con should give you some new material for your blog, and all the celebrities should give you some dirt for *Mermaid Whispers.*"

"Shhhh! Don't out me," Patti said. "You're the only who knows." Patti waved both hands downward like she was trying to keep her secret from escaping.

"Knows what?" Bernie asked, stepping through the back door and sending Chloe into a barking jag until she recognized her friend. The store's Santa doppelganger looked ready for a fishing expedition in his cargo pants and his Hawaiian shirt covered in bright pink flamingos.

"Nothing," Jade and Patti said in unison.

He rolled his eyes and headed for the coffee machine. "I thought I'd stop by before lunch and make sure everything's in place for me tomorrow. I didn't know if you needed help moving the Santa set."

"Nope, all ready for you in your jolly outfit," Patti said. "Jade and I set up your throne yesterday. "We are good to go for Saturday for the big artisan show and, of course, your appearance. Everyone loves you."

His cheeks turned rosy. "You gals took care of everything. I saw the advertising on IG. That's Instagram, you know." He grinned from ear to ear. "My granddaughter told me that it was not TwitterFaceGram or whatever I was calling it. I'm getting hip on all this social stuff. Gotta keep up with the times. Next thing you know, I'll be on ClickClock."

Patti nodded. "Yep. Quite the hipster. But you better brush up on your cryptids before the CreatureCon starts."

"Smarty pants," he said, reaching for his mug of coffee. "I know they're undiscovered creatures that people seem to spot all the time. You know like Bigfoot, the Loch Ness Monster, the Swamp Thing, the Tasmanian Tiger...I've been watching classic horror movies since the nineteen fifties and all those 'In Search of' shows. I know my mysterious creatures."

Patti patted him on the back. "Then you're all ready for our con guests. There's no telling who or what you'll see around town."

"You're not kidding. I've seen all kinds of weird costumes already, and I'm taking pictures of everything. I have a fan page now. People like to follow the adventures of a Santa-actor," he said, tapping the screen on his phone.

"I heard you and the guys at the pier are doing boat excursions for some of the guests," Jade said.

"Yep. We met Angel Cruz. Cecil's planning to take his team out to look at wreck sites in the bay. They may do some filming here. Cecil had to sign an NDA and promise not to talk about where they wanted to visit. It's all hush-hush. This is our second filming in town in so many months. Cecil and Lester said they're also booked some other tours, and Joe Herring, the new guy on the block, is doing some fishing charters for some of the marine biologists who are in town. Mermaid Bay is a hot ticket."

Jade nodded. Before she could reply, he continued, "And we met this guy called the Xplorer. He's a professor or something and a podcaster. His real name is Ernie Something, but don't go around talking about that. He only likes people to call him the Xplorer, with an 'x'. Anyway, he's talking about this big announcement at the conference. He's hired Joe to take him out on the water, too. It would be cool if he and Angel had dueling discoveries. It's all very exciting. Anyway, the Xplorer is interested in the ships scuttled in the York River and the rumors of some giant fish that no one's been able to catch in the bay. Sounds like lots of material for shows and podcasts." Looking up, suddenly, he said, "Jade, you need me to do anything while I'm here?"

She shook her head. "No, we're good. You're the best handyman around. Everything is buttoned up tight around here."

He grinned from ear to ear and waddled down the hall to make sure his Santaland was the way he liked it.

Jade glanced over at Patti, who was furiously scribbling in her notebook. "I wonder what will show up on Mermaid Whispers next?"

Patti shrugged a shoulder, but before she could offer a retort, the bells on the front door jangled like a nor'easter was blowing up the coast.

All conversation stopped when a woman with a long, thick braid shoved open the door and stared at Patti and Jade with a pair of piercing blue eyes.

Chapter Three

"Welcome to 'Tis the Season," Jade said to the slender woman and the tallish man behind her. The woman's long, sandy blond hair hung in a long braid that reminded Jade of a rope. The woman shoved her phone and keys in the pocket of her navy blazer and stepped closer to her as her gaze flitted around the room like she was doing some kind of inspection. "We're from out of town." She looked down her long, ski-sloped nose and curled her lip slightly.

The man with sun-kissed hair sidled up next to her and let loose with a dazzling, megawatt smile. He ran his hand through his hair that was a hipster version of a pompadour. "Yep, we heard about your store from Ruby at the bed and breakfast. Thought we'd stop by to check it out for ourselves. Interesting concept."

The woman continued to scope out the room like she was inventorying all the decorations or casing the joint. She turned and looked at Patti and Jade up and down like she was continuing her inspection.

"It's Christmas here all year long," Jade said, trying to shake off the unsettling vibe from the woman with the ice-blue eyes. "On Saturday, the town is celebrating Mermaid Day, and we'll be showcasing local artisans for the festival."

"And we'll host Santa and have lots of cookies," Patti added.

On cue, Bernie popped his head in and waved.

"Charming," the woman said with another lip twitch that looked like a sneer. She reached for the green basket that Patti offered. "I think we have plans that day."

"Feel free to browse through the showrooms. If you see an ornament you like, they'll be in the peach baskets at the base of each tree. We've decorated these two with our creature ornaments in honor of the convention that's in town," Jade said.

The man smiled again and led the woman over to the two trees that bookended the front door. "Hey, look. Bigfoot and the Creature from the Black Lagoon. We need these." He loaded several into the basket.

The woman pointed her chin toward the showroom and nodded several times. He dumped a few more ornaments in the basket and followed her like a puppy into the rainbow room, where each tree was themed with ornaments of a single color. All the trees together reminded Jade of a magical, kaleidoscope, and the Land of Oz.

"Interesting folk," Bernie said when they were out of earshot.

"Look, look," Patti whispered loudly, pointing at the brochure. "They're kinda famous. They're on the panels at CreatureCon. That's Dr. Meredith Echols. She's a marine biologist who has written lots of books on sea life. And he's Dr. Randall Medlin. His degree is in cryptozoology. He made his name on YouTube, and he has like a bazillion followers." She paused long enough to tap on her phone. "Oooh, look here. This chat site says she's popular at the conventions as the one that the fans love to hate. That doesn't sound nice, but we could kinda tell that she wasn't as friendly as he was. Let's see, it says she debunks the theories of cryptozoologists and armchair researchers, and she likes to rile up the conference audiences."

"A scientist and a cryptozoologist. That's an interesting combination. It sounds like they would be polar opposites," Jade said.

"From some of the comments I skimmed, many describe Dr. Echols as very stuffy and unapproachable. The conference goers like to boo her, but her friend, Dr. Medlin, is very popular. He has such a nice smile. And I liked their matching bracelets. Did you see those? Very beachy bracelets. Do you think Simon would like a braided rope bracelet like that? I could figure out how to make them online." She returned the conference brochure to its stack and busied herself with a search on her phone.

"Everything looks great as usual here," Bernie said. "I'll see y'all bright and early on Saturday. Oh, wait, you want help setting up tables and tents tomorrow?" Jade nodded. "Well, in that case. I'll see you then." He saluted and shuffled toward the back office by way of a detour to the snacks on the table.

Before Patti and Jade could continue their conversation, Drs. Echols and Medlin returned to the checkout desk. He plopped the plastic basket on the counter and whipped out a black credit card. Patti rang up the purchases as Jade wrapped them. "Fun store," he said, taking the receipt and his card. The woman who didn't say anything reached for the bag and bolted for the exit like she was afraid of being contaminated by something.

Patti shrugged when the door closed behind them. "They are quite an unusual pair. I may have to pop into one of their panels. And if she's not careful, she may make a Mermaid Whispers' post. Who knows? Everybody loves a villain. I'm sure it'll be a spicy story."

A shriek ricocheted across the parking lot, and a second sounded like it came from the porch. Jade flung open the door, and she, Patti, and Chloe tried to squeeze through the opening at the same time. Jade scooped up the Frenchie so she wouldn't dart out and join the ruckus.

Several feet away on the porch steps, Meredith had her index finger inches from a man's nose. The guy in an olive hoodie held his phone up, recording the altercation. Randall tugged at her arm, and her head snapped toward him. She made a face that looked like she was gritting her teeth. Meredith screeched something that made Randall step back.

The hoodie guy said something that Jade didn't catch, and Meredith lunged toward him, grabbing for his phone. The guy did a quick ninja move to skirt her reach, and she stumbled. She righted herself on the bottom step, and the small crowd in front of the store started to boo as she stomped off toward the bookstore.

Randall looked around and waved to the onlookers. Picking up the bag that Meredith dropped, he followed the sidewalk to the edge of the street. The small crowd and the hoodie guy scurried off when there was nothing else to see on Jade's porch.

"Well, that was quite the drama," Bernie said, poking his head through the doorway. "I see someone has made my naughty list this year. Tsk. Tsk."

Patti giggled and scrolled on her phone. "You never know what's going to happen around here. Hmmm. This is a little nugget that might come in handy later." Without waiting for anyone to comment, she continued, "The consensus of the comments on this page is that Meredith relishes in her smarter-than-everyone-else persona as an expert in marine biology. She lords it over her colleagues and students. And what did I find here? Ooooooo. This is good. It seems that the handsome and affable Dr. Randall and the not-so-lovable Dr. Meredith are married to each other, much to the chagrin of some of his female fans. Definitely an odd couple. I wonder if they argue science versus cryptology at the dinner table."

Chapter Four

Jade's aunt, Lorelei Tucker, breezed into the lobby from one of the showrooms, followed by her shadow and Chloe's nemesis, Neville the Devil Cat. "That's about it," she said, perching on the stool behind the counter. "Here's the inventory. You've moved a lot of mermaid and creature ornaments. I highlighted the ones that need restocking." Lorelei smoothed out her tailored black dress pants and her alabaster cardigan that matched her signature pearls.

"I appreciate it. The online orders have been outpacing the foot traffic. We're doing inventories almost every other day. I'm hoping tomorrow will be another banner day with all of the festival activities. The back room's all set up. I have name tags on the tables, and I'll put the ones on the outside tables tomorrow. We have the whole team scheduled to help us."

"Even Tori?" her aunt asked.

Jade nodded, and her aunt continued, "I'm so excited that Tori decided to go to Christopher Newport next year. She was talking like she was looking to go somewhere out of state. CNU will be good for her. She will be close to home, but far enough away to spread her wings." Lorelei pulled her red Kate Spade bag from behind the counter and rummaged through it.

"She said she'd like to stay on part-time here, so I'm glad that she'll be here for a little while longer." Jade put the receipts and cash in the bank bag.

"What else do you need me to do? The kitchen's cleaned, and all the lights are off in the back rooms." Lorelei jingled her car keys, and Neville wended his way around her ankles.

"Thanks for all your help. See you bright and early tomorrow. Fingers crossed that the shoppers arrive by the busload."

Her aunt scooped up the tuxedo cat and strolled out the door. "Hasta mañana."

Jade double-timed her closing routine. "Chloe, we're about ready as we'll ever be for Mermaid Day." She shut down her laptop and stuffed the things to take home in her messenger bag. "We need to step up the pace a bit. I need to pick up Amy soon."

After a short walk home, Chloe watched as Jade filled her dinner bowl. "You enjoy. I need to go freshen up. What does one wear to a CreatureCon?" Not interested in fashion statements or monsters, Chloe dug into her chicken and veggie chunks with a snort.

Jade settled on a purple tunic and a pair of black leggings. Going for comfort, she pulled out her black high-top Converse sneakers. After a round with the curling iron and her makeup brushes, she cleared the bathroom counter, checked on Chloe, and put on Animal Planet to keep her company. "I'll be back soon. You're in charge of security while I'm out."

Jade jogged to her Jeep Wrangler and zoomed out of the driveway. She had barely stopped in the bookstore lot before Amy flung open the passenger side door. "Hey, let's get this party started. Can't wait to see what's going on at the Con. You look nice. Two hot chicks checking out the creatures of the night. Too fun. Are you ready for an adventure?"

"You're a hoot, and you look good too."

"It's left over from my goth days. You can never go wrong with all black." Amy twirled a strand of her dark hair tipped in aqua and purple. "You think I need more eyeliner for this crowd?"

"You look fine, and I'm glad you didn't make us go in costumes."

Amy smirked. "And that would be amazing. There are still plenty of days left for that. Todd wasn't into it either. He never wants to have any fun." She made a pouty face and sank back in her seat. Jade slowed down and merged into the traffic turning into the Sandcastle Resort on the other side of Suggs Pier, the official demarcation line between the lively town of Seaport and the sleepy village of Mermaid Bay. Giant blowups of Big Foot and a fire-breathing dragon bookended the turrets at the hotel's main entrance, and a smaller Nessie balloon floated aimlessly in the fountain next to the fake drawbridge.

"Okay, what's the plan?" Amy said, shaking Jade from her thoughts.

"Dunno. Don't really have one," Jade said, zipping into a parking space between a minivan and a red Nissan Cube.

The pair hopped out, and as Jade locked the Wrangler, a guy from the Cube pointed at her personalized plate. "Hey, that's pretty cool. Can I get a picture of your Jeep?"

Jade nodded as he posed for a selfie by her "NO GRNCH" plates.

"She owns the Christmas shop in Mermaid Bay. You need to stop by and check out the Mermaid Festival this weekend," Amy said.

The guy waved and jogged to catch up with his friends.

"Okay," Amy said, pulling out a schedule. "I want to spy on the vendor area. I'm curious to see if it would be worth my while to set up a table at events like this, especially if I could get exclusive book dealer status. This way. Let's see what they have to offer." She pulled out two lanyards from her purse and handed one to Jade. "Your creds. Thanks for being my Plus One. Todd bailed to go hang out with his gamer friends. I can't believe game night with the guys outranked all of this." She spread her arms wide and danced toward the crowded entrance.

Jade followed Amy's dark head as she plunged through the sea of bodies and all kinds of costumed characters. She recognized some from *Star Wars, Star Trek, The Lord of the Rings,* and *The Hunger Games,* but there were a bunch she had no idea who or what they were. Jade tried not to lose Amy in the crowded lobby and down the long hallway to the conference center.

Jade followed along as Amy dodged bodies and zipped inside to the conference center, where tables filled with jewelry, costumes, weaponry, and fan memorabilia covered every inch of available floor space. Jade scanned the displays and all the rows and rows of racks full of merchandise.

"I don't see any books. I'm headed off this way. You want to meet back at the entrance in an hour or so?" Amy asked.

"Sure," Jade yelled to be heard over the crowd. *If Amy's idea pans out, maybe I should get a table at events like this, too. So far, I haven't spotted any ornaments.*

There could be a market for my stuff.

Jade browsed through table after table of jewelry and finally settled on a pair of ruby-colored teardrop earrings.

"Hey, you need a costume to go with that. You can't show up here without sporting your colors." Jade turned to see a shaggy-looking guy in a Mandalorian T-shirt waving at her from the next booth.

"I'm just visiting," Jade said, retrieving her card and taking the small bag from the jewelry clerk.

"We all are," he replied. "You sure I can't interest you in a costume or at least a T-shirt to commemorate the event. It's your first con, right?"

"I look that out of place?" Jade said with a half-smile.

"Not really. I thought you were a reporter or something. Come on over. You need to check out my line of fan shirts. You know, so you'll blend next time. *At least he didn't say I looked like somebody's mother.*

Jade browsed the stacks of colorful tees and found a pink shirt with warrior photos of Carrie Fisher's General Leia and Robin Wright's Antiope that said, "My Childhood Princesses Became Generals." She picked up two and handed her card to another staffer who swooped in and bagged the purchases while the other guy rattled off the virtues of a Mandalorian helmet and costume to several wide-eyed fans.

After checking most of the vendors' wares and watching a weaponry reenactment, Jade made her way to the entrance. She found a spot near the doors and a water fountain where she could wait for Amy.

Jade felt like she was in the Mos Eisley cantina in *Star* Wars with all the crazy costumes, each more elaborate than the previous one. She snapped some photos, and two conference attendees dressed as Han Solo and Chewbacca surrounded her for a group shot. "Thanks. Y'all look great." The Wookie made a low growl and saluted on his way out.

By the time Jade posted some of her photos to Instagram, Amy trudged through the crowd, dragging three giant dragons.

"Here, let me help you. Did you win the grand prizes at a carnival game?" Jade asked, reaching for the green and purple one that resembled Disney's Pete. "Let's put these in the Jeep. Wow. You've got quite a collection here."

"I can't pass up dragons, ever. They're going in my children's nook at the store," Amy said, wending her way through the crowd to an exit to the parking lot. "Whew. It's cooler out here. I was getting hot in there. I have no idea how those guys and gals stand it in those full-body costumes."

"Here, I got you one of these," Jade said, pulling out the T-shirt.

"Too cool. Thanks. And I see we have matching bestie tees. Awesome. We can twinsie. Oh, hey look, Angel Cruz, the treasure-hunting hottie, has a panel in twenty minutes." She pointed to something on her phone screen. "I reeeeeeeally want to go and see him. Come with me? He's teasing on TikTok that he's got some big announcement that will rock the cryptid world. You know scary monsters, weird creatures, and all that. Whoooweeee."

"I thought he was a treasure hunter," Jade said, locking the Jeep after Amy placed the dragons in the backseat.

"He is. I have no idea what the big news is. We gotta hurry. I want to get a good spot. This is going to be soooo worth it." Amy grabbed Jade's arm and pulled her back toward the hotel.

Amy stopped suddenly at the pretend drawbridge where a gang of costumed characters blocked the sidewalk. Most were vaping and chatting. While Amy stood on her tiptoes to see what was going on, Jade caught snippets of conversations about Angel's expeditions that included a recent haul of gold and jewels from a spot off the Florida coast.

A guy in a fuzzy blue costume said, "That's nothing. Dr. Randall Medlin has an announcement, too. It sounded epic. He found a plane in the Bermuda Triangle when he was looking for a new kind of squid. He even found bones on the shipwreck."

"You just said it was a plane wreck," the guy in the Lorax-looking outfit said, punching his buddy in the arm.

"Whatever. Some announcement is coming, and we get to hear it first," fuzzy blue costume said.

"Dr. Medlin is so cool. I want to major in cryptozoology under him, but my dad is giving me crap about it not being a real major," the gal in the warrior outfit added. "He said I had to major in something that would turn into a paying job."

"I heard Dr. Echols badmouthing Dr. Medlin, saying that same thing. She's the worst. And for the record, I think you should major in what you want to," a guy in a red cape added. "I don't know why she even bothers showing up at these events when she knows she's not wanted."

"She gets paid, stupid," the warrior gal said, jabbing him in the arm with her spear.

Not being able to see what was going on, Amy let out with a shrill, two-fingered whistle. "Excuse me, folks. I need to scooch past you. Don't want to be late for the next set of panels and Annnnnngel Cruz."

The crowd parted, and Amy grabbed Jade's arm again and hustled her through the costumed gauntlet. "Angel Cruz awaits."

Inside, Amy barreled through the crowd and headed for another large room on the opposite side of the vendor hall. "Whew, we made it. I'm so glad they're still seats." Amy pointed and led her to two empty chairs. She waved to Angel, who looked relaxed in one of the side chairs on the stage. The set resembled one for a daytime talk show, complete with comfy chairs, a coffee table, and three large potted plants all arranged on a large oriental rug.

"He's coming to my store to do a book signing. I can't wait," Amy whispered in Jade's ear. "It will be amazing. He's the whole package."

Before Jade could comment, Angel jumped off the stage like an Olympic gymnast and bounded over to the pair without losing his Indiana Jones hat. "Hey, how's my favorite bookseller?"

Jade cracked a smile when Amy swooned. "Be still, my beating heart. We are so excited to have you talk to your fans and sign books at the store. I can't wait to hear all about your adventures. And if you need an assistant to help on the dives, sign me up. Jade, get a picture of us. Angel Cruz, this is my very close friend, Jade Hicks."

"It's nice to meet you," he said, flashing a dazzling pearly white smile and tipping his explorer hat.

"There," Jade said, tapping her phone screen. "I got some fun shots. I sent them to you."

"And don't forget to tag me," Angel said. "And you've come to the right place for adventure. I'm planning to do a quick overview tonight, but don't worry. I have plenty of new material exclusively for your event."

Before Angel could say anything else, a rail-thin woman in a magenta pantsuit with long corkscrew curls sidled up next to him. "Excuse me, but they need you in the green room for a quick minute."

Angel nodded. "Thanks, Marcella. See you all around. And thanks for coming tonight." He walked out of the room with a swagger that reminded Jade of some kind of general or maybe a pirate.

Before Jade could get comfortable on the plastic chair, the lights dimmed, and a woman in a cream-colored suit and ruby red lips strode across the floor and lowered herself into one of the chairs with feline grace. She crossed her long legs and adjusted her clip-on microphone. "Good evening, everyone. I'm Alana Green from WVEC in Norfolk, and I will be your host this evening. Without further ado, I'd like to introduce our guest for the evening, the multi-talented treasure hunter, author, and podcaster, Angel Cruz."

Angel strode across the stage, waving with both hands. When the applause and cheers finally died down, Alana began her interview with a series of softball questions where she gushed about Angel's accomplishments.

The treasure hunter spent the next hour talking about his team and their big finds in Florida, Bermuda, and the Bahamas. He and Alana paused only to show a fifteen-minute video of his dives and piles of gold coins that the audience oooed and ahhhed over.

"Well, that was dreamy," Amy said when the lights came back up. Angel took a bow before trotting off the stage.

"I thought there was some big announcement about his latest find," Jade said, following Amy toward the lobby exit.

"Who knows? Maybe he's saving it for my event. Wouldn't that be a scream if he broke the news in my little ol' store?" She fanned herself with her hand and put on her best southern accent.

Jade hoped she didn't roll her eyes. Amy's Bostonian accent never came close to a southern drawl.

As they neared the exit, Jade was bumped from behind, and she braced herself with two hands on Amy's shoulder, so she didn't completely fall into her friend, who was pushed like a three-car pileup into the woman in front of her. The woman's head snapped around, and her face scrunched into a snarl. Meredith Echols demanded, "Watch where you're going. Don't you know how to walk?"

"Soooo sorry," Amy said. "Some ruffian barreled through the crowd."

The marine biologist flipped her long braid over her shoulder and pushed her way through the throngs of people milling about in the lobby.

Before Amy could comment with some snark of her own, all heads turned when a guy in black tactical gear hopped up on a table and yelled, "I see you. Don't try to slink away. Or maybe you should. You have no business being here. You're a fraud, and your only claim to fame is belittling other people's work. Merrrrrr-i-dith, you know I'm talking to you."

"Oooooh, it's the Xplorer," some guy in the crowd yelled, and whoops and cheers surrounded the burly guy balancing on the table as the crowd whipped out their phones to capture the excitement.

The crowd parted to reveal Meredith Echols with both hands on her hips. "Get down from there, Ernie. You're making a fool of yourself as usual. And my CV supports all of my research and study. No fraud or plagiarism anywhere. Yours is made up like your stupid title, which is as dumb as that costume. You look like some kind of Guardian of the Galaxy who bases his whole marketing campaign on a spelling error." Her bright blue eyes flashed, and she stared daggers in Ernie's direction.

Someone made a third-grade oohing sound, and all eyes were on the Xplorer, who waved a fist around like he was preparing for his next wave of attack. "You really do need to take a hint. Nobody wants you here. You're rude, mean, and class-A hack. There are so many people that hate you for taking credit for their work. Face it. You're a pretender. You better watch your back, or something might happen to you."

Meredith flapped both of her hands like she was trying to suppress the catcalls. "Enough. I'm not going to dignify this inane outburst any longer. If you want to debate, that's fine. We'll do it properly, and I'll wipe the floors with you. Bring it." Her piercing eyes flashed like a storm was brewing behind them. She turned, and her long braid bobbed as she strode toward the bar.

The crowd started cheering Ernie the Xplorer, who did a victory dance on the wobbly table.

"We need to see where Miss Prissypants went," Amy said as the crowd continued the spontaneous dance-off around the Xplorer.

Chapter Five

Amy and Jade paused at the smoky glass windows of The Dungeon. The hotel bar's thick wooden doors, decorated with chains, sported a heavy, ornate iron handle. "I can't see anything. It's so dark," Amy whined, pulling Jade inside the bar. The pair blinked slowly to get their eyes to adjust to the dimness of the dark-paneled room with wine-colored vinyl chairs.

"No Meredith," Jade said after she took in the long mahogany bar and the handful of bar-top tables scattered around the room full of suits of armor, swords, and battle axes.

"Maybe she snuck out the other exit," Amy said. "What an evening. There's lots of drama around here. Maybe too much. I'm about ready to head out. What about you? This place is dark and spooky, perfect for all the creatures running around here or the ideal spot to plot mayhem."

Jade nodded and pulled out her keys. "Yep. We've got a big day tomorrow. Let's hope for fabulous weather and lots of shoppers."

The pair walked to the lobby, where a flash of a blue blazer caught Jade's eye near the elevator. She grabbed Amy's arm and pulled her over behind the woman with the long braid. Giving Amy a head tilt and a glare, Jade hoped she got the message to follow her. *I thought Dr. Medlin said they were staying at Ruby's bed and breakfast.*

Meredith jabbed the button and waited for the door to close. "What floor?" she asked when Amy followed Jade inside.

"Six is good for us, too. Thanks. Are you enjoying the con?" Jade pointed to the woman's lanyard.

"I'm so excited to meet all the panelists and the authors. I love all the costumes," Amy gushed.

Meredith shrugged. "They're all about the same. Usually, they're tedious." Seconds later, the bell dinged, and she stepped off as soon as the door opened on the sixth floor. Jade nudged Amy forward. *I hope we don't look like we're stalkers. Just be cool. She didn't act like she recognized us.* She and Amy dawdled a few feet behind Meredith, who strode toward the "T" at the end of the hall. *Let's see how my acting skills are. This is me pretending to search for my keys. What's she doing up here?*

When Meredith stopped abruptly halfway down the hall, Jade casually strode past with Amy on her heels. Meredith didn't seem to care what they were doing. She swiped a room key and let the door slam behind her.

When Jade was sure they were out of range of the door's peephole, she slowed down and pulled Amy into the room across the hall with the vending machines and the icemaker.

"What is she doing here? This doesn't make sense," Amy loudly whispered. Before Jade could comment, Amy said, "Maybe she's meeting someone that she doesn't want people to see. You know something business or conference related, or she's got some kind of secret rendezvous. She and her husband are staying at the Pearl, right?"

Jade signaled with one finger to her lip for them to lower their voices. It was hard to judge how loud they were talking with all the background noise from the icemaker's rumble.

"Yep. She and Randall have rooms at Ruby's. I'm curious about what she's doing up here, too, after her big fight with the Xplorer," Jade said.

"Maybe the hotel comped her a room here since she's on panels," Amy whispered. "It's six-twenty-four by the way, in case we want to make prank phone calls or send some kind of joke to her room."

"Let's give her some time to see if she goes anywhere else. And if not, we'll bag it and head home," Jade said, peeking out the doorway.

"I hope she doesn't get a hankering for snacks or ice. That would be awkward to explain," Amy giggled. "We already slammed into the back of her earlier, and now we've followed her to her room. Totally creepy and stalkerish. She'll think we're crazed fans or serial killers. Wait, from what everyone says, she doesn't have any fans." Amy raised one eyebrow, and her mouth formed a small "o."

Amy and Jade took turns watching the hall for any movement near the door of six-twenty-four. Time felt like it was moving in slow motion.

"I don't think I'm made for stakeouts," Amy said, dropping some change in the vending machine. "At least we have sustenance in here." She selected a Snickers bar. "Want half?"

Jade shook her head. "If nothing happens in the next couple of minutes, we should bag it. We need to find another way to figure out whose room it is."

"Ooooh. Secret rendezvous. This could be spicy," Amy said, rubbing her hands together. "This place is full of all kinds of clandestine activities."

About the time Jade's legs were getting stiff from standing on the tile floor in the snack closet, Amy hissed in a loud whisper, "There she is. It's her." The door down the hall slammed, and Meredith strode to the elevator. "Follow me." When the elevator doors closed, Amy darted out into the hallway.

"She's probably headed to the lobby. Let's catch the next one," Jade whispered.

"I have a better idea," Amy shoved her across the hall to the stairwell. "If we hurry, maybe we can catch up to her. The elevator will take too long. I don't want to lose her."

Six flights of steps later, Amy burst out the door that opened near the registration desk. Not pausing to catch her breath, she said, "We can still find her."

As the pair scanned the lobby near the bank of elevators, someone yelled, "There she is. Get her!"

An icy chill streaked through Jade as she frantically looked around to see what was happening. *I think we found her.*

A crowd of costumed cosplayers ran past Amy and Jade and surrounded Meredith on the marble tile near the elevators. A moment of panic crossed the marine biologist's face as the crowd tightened around her.

"We need to see what's going on," Jade said, pulling out her phone. "This could get ugly. We have to do something before this gets out of hand."

Amy waded into the mob of costumed figures to get closer to Meredith. The crowd squeezed in tighter, and the space around Meredith was reduced from feet to inches. Not sure whether to run to the desk or call the police, Jade waited a beat or two to see what would happen.

"Leave the Xplorer alone," a guy in the back yelled.

"You're such a bully. Nobody asked for your stuck-up comments on everything. Take your nastiness and go back to your little college in Florida. You're not welcome here," someone else yelled.

There were cheers and boos, and the crowd seemed to grow by the minute. Jade inched around the perimeter to the main desk, where the clerk chatted with someone on the phone about a reservation. He looked oblivious to the noise and chaos that was erupting on the other side of his counter.

Before Jade could call the police, the loud voices suddenly dropped from shouts to murmurs as the people stepped back. Two burly security guards bookended Meredith and guided her out the front door into an awaiting cab. The conference goers milled around, but when there was nothing interesting to see, they scattered.

Definitely lots of anger, and that crowd mobilized fast. It got a little scary for a moment. Hopefully, this is the end of whatever this was. Vivian will have a stroke if it spills over into our Mermaid Day activities. I'm surprised that there is this much bad behavior at an event that is supposed to be fun.

"Well, that was something," Amy said. "I bet your evenings weren't as lively as this until I came along. We always have fun girl nights. Though I was a little concerned when the audience turned into a mob. I was waiting for the torches and pitchforks to come out." She jabbed Jade lightly in the ribs. "Anything else you want to see? I think that was the main event."

"Just a sec. I want to see if I can find out about the mysterious owner of room six-twenty-four." Jade looked up the hotel and pushed the link to the phone number. After a couple of rings, it connected with a male voice. "Good evening," she said. "Could you connect me with Dr. Meredith Echols's room, please?"

"Echols, E-C-H-O-L-S?" he asked.

"Yes. That's her."

"I'm sorry, we have no one registered here by that name."

"Hmmm. How about Ernie Post?" Jade asked.

"One moment, please." Light classical music blared in Jade's ear until the voicemail's automated message connected. She hung up. "How can I find out who has room six-twenty-four?"

"I have an idea. Let's see if this works." Amy checked her lipstick and fluffed her hair. "Be right back." She slinked toward the front desk and waited until the young guy finished his phone call. Jade stepped closer to see what she was up to.

"Hi," she said in a breathy tone. "I need your help. I met this guy in the bar at the conference, and he gave me his room key. He said it was on the sixth floor, but I can't remember the number. He went upstairs already, and I don't want to have to knock on doors until I find him. That might disrupt a bunch of your guests. Could you help a girl out? He's really cute with dreamy eyes, and I don't want to blow this by ghosting him. I got so excited when we bonded over drinks and some yummy cheese appetizer. But stupid me can't remember his room number. I feel like such a dolt. I am so embarrassed to tell you this." Amy poked out her bottom lip and gave him a sad, pouty face. "I don't know what else to do."

"I'm sorry. We can't give out room numbers."

"But he gave me the key. I'm not some random person. Ernie Post gave me his key," she insisted, rummaging through her purse. "Here. Can't you check it for me?" She waved a white plastic card in front of the lanky guy with the bored look.

"Ma'am, this looks like it's a subway or a bus pass," he said, handing it back to her.

She clapped her hands lightly to her cheeks and widened her eyes. "That jerk. He told me how fabulous my smile was and that I could be on his podcast. And he gave me a stinking bus pass when I thought it was his room key," she said, raising her voice and pounding on the counter with both fists. "I am mortified and totally cheesed off. Just wait until I find him. I'm going to knock on every door on the sixth floor until I find that sneaky, no good, sorry…" Amy waved her arms around. "He will be so sorry he ever tried this with me. You know what they say about a scorned woman."

Trying to calm the outburst, the clerk spoke to her in a low, soothing tone. "I'm sorry you had a conflict. Maybe it's better if you move on and away from him. He's probably not the caliber of a catch that you want. You saved yourself some trouble by finding out now. Someone like you deserves to be treated better."

"But he promised to put me on his podcast. He said it would go viral, and I'd be a hit. I can't believe it was all a sham." Amy wiped her eyes and sniffed for effect. "I can't believe I fell for his stupid, your eyes are like shimmering pools in a mirage crap. Ooooooh. I'm going to find him if it's the last thing I do." She turned in a huff toward the elevators. "This is so unfair."

"Wait a minute," the clerk yelled. "I may be able to help," he said quietly.

"You can?" she whimpered and zipped back to the desk. "That would be so lovely. Jerks like this can't get to win. You know, karma and all that. He can't treat people like dirt." She put both hands on the counter and rested her chin on them. Then she did her best imitation of Chloe's puppy eyes.

"Here, I can dial Mr. Post's number, and you can leave a voicemail for him. That would be better than you storming the sixth floor and causing a disruption. Plus, you won't have to confront him in person. Win-win," the clerk said.

"You're the best," Amy cooed as he punched in the numbers and handed her the phone.

"Ernie, this is Belinda. We met in the bar. It seems the key you gave me will get me a round-trip bus ride. I don't appreciate that you ghosted me after all those promises and sweettalk at the bar. I will certainly see you around. And watch your back." Amy made a harrumphing sound and handed the phone back to the clerk. "Thank you so much. What's your name? I want to make sure I note it on my survey."

"It's Josh, and it's not a problem. We want everyone to have a memorable experience when they visit with us." The desk phone rang, and Amy used that as her cue to flounce over to where Jade stood.

The pair sat on an empty loveseat surrounded by potted palms. A Cheshire cat grin crossed Amy's face. "Ol' Josh came through for me. It's Ernie's room. And now the besotted Belinda doesn't have to go and raise a ruckus on the sixth floor."

"What an Oscar-worthy performance. You make a great jilted girlfriend. You've got skills."

"All those years in drama club paid off," Amy said, patting herself on the back. Then she looked over her shoulder and whispered, "What is Meredith doing in Ernie Post's room after she had that verbal brawl with him? Was she sneaking around to do something nefarious? Should we warn him?"

"Maybe Ernie and Meredith are a thing, or at least, they're friendly enough for her to use his hotel room. Was that whole shouting match for show?" Jade mused.

"Vavavoom. Dern that the whole argument was an act. There are some serious shenanigans going on around here. Well, that's about as much fun as I can stand for one evening. Let's say we head out? Maybe we should leak it on social media that the Xplorer and Meredith are a thing. That would surely send this crowd into a tailspin. Can you imagine what kind of shock and awe that would create?"

Chapter Six

"Wheweeeee," Peppermint Patti said, leaning against the front counter. "By my count, three busloads came through those doors. And that doesn't count all the other folks who came to visit for Mermaid Day. And it's not even lunch time yet. Wow!"

Jade smiled. "I'm not complaining. I love it when it's this busy, but I'll probably be exhausted by the time I get home." She pulled her phone out of her pocket and glanced at the string of panicked texts from Amy.

"What's up?" Lorelei asked, returning a bunch of empty shopping baskets to the stack.

"Amy has her big book talk with Angel Cruz today, and her photographer bailed on her. And Todd is swamped over at the restaurant."

"Go, go." Lorelei shooed her toward the office as Patti nodded. "We've got this. We'll text you if anything urgent comes up. Go help her out."

Jade rummaged through her desk and pulled out her digital camera. She let out a little whistle, relieved that the camera still held a charge. "Thanks, y'all. Do you want me to bring back lunch?"

"Nope. I brought mine," Patti said.

"I'm good too. But thanks." Lorelei perched on the stool behind the cash register.

Jade jogged across the street to the bookstore and dodged groups of slow-moving visitors who congregated along Neptune Road. It looked like July Fourth weekend without the summer heat and humidity.

The line of customers at the bookstore circled the building and almost reached the nearby pier. The sandcastles that now blocked the view of the bay had taken shape over the past couple of hours. Many of them were already over ten feet tall with ornate bases and intricate decorations, all carved out of wet sand.

Jade took a deep breath. The hint of brine and the tangy salt on her lips reminded her of why she loved this place. It was her peaceful spot. Knowing that she was going to get some glares and comments about cutting the bookstore line, she took one more deep breath of sea air and squared her shoulders. She said, "Excuse me" at least twenty times as she moved through the crowd and up the wooden stairs to Amy's store.

The large glass doors flew open, and Amy hollered, "Folks, we'll be starting in a few minutes. Thank you for your patience. Please make way and let our crew in. We'll open the doors in a hot minute, and you all get to meet Angel and his team." She smiled and waved. When Jade was closer, Amy whispered, "Thanks for jumping in during my hour of need. Come on back. We're almost ready to let that awesome mob of people in."

Jade spent what felt like hours taking photos of Amy with Angel's team and lots of candid ones of his interactions with fans. His display looked like Hollywood had come to town again. A monitor played his videos on a loop for those waiting in line, and the table was surrounded with life-sized posters and flags and a giant banner of Angel in his signature outfits, complete with black leather, metal studs, and an Indiana Jones-style hat.

Jade waved when the East Coast Paranormal team stepped up to Angel's table. Eliot said with a grin, "Mr. Cruz, we're super psyched that you'll be our guest on the podcast, and you'll be at an investigation with us. And we can't wait for the tour of the creepy presidential heads."

"I'm looking forward to it," Angel said.

"It's going to be awesome. Near the farm where the statues are, there's a cool bridge that's haunted and another abandoned building where all the sightings of a creature with burning red eyes have occurred. We're stoked to see what kind of contact we can make. Suz will text your assistant with the details for scoping out the property ahead of the tour. She said we can do the podcast and publicity spots then."

"I'm glad we can partner. I'm interested in what you all do," Angel said, signing Eliot's book with the flourish of John Hancock. Suz stepped closer and snapped some photos. "Marcella will walk you through the schedule, and we'll be ready to go." Angel handed off the ghost hunters to his publicist and turned his megawatt smile to the next two women in line.

As Jade made her way to the counter, she noticed the Xplorer moving with the line toward Angel. She tried to get Amy's attention in case she needed to tamp down any altercations like what happened the other evening, but her friend was laser-focused on ringing up book sales and chatting with her customers. Ernie the Xplorer laughed and chatted with the people in line in front of him.

Jade stepped closer to the table and pulled out her phone in case backup was needed. Over the buzz of the crowd noise, Jade felt her heart pounding in her temples. *Come on, girl. Just breathe. Let's see what he's planning to do before you freak out like Vivian.*

He didn't look riled up like he did at the con with Meredith. The more she watched him interact with the fans, she relaxed slightly.

Ernie paused for a couple of beats in silence and then stepped forward and slid his copy of Angel's book across the table. He thrust his right hand out for shaking and spent his two minutes with the star, gushing about how much he liked his brand and the show. *So, Ernie the Xplorer is a fan boy.* Jade let out a sigh of relief.

Not wanting to interrupt her friend who was holding court with a gaggle of customers at the front counter, Jade tapped out a quick message to Amy. **See that you're super busy. I got some good photos. I'm heading back to the store if you don't need me for anything else.**

Thank you sooooo much. I owe you big time. Make sure you've got our ghost tour on your calendar. You won't be sorry. Amy followed her reply with a string of ghost emojis.

Jade turned and almost ran into a scowling Meredith Echols. "Hello. How are you doing? Are you here for the signing?"

"No. I'm checking out the competition and waiting for someone." She turned and pushed her way through Angel's fans.

At least she was honest. Is she waiting for Randall or Ernie? Jade paused and let out a squeak. One of Angel's giant posters near where Meredith had been lurking now sported a black marker mustache.

Jade tried to suppress a snicker as she swung by the counter where Amy was unloading another box of books. She motioned for her friend to come closer. "Sorry to bother you, but I think you need to take care of one of Angel's posters. Someone decorated it with a marker."

Amy's eyes widened, and she let out a nervous giggle. "I may have to keep that one as a souvenir. I'll take care of it. Thanks for the heads up. Who would deface such a stunning face?"

Jade made her way through the crowd and down the steps, where Eliot and the Ecto-mobile were surrounded by a crowd. She waved at Noah and Cliffy.

"I hope you're going on the tour Monday. It's going to be epic," Eliot said in a booming voice.

"I'm looking forward to it," Jade replied. Eliot lumbered over next to her, and she continued, "I've never been on a paranormal investigation before."

"It'll be a blast. But it's also informative and educational," Eliot said. "We'll demo the tools and techniques we use, and if we're lucky, we'll make contact. Suz, here, is an expert at making the spirits comfortable. And the area's supposed to be rife with activity, so it should be an interesting evening for us. And there's nothing more exciting than connecting with another realm."

Suz nodded with her normal sullen look.

"The whole big heads thing sounds weird, but cool. The pictures of how they look now are apocalyptic," Cliffy said. "I'm fascinated that that was a thing back in the day?"

"Sort of," Jade said. "I remember when the park opened. The giant heads weighed thousands of pounds, and each were the size of dump truck. The park owners spent millions of dollars on the statues and the landscaping. It was a self-paced walking tour thing. The park eventually closed, and they moved the statues, and most of them were damaged during transport to their current resting place."

"That adds to the creepy factor," Cliffy said, wiggling his fingers on either side of his face.

"It's eerie looking," Eliot added. "Suz did some research, and there are some spooky spots nearby in Croaker and Norge. They go back in time to the indigenous peoples and the early days of the colonies, not to mention all the battles that were fought around here. Lots of death and destruction over the years."

Suz nodded and continued to stare at her phone.

"And Amy and Todd are bringing the hearse for the tour. With that and our baby here, this will be lit," Cliffy said.

It'll definitely be something. "I'll see you all then. Can't wait." Jade hoped she didn't look or sound as skeptical as she felt about making contact with the spirit world.

On the way back to the store, thoughts of Randall and Meredith pushed their way to the forefront of her mind. Jade mulled over what she knew about the couple and the Xplorer. *Is something salacious going on here, or am I jumping to conclusions? They all have tempers, and love and hate are a two-sided coin.*

Chapter Seven

"Laaaaaah dah di di dah," Patti sang as she ping-ponged through the showrooms with her feather duster.

"What's got you in such a good mood today?" Jade asked as she checked inventory in the toy room. "It looks like the bears and the cats are selling well again." She made notes on her clipboard and moved to the next tree.

"Simon and I are off to the CreatureCon. Whooopie. It should be a hoot. We're excited to see some of the monster movie and television actors from the seventies and eighties. Simon is such a fan, and I'm looking forward to it too." She looked over her shoulder and lowered her voice like someone was nearby to overhear their conversation. "Who knows, maybe I'll get an idea for the blog." After a couple of flicks of the duster, she flitted to the next room, humming as she looked for any dust or cobwebs on the ornaments.

When Patti joined Jade later in the back office, she said, "That crowd today cleaned out some of our baskets in the rainbow room. That's a good problem to have. Do you need for me to get anything out of storage?" Patti pulled a mirror out of her purse and checked her lipstick.

"Nope. I'll do some restocking before I head out. The multipurpose room is all cleaned up, and Bernie and I will take care of the tents later. I'm glad we had such a healthy turnout today." Jade tapped the receipt report that proved her point.

"I'm heading out," Patti said with a finger wave. "It's monster night, and I'm psyched."

"I'll be watching to see what appears on the Mermaid's blog." Jade raised her eyebrows. Before Jade could tease Patti about the gossip blog, her phone buzzed, and Nick's photo popped up on her screen. "Good afternoon. How's life at the Sheriff's Department?" she asked.

Patti waved with both hands and said in a sing-songy voice, "Hello, Sheriff Driscoll. How are you?"

"Tell Patti I said hey," he said.

"Nick said to tell you hey," Jade yelled right before the front door shut and the bells jangled.

"Life here is peachy. One stolen bike, a barking dog, a handful of parking tickets, and one found lost kid. All in a day's work. I'm getting out of here on time tonight. Wanna grab dinner if you're free?" he asked.

"Sounds like fun. What did you have in mind?"

"Seafood? The Red Herring is always my go-to place. Nothing's better than fresh seafood," he said, shuffling papers. "Is six or six-thirty okay?"

"Let's do six-thirty. I have to clean up out front and get Chloe fed."

"Sounds like a plan. I'll pick you up then. Love you."

"I love you too." A warm feeling gushed through her, and she could feel the flush in her cheeks.

Jade hustled through her restocking tasks and found herself humming like Patti. By the time she had emptied three shelves in the storage closet, Bernie and his fishing buddy, Cecil Jacobs, bustled through the back door.

"Hey, Jade. We took down all the tents. They're all in the shed with the tables and chairs. Do you need us to do anything in here?" Bernie, her part-time Santa and handyman, asked.

"Nope, the multipurpose room is back to normal, and I finished the restocking. Can I interest either of you in some of Patti's goodies?"

"Don't mind if I do," Bernie said, scooping up a handful of cookies and a brownie. "These look like Nessie. I like 'em."

"Mmm," Cecil said, taking a bite of Patti's mermaid bark and wiping crumbs off his stubbled chin. He reached for another piece of the candy.

"I heard you were taking some of the folks from the Con on of boat tours," Jade said, picking up a mermaid cookie covered in pink and purple sprinkles.

Cecil nodded so furiously that she was afraid for a moment that he might jar something loose. "It's been great. Me and the guys took out Angel Cruz and his team. He wanted to see some sites rumored to hold clues to some shipwrecks. He hinted that he wanted to come back and see some places along the York River. I can't reveal the exact sites. It's top secret, you know. We had a great time, and Angel's crew was all into the stories about the ships that sank around here during the Revolutionary War. We're planning to do it again next week when his producer arrives. This could turn into something big," Cecil said with a wink.

"Angel strongly hinted that he wants to do an episode or two about it on his show. Woooo doggie. He promised to hire Cecil here to captain the boat for the filming. That's the most exciting thing since those Love Channel Hollywood folks spent time here," Bernie said.

"We also took a marine biologist and her friend the Xplorer out for a tour of the bay. She wanted to see if there were any whales in the area. We saw a couple of dolphins and a bunch of seagulls, but no whales. She promised to come back for another try." Cecil reached for a cookie. "Business is good. I hope it's a harbinger of a profitable summer season."

"Hey, if y'all are going back to the pier, why don't you take the rest of these?" she said.

"Don't mind if we do. I'll bring your dish back later this week," Bernie said.

"Thanks so much for breaking down the tents out front. It sounds like Mermaid Bay had a great day. Sales were incredible here," Jade said, settling in her office chair.

"The town was hoppin'. And I didn't hear about any problems even though your beau and his team were on regular patrols. Tell Nick his guys did a great job. I didn't hear any fussing or grousing from anyone. And we'll be sure to take care of these sweets for you," Bernie said.

"I appreciate all you do," she said as they shuffled toward the back door.

When the door shut behind the two, Jade double-timed her closing routine. "We gotta hurry, Chloe. We need to get you fed before Nick arrives."

The round little dog's ears shot up, and she danced at the door until Jade clicked her leash to her collar. Juggling her messenger bag, purse, and the leash, Jade set the alarm with one hand and pulled the door locked behind her. The pair trotted across the empty lot and crossed Neptune Road, where the traffic was almost back to normal.

After a quick shower, Jade changed outfits three times before she settled on a white blouse with flowers, a pale pink shrug, and black stretchy pants that looked like dress pants. She pulled her long red curls into a messy bun and did a couple of quick swipes of lip gloss and mascara before a rap on the door sent Chloe into attack mode.

The French bulldog went from killer beast to huggy-bug in less than three seconds when she saw Nick and did a happy dance on her back legs to get his attention. "Hey, cutie." The little dog melted like butter when he picked her up. "You look good, too," he said, kissing Jade.

"You're looking mighty fine in your civvies. I'm glad to see you. Hopefully, the first day of the Mermaid Festival didn't cause y'all too much chaos. Oh, and Bernie said to tell you how great your guys are."

"Nah, today was easy peasy compared to some of the stuff that goes on here in the summer. You ready for dinner? Is the Red Herring still where we want to go? I'm in the mood for a full dinner and not something out of the snack machine." He set Chloe on her blanket on the couch and followed Jade outside.

Pulling the door shut, he jiggled the handle. When she locked the deadbolt, a slight grin crossed his lips. *Always the cop, even if he isn't in uniform.*

He held the door of his behemoth truck, and Jade did a little hop and grabbed the panic bar to swing into the passenger seat. By the time she buckled in, he fired the massive engine and sped down her driveway backward. She clutched the bar again to steady herself as they rocketed to the nearby restaurant.

Outside the weather-worn building that had been a fixture near the pier for years, Nick held the rustic wooden door of the restaurant and said, "It looks like we beat the rush." Wooden paneling covered all the walls of the family restaurant, and framed posters of famous hard-boiled detective and noir films were the chief decorations. The dark wood and the low lighting reminded Jade of shadowy bars in the Philip Marlowe and Sam Spade stories of yesteryear.

"Welcome, y'all," Anji Kelso hollered from behind the bar. "Sit anywhere you like. I'll be right there to get your drink orders."

The pair slid into one side of a booth that faced the large windows overlooking the bay. Gulls glided on the breeze, and several boats bobbed up and down on the horizon. Small clutches of visitors watched the builders put the finishing touches on the sand designs.

"Hey, Jade. Hey, Sheriff," Anji said, whipping out an order book and pen. "What can I get you to drink?" She batted her false eyelashes at Nick. *How does she see clearly through those lashes that look like centipede legs?*

"I'll have an unsweetened tea. No lemon," Jade said.

"Me too. And I know what I want to order. What about you?" Jade nodded, and he continued, "I'll have the crab cakes with a side salad and a baked sweet potato."

"I'll have the popcorn shrimp, with a Caesar salad, and a baked potato with butter."

"They both sound good. I'll be right back with your drinks and some hushpuppies before you miss me." She winked and trotted off toward the kitchen.

Nick rolled his eyes. "How were the crowds at your place? I saw some folks walking around with your bags."

"We had a successful day. Hopefully, it'll continue all the way through the summer season. From what I heard from Bernie and Cecil, things ran pretty smoothly today. I'm sure Vivan's pleased."

His head bobbed in a slow nod. "We both know Vivian, right? She only called me four times today. That's down from other days when she's on a tear about something. For my team, the big ticket items were traffic control and some parking violations. Nothing major. The way it should be." He paused and pointed toward the window. "Those look elaborate. We should go for a walk later and check them out. The last time I looked at them, they were working on the bases."

Jade nodded and stared out at the huge mermaid and a nearby depiction of Neptune and his trident.

"Here's a basket of hushpuppies, butter, and your salads. And your drinks," Anji said, taking two plastic cups from the bartender behind her. "Your dinners will be out shortly."

When the waitress moved on to a couple at a high-top table near the bar, Nick stabbed a hushpuppy with his knife and sliced it open. Slathering it in butter, he asked, "Want one?"

"They smell good." She pulled a crunchy one out of the basket he offered and dropped it on her napkin. "Hot. Hot. Hot."

"Here, butter'll cool it down. You okay?" He grabbed her hand and held on long after she nodded that she was fine. They stared out at the waves breaking on the sand as twilight started to descend on the bay. The fiery reds and oranges melted into a purply pink, and little dots of light from passing ships on the horizon bobbed slowly across the bay.

Nick spoke and caused Jade to startle. "Vivian looked like she had a bit too much caffeine today. She seemed to be there every second, making sure all rules were followed and all events stayed on schedule. Sorry, I didn't mean to make you jump."

"That's her normal speed." Before she could continue, Anji arrived with steaming platters. "Here you go. Let me know if y'all need anything else. I'll be back to check on you in a bit and to get your dessert orders. Save room. Strawberry pie is tonight's specialty."

Conversation paused as the pair dug into their dinners and watched the joggers, dog walkers, and seagulls in the twilight that faded to a gray that matched the color of the bay.

"This tastes great. Lunch was fast food in my vehicle, so it's nice to sit down at a table with excellent company. What else do you want to do tonight?" he asked.

"A walk on the beach sounded nice and romantic after dessert," she said with a wink.

"Of course. I always save room for pie."

When the pair pushed their plates to the center of the table, Anji swooped in and cleared. "Okay, what'll y'all have for dessert?"

"You want to split something?" he asked. "How about that gooey brownie with caramel sauce and ice cream," he replied. "And two spoons."

"Perfect," Jade added.

"Be back in a flash," Anji said.

Nick's phone jangled. "Driscoll here. What's up? Yep. Be there in a few. Call Sebastian. We're going to need some help with this."

He clicked the red button. "I'm sorry. I've got to go. There's an accident over in the neighborhood near the Pearl, and it looks bad." He pulled out cash from his wallet and dropped it on the table.

She let out a sigh that she hoped wasn't too loud. "It's fine. Go be a hero. You have work to do. Somebody needs you. I'll be home with Chloe if you finish early, but I can't guarantee all this brownie will be there."

"Here. I gotta run. Keep the change," he said, pointing to the cash after Anji set the dessert down. He kissed Jade. "Love you. See you later."

"I'll need a box," Jade said to Anji, who was still lurking nearby.

Jade boxed the dessert, licked her spoon, and hustled home as the streetlights and the lights in nearby windows popped on. When she opened her front door, Chloe shot out like a steely ball in a pinball game. "Okay, okay. Thanks for the kisses. Let me put this in the fridge, and we'll take a little walk to burn up some of that energy. I didn't get to see the sand art. We'll see what we can see even if it's dark."

Grabbing her keys and phone, she juggled them with the leash, and Chloe clamored down the steps. The pair trotted down the dark pathway to the beach. When the space opened to the dunes and the seagrass, Jade was surprised to see the sand sculptures and the pier lit up like it was Christmas by large portable lights. Jade had to blink to get used to the brightness.

Chloe and Jade cruised by a giant castle, the mermaid, Neptune, an octopus, and a giant sea dragon. *The judges had their work cut out for them. They're all amazing.*

Noise from the nearby pier caught her attention. Jade coaxed Chloe in that direction and away from a tiny white crab that was taunting the curious dog. They found a bench and creature-watched. All kinds of aliens from *Star Wars* and *Star Trek*, a yeti, and tons of zombies strolled by in the cool night air. Jade pulled her shrug closer to her and snuggled Chloe.

When the little dog started to get restless, Jade said, "Let's head back, baby. We'll see what's on the DVR, and maybe Nick will be done with the accident soon. That brownie is still in the fridge."

Red and blue lights streaked by under Suggs Pier. They bobbed and weaved, and Jade had no idea what was going on. She scooped up the Frenchie and stepped closer for a better look. The lights jumped around like some kind of frenetic game. They would disappear and then reappear like slashes in the darkness.

Jade moved closer to see what was happening. Deep under the pier, two caped characters were having an epic play battle with light sabers. The pair kicked up sand and zipped around the massive pylons like it was a giant game of tag in the dark. Chloe yipped, wanting to get in on the action.

As Jade turned to leave, the guy with the blue lightsaber tripped and landed in the loose sand with a whomp and a groan that turned into a blood-curdling scream. The blue light fell on the ground and illuminated something that looked like a pile of trash bags or clothing. Jade paused and reached for her phone. "Are you okay?" she yelled.

One of the guys whined, "Call the cops. I am totally freaking out over here. I tripped over a body. It's not moving. And I think I twisted my ankle."

Chapter Eight

Jade shifted Chloe to her hip and dialed 9-1-1 with one hand. "Do I need to ask for an ambulance?"

Both of the guys backed away from the light sabers they left in the sand next to the body. "I dunno. He didn't move when I landed on him. Ewwwww. It smells funky over there. I don't think he's breathing," said the guy who limped behind his friend.

When the call connected, she said to the dispatcher, "This is Jade Hicks. I'm under Suggs Pier. Two guys who were playing under the pier tripped over something, and they think it's a body. Could you send the police and an ambulance?"

"A body? Okay, sure. Where exactly are you?"

"We're about mid-way down the pier. There's a crowd gathering. They'll see the people."

"Okay, I've got a unit nearby, and the ambulance is on its way. Stay on the line with me until you see the deputy."

"I'm gonna be sick," one of the guys yelled.

"Sit down and take a deep breath," Jade said, covering the phone. "Deep breaths. Help is on the way." Both of the guys plopped down in the sand and whipped out their phones. None of the bystanders offered any help.

"Who was that? Are they okay? Are you in a safe place?" The dispatcher asked.

"It's the two guys who found the body. They're sitting in the sand. One of them said that he twisted his ankle when he fell. Hey, I think I see blue police lights on the other side of the dune."

Moments later, a deputy with a large flashlight hiked over the sand dune. Jade lost him in the crowd, but she spotted him edging around clusters of the people seconds later.

"Y'all step back, the deputy said. "The EMTs will need to get through here. Back it up, please. I need everyone to step back and stay put until we can get this under control."

"He's here," Jade said to the dispatcher. "You may want to send backup for him. If the police are planning to question people, there's quite a crowd gathered here already."

"Two other units are on their way. The ambulance is also about two minutes out."

"Thanks for all of your help." Jade disconnected and watched the deputy and his giant flashlight duck under the pier.

Two deputies and Nick arrived minutes later. "Jade waved as he rushed under the pier. Seconds later, two EMTs jogged over the dunes with large orange tackleboxes. The first responders swarmed the body, and more deputies arrived and set up portable lights on stands under the pier. Deputies Kate Abernathy and Sebastian Sanchez quickly corralled the crowd and started taking statements.

After what felt like hours, Jade plopped down in the sand, and Chloe curled up in a fuzzy ball in her lap. Kate finally approached with her notebook open. "Hey, Jade. What happened?"

"Hey." Jade picked up Chloe and stood. "Chloe and I were looking at the sand sculptures, and I saw some flashing blue and red lights under the pier. So we came over to see what was going on." She dusted the sand off of her pants with one hand.

"What was it?" the deputy asked.

"Two guys having a light saber battle around the pylons."

Kate nodded, and a slight smile crept across her face. "And…"

"One of them yelled. He said he tripped over something. All I could see was something that looked like a pile of clothes. Is it really a person?" she whispered.

The deputy nodded slightly as she scribbled notes. "We'll know more details about what happened after the medical examiner gets here. Anything else?"

Jade shook her head. "No. I called it in right after the guy yelled. The crowd moved this way when they heard the commotion."

"Thanks." Kate capped her pen and stepped over to the next cluster of people.

By now, police from Mermaid Bay and nearby Seaport, a forensics unit, and multiple EMTs tromped around under the pier. Jade stepped closer to the yellow tape a deputy had strung around the pier's massive pylons. The tape fluttered in the breeze as forensic techs took photos and measurements of every inch of space.

Yards away, Sebastian stood next to the two costumed light saber guys who sat in the sand. One of the twenty-somethings waved his arms around, but Jade was too far away to hear him. The other one had his head between his knees. The EMTs blocked the view around the body. Jade picked up Chloe and hugged her closely.

"Hey, you doing okay?" Nick asked, resting his hand on her shoulder.

"Hi. I'm fine. Chloe and I came out to see sandcastles. We didn't expect all of this. Everything all right from the earlier accident?"

Nick nodded. "A tourist was speeding. He took out a couple of mailboxes, hit a parked car, and met an ancient oak tree head-on. He's at the hospital with a bunch of broken bones and a head injury."

"That's awful," she said.

"Better than this vic. How come you always seem to be around when someone finds a body?" he asked with a slight grin.

"It's a small town. It's not like I went out looking for trouble." She gave him a scowl. "And I always call 9-1-1 and report stuff. The rest of this group was too busy making videos of what was going on to be bothered."

"Calm down, slugger. I was kidding. Your timing is always impeccable." He patted her shoulder. "Anything I need to know?"

"I can't think of anything. I told Kate everything I could remember. Who is it?" she whispered, hoping it wasn't a local.

Nick looked over his shoulder and lowered his voice. "It's one of the conference speakers. He's still wearing his lanyard. It's Ernie Post."

"The Xplorer," she said a little too loudly. "Sorry," she said, covering her mouth. "If it's him," she whispered, "Amy and I and about a hundred other people saw an altercation he had with Dr. Meredith Echols at the hotel. He's a podcaster with a pretty big following."

Jade looked around and leaned closer to Nick. "This may be nothing," she whispered. "But Amy and I also saw Dr. Echols go into Ernie's hotel room after the fight…she's married to one of the other speakers at the conference."

"I won't ask how you knew that. You can tell me later."

Jade shrugged both shoulders and tried out her best "who me" look.

"We'll wait for official confirmation before we release the name. Kate's trying to reach his relatives. That'll give us a jump start on the investigation before word gets out," Nick said.

"I'm sure the news that they found a body is already out on social media. This crowd whipped out their phones as soon as they heard the guy shriek… so, I'm guessing it wasn't natural causes or some freak accident?" she whispered.

He shook his head. "There were signs of strangulation, ligature marks on his neck. But keep it to yourself." Nick closed his eyes for a beat. He suddenly looked five years older. He ran a hand through his dark, wavy hair. "It's going to be a late night. I'll call you when I can, and we'll do a redo on dinner and dessert. I may be tied up on this for a long time."

She blew him a kiss. "Go save the world. And when you're done, you'll know where I'll be. But I can't guarantee any of that caramel brownie will be left. After the shock of the body under the pier, I may need the comfort food."

He winked and jogged under the pier.

Who would kill Ernie the Xplorer? Was it related to his altercation with Meredith, or was it some rando thing? And what is going on between Meredith and Ernie, and Meredith and Randall? Thoughts of all the people she met at the con bounced around Jade's head and gave her a slight headache. Chloe got her second wind and started digging in the sand. Jade tried to hurry the pudgy dog along, but the Frenchie had other ideas. She was on a sniff tour of the sand dunes.

The chilly night air off the bay and Ernie's murder sent a shiver through Jade. She pulled her shrug closer to her with one hand and nudged Chloe along with the other. "We have some things to do before we call it a night. Time to go."

Chloe reluctantly acquiesced and trotted beside Jade to the bungalow. Once inside, Jade rubbed her arms and made herself a coffee to warm up. She pulled the brownie out of the fridge and settled in one of her dining room chairs. Jade opened her laptop and made a spreadsheet of all the people they had encountered from the con. Then she added any details she could remember.

"Chloe, somebody said that Ernie the Xplorer had some kind of thing going on about a discovery or a hypothesis that was hush-hush with Angel Cruz, but at the book signing, he turned into fanboy when they talked. It didn't seem like they were colleagues with a shared project. It was almost like they had never met. He also had a full-on word brawl with Dr. Meredith Echols." She tapped her capped pen to her lip. "And we find out that Meredith, who is still married to Randall, went to Ernie's hotel room after the altercation. She seemed casual and relaxed, so I don't get the sense she was breaking in to do anything nefarious. It wasn't like she was sneaking around. Wow. Lots of players with all kinds of possible motives. Let's see what we can find on Angel, Meredith, and Ernie."

On a whim, she pulled up the *Beach Comber's* website. The town's weekly was the primo source of gossip for the locals and popular among the tourists for coupons and discounts on things to do. "Nosy" Nell Jones usually had her finger on the town's gossip pulse and an ear on her police scanner. Nothing on that site or on Patti's *Mermaid Whispers* page yet about the body under the pier. Jade fired off two quick texts about the body to Patti and Nell. "Chloe, don't give me that judgy look. I didn't reveal who it was." Jade smiled when Patti's response was almost instantaneous.

Thanks for the hot lead. Hadn't heard anything about it here at CreatureCon.

Her phone beeped again with Nell's reply. **I'm en route to get the deets.**

Thx.

"Well, Ernie is a podcaster and a cryptozoologist. He's very vocal on social media about anyone who tries to debunk tales about mysterious creatures. He's also a fantasy writer with a series about sea monsters." She googled his books and found his website with a string of outdated blog posts. The last book came out three years ago. "Hmm. From some of his posts, it seems that he and Randall are good friends. They're together a lot in his pictures. Uh, oh. This must be related to the fight with Meredith." Jade pulled her laptop closer and read quite a few of Ernie's disparaging posts about Meredith, who he claimed had a bad habit of co-opting others' research. I wonder if I can find anything to corroborate his accusation. That might be a reason to want to hush him up. Right now, Meredith's relationship with the Xplorer seems to be my biggest lead.

* * *

Jade jumped and woke with a start. Her laptop had gone into sleep mode hours ago. She touched the keyboard. "Four-thirty. Chloe, why'd you let me fall asleep here? And now I'm stiff as a board." She stood and stretched her arms, legs, and neck.

Her guard dog snored softly from under the lap blanket on the sofa. "I see you nodded off, too."

She moved the mouse and closed her spreadsheet, but paused when she saw the paragraphs about Meredith and Ernie. *Why do thoughts of those two keep banging around in my brain. This whole thing is like a giant onion. Lots of layers upon layers.*

Jade spent the next hour searching for more about Ernie and Meredith. "Ah ha," she said loudly enough to disturb Chloe's Zzzzzs. "Ernie was once a teaching assistant for Meredith in her marine biology department. He wrote scathing blog posts about how she abused her staff, stole students' ideas, and lashed out at anyone who didn't meet her prissy standards. He had a celebratory vlog post on the day he left her tutelage and transferred to another school with a cryptozoology program."

Still not interested in any of this, Chloe rolled over. This time, Jade shut off her laptop and the lights. She picked up the snoozing dog and padded off to bed. Thoughts of all the players banged around in her head and pushed the urge to sleep out of the way.

Chapter Nine

Foot traffic in the store on Sunday was nonexistent. *Everyone must be on the beach or at the CreatureCon.* Jade cranked up the Christmas rock tunes to keep her company while Chloe snored in her bed. When there were no more online orders to fill, Jade did a quick walk-through. The Nessie, Bumble, and Yeti ornaments were selling well. She put in another order to make sure they didn't run out.

Jade settled in at her desk and pulled up her spreadsheet of notes on the Xplorer. Her brain flitted to thoughts of Meredith and Ernie. What would cause someone to kill him and then abandon him under the pier? *I guess it could be a random crime, but my gut tells me that this was personal. Someone got close enough to choke him.*

Footsteps resounded on the wooden porch outside and interrupted the discussion she was having in her head. More rustling on the other side of the door caused her to make her way to the lobby. When no one entered the store, she shooed Chloe behind the dividing door. Jade peeked out the front window. No one in sight. One of her white rockers moved like it had been recently abandoned or a ghost had taken up residence on her porch. Jade pulled open the door.

"Oh, hi," Randall Medlin said from the other side of the porch. He was leaning over the railing. She almost didn't recognize him with his bedhead and rumpled clothes. "I was gathering my thoughts before I came in to see you." He looked nothing like the suave professor who charmed everyone the other day.

"What kind of thoughts?" she asked, trying to figure out what he wanted.

"I, uh, I heard from Josie over at the B and B that you were adept at solving murders. I need your help. I mean, we need your help. Josie said you've helped solve at least three murders. You're quite the detective."

Before Jade could respond, he continued, "I've been at the police station for hours. They woke us up in the middle of the night and dragged us over for questioning that went on forever. They let me go before Mer, but I hung around until she was finished. She looked like she'd been run over by a herd of wild horses when we were done. I have known her since college, and she is always the cool and collected professional with the sharp tongue, but she looked whipped today. I've never seen her this scared before." He paused and stared at something across the street. He ran both hands through his hair, causing it to stick up in all directions. "I fell in love with Meredith's spunk. She never backs down from a fight. It was the classic love tragedy. We got married, focused on our careers, didn't pay enough attention to each other, and eventually went our separate ways." His voice faded as he stared at the bay in the distance.

Before Jade could comment, he cleared his throat and continued, "When she realized I was making tons more money on the con circuit than she was with her precious research, she came along and reaped the rewards. For a couple who's separated, we spend quite a bit of time together. It's been good. We're talking about reconciling. That is if she'd make up her mind." A slight smile tugged at the corners of his mouth, and he continued to stare across the street.

"I need your help," he repeated before she could get a word in. "The police told us not to leave town, and they want to talk to her again today. And if that's not enough bad news, she notified the university about the situation, they put her on unpaid leave until all this gets sorted out. They told her they didn't want this to be a distraction for her students. She's devastated. I've never seen her this torn up. Her career and her reputation are her life. Meredith's had her share of fights over the years, but she's not a murderer. You've got to help us. Josie said that you also have the sheriff's ear. We need all the assistance we can get right now. Would you think about it?" He pulled out a business card and jotted a number on the back. "This is my cell. Call or text me anytime. I don't have a clue what to do next. This is way out of my wheelhouse." He blew out a large puff of air and sank into the nearest rocking chair.

Randall buried his head in his hands. "I know Meredith. She didn't kill Ernie. Ernie was my friend. We worked together on a couple of projects. He's fun, but he liked to stir up controversy, and he had no qualms about going after anyone who thought too highly of themselves. He kinda took it on as his mission to take them down a few pegs. I'm scared that the police will see Meredith as an easy target because she and Ernie squabbled constantly, and they have a history." His grimace took on a pained look. "They can't see the real killer because they can't look past us. I'm not going to let them railroad either one of us. We don't need this right now. Just when things were improving between us." He blew out another breath through his nose and slouched in the chair.

Jade fished a card from her phone case. "I'm not sure what I can do, but I can take a look into a couple of things."

"Thank you." He jumped up and grabbed her card. His countenance brightened, and he shook both of her hands. The grimace melted away, and the sparkle returned to his eyes. "You don't know how much I appreciate this. Let's have lunch or dinner soon, so I can fill you in on everything."

Gently freeing herself, she asked, "Would you like to come inside for some coffee or tea?"

"Coffee sounds good." Randall held the door and then followed her inside. "I like your store. The monster ornaments will be perfect on my desk." He fingered a sparkling Nessie as he walked by the two large trees in the lobby. "I bought this one for Mer when we were here the other day. She'd never admit it in public, but the famous inhabitant of the Scottish Loch is her favorite."

"You said you and Meredith met at college," Jade said, pulling out two 'Tis the Season mugs and coffee pods.

He nodded as the coffee maker sputtered and roared to life. "We were both in the science program. I started off with a traditional degree. Cryptozoology took off much later. There's still a stigma around it at most universities, but I don't care. I'm laughing all the way to the bank. It pays way better than what tenured profs make, and I don't have to jump through all the hoops of scientific academia and the publish or perish requirements. Even Meredith realized that. She joined in on her own terms as the naysayer of the circuit, but every good wrestling match needs a villain, right? She was cashing in and socking funds away for retirement. If her beloved tenure slips away, it may be all that she has left." He let out a heavy sigh.

"I'm sorry. I'm new to all this. I just learned what cryptid is. What is cryptozoology actually?" she asked.

"It's a subculture of the sciences. Most of the snotty academics consider it a pseudoscience." The corner of his lip curled into a slight sneer. "But according to the Oxford English Dictionary, 'it's the 'study of unknown, legendary, or extinct animals whose existence or survival to the present day is disputed or unsubstantiated.'" *Sounds like he has used his elevator speech before.* Jade nodded, and he continued, "Meaning we're always looking for the presence of extinct species or things people think are extinct. Or creatures that have never been cataloged except in legends."

When the machine finished gurgling, Jade handed him the mug. "There's creamer and sugar over there."

He tipped his chin and reached for the sugar. Three teaspoons later, his frantic stirring created a small vortex in his mug.

While she waited for her drink to brew, Jade continued her probing. "Who would want to kill Ernie? From what I read, he's an author, public speaker, and a podcaster."

"I honestly have no idea, but I'm sure he's ruffled feathers along the way. He has no filter. I've been racking my brain for hours thinking about it. He was a showman who felt even bad publicity was better than no publicity. He was always jumping on projects to get his name in the headlines. And when he wasn't out there mugging for the cameras or the microphones, he was insulting people on his blog. If I were you, I'd start there. I'm sure there's no shortage of haters. I heard he had some epic Twitter battles years ago."

He took a couple of sips of his coffee and set the mug on the table. "Meredith doesn't shy away from a conflict either, and she digs in when she knows she's right. She's back at the Pearl talking to her lawyer and publicist about how to spin this. She can handle herself blindfolded in an argument about science and the viability of a theory. I'm worried that she's not ready for all the police scrutiny, and she won't handle it well when she can't control the situation. She'll be backed into a corner. Mer is usually large and in charge when it's her specialty, but a murder investigation is a whole 'nother animal. She's lying low for a couple of days. She's tired of the press chasing after her already."

He rose suddenly. "I have to get back and check on her. Call me as soon as you hear anything. I appreciate you helping us with this. It's a matter of life and death. I can't let this police investigation derail our plans. We had everything nailed down, and now this." Randall jammed his hands in his pockets and strode through the door. The bells jangled and sent Chloe into security mode until she realized no one but Jade was there.

Chapter Ten

"Well, that was interesting, Chloe." The little dog turned her boxy head like she was puzzled, too. "Let's see what we can find on the big wild web."

Jade handed the pudgy dog a peanut butter treat from her stash in the cabinet and settled in for another search of all the players. Was Ernie's murder related to something in his personal life or from his complicated, very public life in the spotlight?

After a couple of hours, she stood and stretched. "I found a ton of stuff, but nothing that points to any single theory. Randall was right about all the vitriolic comments on the Xplorer's blog and social media platforms. I felt like I needed a shower after reading all that dirt."

Not really that interested, Chloe rolled over in her puffy bed and let out a snort.

"Thanks for that feedback," Jade said. "Most of Meredith's info is the polished stuff on the university's webpage or her own website. It's chock full of her papers and research. The academic stuff is so boring compared to all the back and forth on Ernie's blog. Then, there are the Meredith mentions on the other cryptid pages. She is the evil witch of the cryptozoology circuit. The biggest complaint is that she's a nonbeliever, and she goes out of her way to be high and mighty when she attempts to debunk things. She's not likable. The articles about Ernie are in two camps, too. They are either doting fans who follow him from con to con or from haters who think he jumps on the bandwagon of every hot new trend in order to cash in." *Some of the comments are over the top. The devotion feels almost cult-like, and the criticisms border on threatening. How does anyone live with all of this all the time?*

"Interesting," Jade said, hopping up for a drink of water. "I think I've exhausted what mere mortals can do on the big web unless I want to dive deep into the sightings and theories of the creatures. I'm not ready for a bunch of hair-raising stories that will give me nightmares. I think I'll save that stuff for later. I'm more interested in the real characters at CreatureCon."

She pulled out her phone and texted Todd's friend Delia.

Hey, lady. I have another puzzle. Would you have some time to do some creeping around the dark web for me?

Almost instantly, the little dots started flashing, and Jade's pulse ticked up a couple of beats. If anyone could find out dark secrets, it was Delia Simmons. She had helped Todd last summer when a cyber-stalker tried to ruin his business. She knows the ins and outs of the dark web and a lot about the secret hiding places.

I'm between projects, so it's perfect timing. Whatcha thinking about? Delia responded.

You always find good stuff. We have a CreatureCon going on. One of the speakers was found dead. I'd like to know what you can dig up on Dr. Meredith Echols, Dr. Randall Medlin, and Ernie Post, aka the Xplorer.

Who's the victim?

The Xplorer, Jade typed.

Awww. Folks who will be shocked. He is a name that I recognize. I'll see what I can find for you.

You're the best. Let me know how much I owe you. I appreciate your superpowers. And I need you to keep this on the down low until the police notify the next of kin.

Not a problem. Your quests are fun. I'm glad to help.

You made my day. I can't wait to see what you dig up, Jade tapped into her phone.

Delia replied with a string of smiley faces and monster emojis.

Jade set her phone down and rested her head on her folded arms. Delia had a knack for finding the dirt. She helped Todd when his hot dog stand was attacked by a flood of bad reviews. She used her freaky computer skills to find all kinds of information in the dark corners of the web where mere mortals fear to tread. *Hmmm. That sounds like a great voice-over for some kind of documentary on Delia's special skills. Nope. She wouldn't like the spotlight. Delia, whose real name is Lakeisha, likes to fly under the radar. For someone who lives with technology twenty-four-seven, she has a very small social media presence. She's kinda like one of Randall and the Xplorer's elusive creatures.*

Jade stood and stretched. "I'm pretty much done for the day. I don't think anyone will miss us if we close up a bit early. Let me do my walk-through, and we'll head out."

Chloe raised one eyebrow. "I'll take that as tacit agreement. Be back in a flash."

After she grabbed her things, leashed up Chloe, and set the alarm, the pair hustled down the back steps. Chloe, recharged from all of her naps, took off like a shot. She wanted to explore the vacant lot next door.

After the chubby dog smelled everything there was to smell, she finally conceded to Jade's coaxing to move in the direction of home. Stopping suddenly on the sidewalk, Chloe snorted and sniffed the air and stared at Hot Diggity Dogs across the street.

"Todd's place smells good. You hungry?"

Chloe yipped and trotted down the sidewalk. "Dinner it is," Jade replied, picking up her pace to keep up with the energized Frenchie.

While they stood in line at Todd's front counter, Jade mentally flipped through the players who had interactions with Ernie. Were Randall and Meredith really ready to reconcile or was that wishful thinking on his part? And was Meredith leading a double life outside of her professional persona and her resting Grinch face? The murderer could have been any one of the hundreds of con attendees or the online detractors who had a beef with Ernie. Jade made a note to go through the con staff and presenters again when she got home. *I've got to find a way to narrow this pool of people down.*

"What can I get for you?" a magenta-haired teen behind the counter asked, interrupting Jade's planning.

"Oh, hi. Could I get a regular dog with only mustard and a giant pretzel to go?"

The teen nodded, and Todd yelled from the back, "Hey, Jade. Tell Chloe I put her favorite on the grill to go with your order."

"She said thanks. Stopping by was her idea tonight."

The teen at the register with the Bethany nametag had a puzzled look on her face as she handed Jade her card.

"Chloe, my four-legged sidekick," Jade said, pointing down.

Bethany looked over the counter and smiled. Then she greeted the next customer.

Jade sat in an empty booth to wait for the order, and Chloe sniffed around on the floor in search of any discarded yummies. A dark memory flashed across Jade's brain when she glanced at the large plate-glass window that a guy broke last summer when he tossed a weight through it. Closing her eyes for a second, she reminded herself that no one was hurt. But Jade could still hear the crack and the tinkling of the broken glass raining down on everything. That day was terrifying, but she calmed her racing thoughts by reminding herself that she was able to follow the clues that eventually led her to the person who was behind all of the attacks on Todd. She let out a long breath. That case had seemed impossible at first. Just like this one. *Persistence, girl. That's all it takes—and a little bit of luck.*

Her phone rang, and she hesitated when she didn't recognize the number. "Hello."

"Hey. It's Randall. I wanted to see if you've found out anything yet. I told Meredith that you would help us, and she's happy. Or as happy as she gets."

She pulled out the card he gave her from her phone cases. *That's not the number he gave me.* "I'm working on a couple of different angles. I'll let you know what I find. It may be a couple of days before I can get back with you. There are so many leads to look into."

"That's a good thing, right? I'm glad you're making progress. Mer and I are both a bit edgy about all of this. Regular updates, even if they're texts, would go a long way to ease our minds," he said in a softer tone.

"I'll do my best."

"I know you're up to the task. I've heard glowing things about you from people around here. Plus, we have a bunch of events and a book launch coming up soon, and we don't want to hang around Mermaid Bay if we don't have to. Uh, no offense. Sorry. I'm a little out of sorts today. But you know what I mean. We need to get on with our lives together."

Ignoring his jab about Mermaid Bay, Jade said, "I'll do what I can."

"Jade, hey, Jade, your order's up," Todd yelled from the grill.

"I've gotta go. I'll be in touch." Jade hopped up to get her food. *I know they're stressed out about the murder and the investigation, but sometimes I get the feeling that he's focused on himself and controlling the situation. We'll see how this goes. I hope I don't regret offering to look into this for him.*

Jade and Chloe hustled outside. The promise of food was the dog's only focus as she trotted down the sidewalk toward home. Jade's phone rang again, and she swallowed a sigh when she realized it was Delia and not Randall again. "Hey, lady. What's up?"

"Hey, Nancy Drew, I found some preliminary stuff that was too good not to share. You have some time now?"

"Sure. You work fast.

"There's a lot of stuff out there. Let's see. Where to begin…Meredith and Randall have been off-and-on as a thing for about twenty years. They met in college. He is a hundred percent believer in the cryptozoology world. He left his academic science life behind and never looked back. It seems that Dr. Meredith has only been at her current university job for about six years. She left her previous one quietly after an investigation. It seems she had an affair with one of her students. And drum roll, please. And the other party was none other than Ernie Post. I want to do more research on this, but it sent up red flares in my brain when I found it. There was some spat after that, and Ernie made it his goal to say nasty things about her whenever he got the chance."

"I'm not sure the Ernie-Meredith thing is over. One day at the con, we saw them in a very public argument, and then she went upstairs to his room."

"Interesting. Very interesting. I'll see if I can find out anything about a secret romance," Delia said.

"You have some amazing skills. What do I owe you?"

"Nothing. Absolutely nothing. I love digging up dirt for you. You're all about solving mysteries and righting wrongs. It makes me feel like I'm doing stuff for the good of humankind. I will help you out anytime. I can't decide if I'm Bess or George to your Nancy."

Jade laughed. "You are the superhero. I'm sending you another chocolate basket to keep you sugared up during your research and gaming sessions."

"Deal. I'll let you know what else I find. These characters have interesting lives. I've got to get back online." Delia clicked off before Jade could reply.

Before she had time to put her phone away, it alerted again with a text from Amy. **Don't forget we're on for the paranormal tour tomorrow night at the farm with the big Presidential heads. I'm saving you a seat in the hearse. Can Nick make it in light of you-know-what?**

Probably not. His team is working OT on the murder. But I'll be there.

Sorry he can't make it. Glad you can. Amy ended her text with a string of ghost emojis.

Jade replied with a thumbs up and a skull and crossbones.

So, Meredith and Ernie have a deeper connection and a love-hate relationship that spans many years. What else is lurking from their past? Let's see if I can get Randall to divulge any details that'll help in our search.

Chapter Eleven

Jade spent the afternoon filling online orders as Chloe followed her from showroom to showroom. The foot traffic that was heavy in the morning slowed to a trickle and had all but dried up. "Neville's not here to play with you today. I know you miss your buddy." She reached down and patted the dog's head. "You pretend to be sworn enemies, but you really do like him. Let's go get these ready to ship, and then we'll call it a day."

After the delivery driver took the two bins of orders, Jade locked the door behind him. "That's a wrap," she said, zipping through the store and making sure everything was in its place.

They double-timed it home, and Jade swapped out her strappy sandals for socks and her high-top sneakers. *Maybe I should wear my work boots. I hope the place isn't all overgrown and full of snakes and bugs.* She did a full body shudder and tried to shake off the creepy-crawly feeling.

"Okay, kiddo. You've been fed and walked. You take a nice nap, and I'll be back as soon as I can." She pulled on a black hoodie and fluffed her ponytail.

Chloe opened one eye and rolled over for more snoozes. "See ya, guard dog," Jade said with a snicker.

As she approached Mermaid Books's parking lot, Todd let out a blast of the hearse's musical horn. Bon Jovi's "Dead or Alive" echoed off the buildings and caused heads to turn. Jade raised one eyebrow. *It's a good thing Vivian's not around. She'd have something to say about his vehicle and all the noise.*

Amy bounced around the small crowd like she'd had six coffees. After greeting each person, she marked their names off on her clipboard and handed them a Mermaid Haunts flashlight. She hurried over to where Jade stood and hugged her. "I'm so glad you could come. Like it?" Amy modeled the logoed flashlight.

"Excellent give-away. I didn't think to bring one," Jade said, pressing the button on the handle.

"It's gonna get incredibly dark out there with no ambient light, so voila, and they're newly branded," Amy said. "Todd and I are officially business partners. Delia's doing our spooky website and social pages. I am soooooo excited. It's almost time to launch this thing." She cleared her throat and waved her arms around. "People. Paranormal-loving people. We're heading out for our amazing adventure to the land of the giant presidents. I'm Amy Pemberton, and my partner, Todd Brickman, and I want to welcome you to the inaugural tour. We are so excited that we were able to secure permission to view the site of the giant Presidential busts. These historic sculptures were once part of the Presidents' Park that closed in 2010. We are also so pleased to announce that we have an exclusive presentation tonight with the famous East Coast Paranormal investigators. They plan to show us their behind-the-scenes methods and their cool equipment. And then, if we're lucky, will make contact with the great beyond. So y'all grab your flashlights and find a seat inside the Hauntsmobile. That hunky guy is my partner, Todd, and he'll be our driver tonight. Sit back and relax, and we'll get this show on the road. And be prepared to be amazed."

Amy did a quick count and yelled, "Todd, they're all yours."

Jade slid onto one of the bench seats in the back next to a group of twenty-somethings who were chatting about a guy they met at CreatureCon.

Amy interrupted and stuck her head in the back from the passenger seat. "And another thing. I didn't do name tags because we'll be in the dark, but I want to check names one more time before we head out, and this will be your intro to your fellow travelers if you haven't chatted yet. Nod or wave when I call your name. Callie Owens, Ethan Rogers, Merri Chu, Dave Krebs, Marcus Alexander, Xander Davis, and my good friend, Jade Hicks." When everyone nodded, she said, "Todd, let's roll."

Jade's eyes widened when someone on the other side of the vehicle said, "Did you hear that they hauled Meredith Echols in for questioning for the murder of the Xplorer?"

"I heard it was twice," the gal with the curly hair added. "She's a prime suspect. I also heard that her university may even expel her for violating its code of ethics. She's in serious trouble."

"Serves her right. She is always in the middle of stuff," a guy with a buzzcut said. "It wouldn't surprise me at all if she did it. If you read reviews from her students, they all hate her. I saw her pick a fight with the dead guy." The guy with the fauxhawk next to him snickered. "Well, he wasn't dead when she picked the fight with him. You know what I meant."

"I'm still going to her panel this weekend. I'll be bummed if it's cancelled. I wouldn't miss it for anything. You know the press will be there in droves, and I bet the police even have undercover people in the audience to watch her," the woman with the white-blond hair said.

The talk slowly shifted to multiple conversations about the con and what they were hoping to see or hear tonight at the ghost hunt. The audience was almost evenly split between those excited to make contact with the dead and those who were skeptical and wanted to see for themselves. Jade sat back in her seat and was a little disappointed that there was no more talk of the Xplorer's murder.

Todd pulled off of the main road into the small town of Croaker and followed a paved but rutted road through the woods. The sun slipped low behind the trees as a large metal gate stood sentry where the pavement ended. "Sorry about this, folks," Todd said. "The driveway to the farm isn't paved, so hang on. We're going to give the struts in this baby a workout." He drove slowly through the open gate.

After about five minutes of bouncing around in the back of a hearse with a bunch of complete strangers, Jade tried to brace herself with one hand on the bench and the other on the ceiling. Todd let loose with another horn blast as he pulled in next to the Ecto-mobile, a minivan, and several cars.

Everyone piled out and took selfies next to the *Ghostbusters* replica and Todd's hearse. Anticipation zinged through Jade as she listened to the excited conversations of her tourmates. At about the time the novelty of the vehicles wore off, Cliffy and Norm trudged around the bend. "Hey, guys. We're almost set up and ready for you all. If you'll put on your flashlights and follow us. The ground is kinda uneven, so watch your step," Cliffy said.

Norm waved both arms like he was some kind of giant bird flapping his wings. "This way. We have a ton of equipment to show you, and then we'll give you some time to explore while we wait for it to get dark enough for us to make contact. Watch out for the briars on the edge of the path. They bite," he said, rubbing his forearm.

The group trudged behind the two paranormal investigators in small groups, with Amy and Todd bringing up the rear. When the path curved, they walked around another metal gate that led to a field surrounded on three sides by the woods. "This is what the owner is calling the Ruins, and some people call it Hankins Folly. He wants to open some kind of park that showcases the busts as they are today," Norm said.

"Did any of you see these statues at their original location?" Cliffy asked. When no one responded, he continued, "Well, it was a garden setting that people could wander through and see the monuments of the presidents up to George W. Bush. The park went belly up, and the statues were moved here. Before we send you all off to commune with the former presidents, our own fearless leader, the president of the East Coast Paranormal Society, wants to introduce you to the team."

"Thanks, Cliffy. I'm Eliot Kellogg. You've already met Cliffy Johnson and Norm Wendt. They've been part of the team for about five years now. This is Drew Nelson, our historian, and Noah Jenkins, our tech guy. And last but not least is Suz Brewster. She is our medium or our conduit to the other side. So, what you're about to see tonight is a mix of technology that you can see and the connection with other dimensions that you'll be able to feel. We want y'all to have an immersive experience. Noah, you're up. Let's see some of the cool gadgets that the team uses."

Noah cleared his throat and stepped forward with a device in each hand, and Drew followed him with an armload of other items. "This is an EMF meter, and it registers electromagnetic fields. We use this to see fluctuations that could indicate paranormal activity. We have to be careful and not move too fast with it because it could give off false positives. Like most of our equipment, it's very sensitive. And this here," Noah said, waving another device that looked like a tape recorder, "is an EVP Recorder. It captures electronic voice phenomena, which could be proof that we made a connection. We're pretty far away from manmade things like electrical lines that will interact with our tools. So that's good. I do need to ask everyone to turn off their phones until we finish the investigation. They could disrupt some of our equipment." The crowd pulled out phones from pockets and purses, and shut them off as Noah continued, "Oh, and Cliffy back there has an old, tried but true tool. It's the very basic divining rod. If used properly, the rod and the person holding it become the vehicle to summon the spirits. We'll be using all of these and some other equipment tonight."

Cliffy held up his Y-shaped rod and showed it to the group. "They're very effective and have been used in ghost hunting, among other things, for hundreds of years. They're a simple, forked stick. Some are wooden, and others are made of metal. Sometimes, they're called a dowsing stick or a witching stick. Some paranormal researchers snub them as antiquated, and others shy away from their power. It is low-tech, but it's a strong tool that some people don't know how to harness. The divining rod uses the human body as a conduit, and many people don't want to put themselves in that position when contact is made with an unknown spirit. Our team is made up of Gen-Zers and Millennials, so we tend to gravitate toward the high-tech options. But we'll show you how it's used. Any questions?"

"That rod looks like a big stick to me. Why would someone be afraid to use it? I don't see how it can be helpful," the curly-headed woman across from Jade said.

Suz cleared her throat and stepped forward. "It may be simple, but it's effective. Many people believe in the device's power. They've been used to find water sources, minerals, hidden treasure, and graves. There are also reports that some people have used them to detect or reveal criminals or other evil-doers. But when you use them to summon a spirit, you don't always know its intentions. If your body is the connector between the worlds, you don't know if you're interacting with a benevolent or malevolent being. And it's your body. A lot of people don't want to take that chance and put themselves in a dangerous situation."

"Why did you choose this area?" the blond in a dark hoodie asked.

"This property used to be a family farm, and there's a cemetery plot on the other side of these trees. Who knows what's in these woods? We're close to some battlefields, and we have all those presidents here. Many of them had tragedies befall them. We felt that all those factors would make for a favorable place to explore," Drew said.

"What kind of spirits do you normally encounter?" a tall guy with a thick beard asked.

"Some spirits are trapped in our world and feel lost. Others are mischievous, and some are downright evil," Suz said. "We've encountered all types. Usually, we find the trapped souls, and every once in a while, we get a prankster who likes to play tricks with our equipment. Those make our encounters interesting. The jokester is usually very active and fun to interact with. Though we have been to some sites with malevolent spirits, and that is a whole other kind of experience. Any other questions?" When no one said anything, Suz added, "Then go enjoy your walk through the final resting place of the presidential statues. Be careful where you step, and be back here ready to go in a half hour."

"Thanks, guys," Eliot said. "It'll take us a few minutes to get set up. We took some readings earlier, and this spot is prime for some paranormal activity. We need a couple of minutes to get everything ready, so why don't y'all use this time to explore? The humongous guests of honor are over there." He pointed toward the large white statues in the distance. "They're not in any chronological order, so if you're interested in a particular president, you'll have to look around. See you all back here in thirty. And if you forget, Amy has an airhorn that she's not afraid to use."

Amy caught up to Jade and whispered, "I hope we get the fun ghosts. I don't really want the *Exorcist* experience." She shuddered and pulled her jacket closer around her. "I didn't think about contacting Satan's spawn when I booked this."

Jade patted her arm. "I think we'll be okay. If it's anything like those TV shows, we'll probably hear knocks and whistles and feel an eerie breeze."

Jade squeezed Amy's arm and made her friend jump.

"I don't care what Noah said. If it turns into a seventies horror movie, I'm whipping out my phone to record it," Amy said.

The participants wandered off in small clusters. Jade and Amy followed the beam from Todd's bobbing flashlight through the overgrown field.

"Today has been so cool," Amy squealed. "Angel Cruz and his team were here earlier to do a taping for the podcast and some promotional videos. And he even brought a photographer with him to do a photo shoot on and around the statues. I got tons of pictures of him. The place looked apocalyptic in the daylight, and it looks downright unnerving right now."

"I'm not jealous or anything," Todd said with a smirk. "And the ambiance adds to the mystique of the ghost hunt. It's like the anticipation of going through a haunted house or cresting a hill on a roller coaster that makes the experience."

"And there's no need for you to be jealous, my pookie bear," Amy cooed, pinching him on the arm. "You're my main squeeze."

"Let's get some pics next to the statues. Got a favorite?" Todd asked, pulling out his phone.

"I want to see JFK and Teddy Roosevelt. Let's go see if we can find them. What an interesting quest, and if we add hide and seek. It'll be awesome," Amy said. She smacked Todd lightly again on the arm and yelled, "You're it" before she took off running.

When Todd dashed off after Amy, Jade found herself alone on the path. The size of the statues and the shadows they cast gave Jade the willies. Most of the figures had some kind of serious damage, giving the landscape a dystopian feel like something out of a Mad Max film. Jade froze for a moment. *This reminds me of the scene with the half-buried Statue of Liberty at the end of the original Planet of the Apes. Yep. It's the perfect spot for a ghost hunt.* A tingle of excitement spread through Jade as she hustled to keep up with Amy and Todd on their search for Amy's favorite presidents.

Chapter Twelve

The last rays of the sun disappeared behind the nearby trees. The darkness and the damaged faces of the former presidents created a haunted house vibe that sent a chill rocketing through Jade. Every night noise made her jump. *Girl, you're letting your imagination run wild.* She took a couple of deep breaths to calm the fluttery feeling in her core.

"This way. Come and find me," Amy yelled. "What a cool place to run around. I like this better than the original park. Jade heard pounding footsteps, and Amy yelled, "Olly, Olly Oxen Free."

Jade hid behind a statue and sucked in a mouthful of air when she realized she was hiding behind Lincoln. The damage to the head looked eerily similar to what happened to the real president. Shaking off the creepiness, she ducked behind a statue she couldn't identify and listened for any sign of Todd or Amy. A stick cracked nearby, and footsteps approached. Jade slid behind the next statue. She held her breath, listening for sounds of someone approaching. Jade's heartbeat banged out a drum solo in her head. She tried breathing deeply, but endorphins and adrenaline coursed through her veins and drowned out the night noises around her.

Another twig snapped behind her, and she whipped her head around, looking for any flashlights or movement. She measured the seconds that passed by the staccato beats of her heart.

A scream echoed across the field and seemed to bounce off the statues. It was hard to pinpoint the source. Jade strained to listen for any movement. *Okay, now I'm freaking out.* After what seemed like forever, she flipped on her flashlight and headed in the direction of the scream. *This better not be one of Amy's ploys to win the game. Actually, I wouldn't put it past her and her competitive streak.*

A second high-pitched scream dispelled any thoughts of a prank, and Jade picked up her pace over the bumpy terrain.

Near the edge of the woods, Cliffy pointed at something on the ground and let out another blood-curdling scream. "I can deal with ghosts, but actual cold bodies," he stammered as Drew and Noah surrounded him.

Jade quickly pulled out her phone and turned it on. She stepped closer to the men who continued to stare at the ground. The group grew with each second. Circles of light from the flashlights danced around the body. A female in jeans and a dark T-shirt lay sprawled out between two of the giant presidential statues.

Eliot leaned over and felt for a pulse. He shook his head as Jade let out a little squeak. A long blond braid peeked out from under the woman. Jade stepped closer for a better view as an icy sensation spread through her body and crashed in the bottom of her stomach. Her knees felt wobbly.

Taking a deep breath to calm the bats inside her, Jade called 9-1-1 and waited for what felt like an eternity for the call to connect. "James City County Emergency Dispatch. What's your emergency?"

"I'm Jade Hicks. I'm with a group here in Croaker. We're taking a tour of the farm where the giant Presidential busts are, and one of the guys in the tour group tripped over a body. She's not moving. He checked for a pulse…"

"And she's cold," Eliot yelled. "I think she's crossed over."

Suz grabbed Eliot's arm and whispered something to him as the dispatcher said, "I heard him. I'm sending police and rescue to the scene. It may take a few minutes. Can they get on the property?"

"Does anyone know if the gates are unlocked?" Jade asked loudly.

"The gates are open," Todd said from somewhere behind her.

"Where are you on the property?" the dispatcher asked.

"Near the giant statues," Jade said as Todd reached for her phone. He quietly gave detailed directions to get from the main road to the field. After a long pause, he said, "Yep. There are a bunch of vehicles before you get to the statues. You can't miss the hearse and the replica of the *Ghostbusters* ambulance. I'll go stand by the gate to make sure you can find us." Todd handed Jade the phone and jogged toward the field.

"Okay, police and an ambulance are on their way. I'll make sure that the detective on call is notified. Please make sure that everyone remains where they are and they don't disturb the scene any further. Stay on the line with me, and I'll let you know when they're approaching," the dispatcher said.

Jade quietly said, "Okay," and stared at Dr. Meredith Echols, who lay crumpled between two statues. *What is she doing out here in the middle of nowhere? Meredith, what happened to you?*

The fauxhawk guy across from Jade said, "Oh, that's totally freaky. Don't know if it's a big coincidence or a sign or something, but they found her between Garfield and McKinley." He pointed at the statues with his light, and everyone looked up. "I'm taking it as a sign. Both of those presidents were assassinated, like Lincoln and Kennedy. Maybe this is some creepy message someone left us."

"Or it could be a sign from her spirit to let us know that she didn't die of natural causes," Suz said.

Muffled chatter rose from the group, and then a solemn silence settled like fog over the bystanders. *If Noah's meters were on, I'm sure they were picking up all the tension in the area.* Jade looked around for Amy. She stood near the East Coast Paranormal team, who huddled together near the statues. Suz and Noah adjusted the settings on one of their gadgets that they pointed toward where Meredith lay.

"The first responders are on the property. You should see them any minute now." The dispatcher's voice seemed to boom from Jade's phone.

"Thank you. They should see us near the statues." Jade let out a puff of air that fluttered her bangs. She disconnected the call and stared at the little dots off in the horizon that were bobbing and getting larger as the vehicles approached.

Within minutes, the EMTs hurried in, and two police officers took charge of the area. They shooed everyone back and started taking statements. By the time they got to Jade, more EMTs had arrived. Someone covered the body with a thin sheet.

A wiry officer stepped toward Jade. His gold badge hung off his belt, and he was the only one in jeans. "Evening. I'm Detective Gabe Russo. What's your name, why are you here, and what can you tell me about the deceased?" He moved his phone closer to her.

She cleared her throat. "I'm Jade Hicks. I live in Mermaid Bay, and I'm part of the paranormal tour group. My friends, Amy Pemberton and Todd Brickman, arranged the event. I didn't really see anything. I was over there when I heard the screams."

"A woman's scream?" the detective asked.

"I couldn't tell at first. It echoed. We ran in the direction of where we thought it came from. Then we heard another scream. The screams came from Norm, one of the paranormal investigators," Jade said, pausing to take a breath. "We were looking at the statues while the East Coast Paranormal team was setting up over here. By the time we got here, others on the tour had started to gather. Cliffy, Noah, and Drew were standing near the body. Eliot checked for a pulse, and I called 9-1-1. Suz…" Jade pointed to the slender woman and said, "She's part of that group, too."

"Was the victim with your group?" Detective Russo asked.

"No." Jade stared at the sheet that now covered Meredith. "She didn't come with us, and she's not with the paranormal team either. I don't know how she got here."

"Do you know who the victim is?" he asked.

"I'm pretty sure it's Dr. Meredith Echols. We saw her in Seaport for the CreatureCon. She's one of the speakers," Jade said quietly.

"Anything else that you remember?" Jade shook her head, and he pressed a button on his phone. "Thanks. If you think of anything later, this is my card."

She nodded, and before she could comment, another deputy yelled, "Hey, Gabe. I need you to take a look at this."

When Detective Russo had moved out of earshot, Amy shuffled over and looped her arm through Jade's. "Doing okay over here? This is not how I imagined tonight going."

"Fine, I guess," Jade said. "What about you?"

"Just peachy. In a sick way, a dead body can only make the tours seem super exciting. I hope people don't expect this with every tour," Amy whispered. "And on top of all this, Todd's ready to give up on this venture. I think it's still worth it and pretty cool. Maybe he'll mellow in a day or two. I'll have to work on him with my awesome negotiation skills." She let out a breath that sounded like a leaky beach raft. "Two bodies in one week. Wow. I had no idea that something like this would happen. Do you know, I never saw a dead body until I met you."

Jade wrinkled her nose. "What's next for this evening?" Jade whispered, changing the subject.

Amy shrugged. "Who knows? I doubt they'll let us continue here tonight. It took a while to get permission to visit the property. I'm not sure I can reschedule before the con people go home. I guess I'll do refunds and try again next time. I was kinda looking forward to communing with the other world, but maybe not such much now that there's a dead body over there."

Amy let out a sigh. "The cop asked if I knew how Meredith got here." She raised both her palms, like she had nothing. "I told him Todd and I and the East Coast Paranormal guys were here earlier today with Angel Cruz and his team. I didn't see any sign of Meredith then, but I wasn't looking for her either. So, she had to show up between the time we left and the time the tour arrived. I'm curious how long she's been dead."

"Did you notice any tracks near her?" Jade asked. Amy shook her head. "I didn't either. I'm wondering if she was killed on the property or dumped here."

"Ladies and gentlemen. Is there anyone we haven't gotten a statement from?" The other officer asked.

Whispers spread through the group, but no one answered.

"Okay, then you're free to leave the property. The investigation is ongoing, and we need to clear this area for the forensic team. Thank you for your help. Ms. Pemberton, please send the contact information that we talked about," the officer said. He waved his arm toward where the cars sat in the empty field like he was directing traffic.

When Todd unlocked the hearse, Jade slid inside behind the other two women. The guys spread out on the bench seats on the opposite side. She pulled out her phone and tapped a quick text to Nick. Even though the murders happened in different jurisdictions, the victims knew each other. Her spidey sense had been working overtime since she recognized Meredith. Jade hit send and closed her eyes for a moment. Thoughts of everything she could remember about Meredith and Ernie flashed across her brain like a weird slideshow.

Her phone beeped with Nick's response: **Doubtful that it's a coincidence. I'll follow up with James City County. Be safe. Let me know when you get home.**

"Excuse me, you all. I'm sorry to interrupt. I know it's been a long night and not what you expected or were promised. I've talked with my partner. I'm not sure we will be able to reschedule the paranormal experience for another evening. So, we're prepared to offer you all refunds," Amy said from the passenger seat.

Whispers in the back of the vehicle turned into loud mumbling.

Finally, the petite woman with the bobbed blond hair let out an ear-piercing whistle. "I think what we're all trying to say is that this was terribly exciting, and no one anywhere has had an experience like this. It was like being right in the middle of *Forty-eight Hours*. I can't speak for everyone else, but I don't need a refund. Now I've got to follow this case to see what happens and who did it."

When she finished, the rest of the passengers added a series of "what she said," "heck yes," and "we don't need refunds."

"As weird and hair-raising creepy as it was, it was an adventure," the Gen-Zer with the buzzcut said. "Nope, nobody wants refunds. And we'll all leave you kickin' reviews."

Jade let a smile creep across her face when she saw Amy do a quick fist pump before she turned around as the hearse bounced along the uneven turf.

The silence quickly morphed into a groupthink discussion full of theories about how Meredith ended up next to the statues and the reasons for her demise.

The blond woman said, "I'm sure the body was Dr. Echols, and I told the cop that. I didn't see any blood or evidence that she was dragged there. Maybe she met someone here for a secret rendezvous that went bad."

"More likely an argument with someone. Now that's believable," the fauxhawk guy said. "That woman would argue with the devil if he told her she was beautiful. I bet she was here to pay off someone who was blackmailing her. It's the perfect place for a shady deal."

"Or she could have been blackmailing someone. That's not out of the realm of possibility either," the guy with the beard said.

"When they turned her over, did you see what was under her?" the guy with the spiked red hair who had been quiet most of the evening asked. Before anyone could answer, he jumped in with, "A pile of Pogs. Is it some kind of symbol, or was she out in the woods playing some weird game? Maybe it was some ritualistic thing that turned deadly."

"Pogs? You sure? I haven't seen them since I was in elementary school. Aren't some of them collector's items these days?" The guy next to him said. "What does that mean?"

"It wasn't accidental," the curly-headed gal replied. "There's a real mystery here, and I don't think that ghosts have anything to do with it."

"Maybe it was something the killer left on purpose, you know, like the Joker who always left a playing card," the bearded guy said without looking up from his phone.

"But wait. How did she get back there? It's not like it's close to the hotel or it's even a place that people would think to go," the blond woman added. "The Pogs add a weird twist to it. Now, I'm super curious."

"The paranormal extravaganza was advertised all over the conference. It was on the daily activities list and the electronic boards, and I saw flyers everywhere. Anyone at the hotel could have known when and where the tour was," buzzcut said.

"That would be my fault," Amy said quietly from the front. "I got a little carried away with the marketing. I wanted to get the word out."

"But this location is the perfect place to hide a body. Well, if they had actually hidden it. I wonder how we can find out when the time of death was," the fauxhawk guy said.

Jade sat back in her seat. Two people, who had a tumultuous history and happened to attend the same conference, ended up dead within days of each other. This is no coincidence.

Chapter Thirteen

As Chloe and Jade returned from their evening walk on the beach, her phone rang. "I got your text that you made it home," Nick said. "You okay?"

"I'm fine." Jade opened the door, and Chloe took off like a shot. "Now, the paranormal guy who found Meredith screamed like a little girl. He said he was used to spirits and not dead bodies. The whole evening was kind of creepy."

It sounded like Nick was trying to stifle a laugh. "What exactly happened?"

"When we got to the property in Todd's hearse, the paranormal investigators showed us their equipment, and we were walking around looking at the giant statues when the guy screamed. We all rushed over, and there she was lying on the ground."

"Todd and Amy doing okay?" he asked.

"I guess. They offered refunds, but no one wanted one. The people on the tour were excited to be front and center in a murder investigation. Oh, I almost forgot, one of the guys on the tour was talking about Meredith. He said that when EMTs moved her, there were Pogs under her body. And the body was located between two statues of presidents who had been assassinated. That's when the conspiracy theories started flying."

"Pogs like the game tokens?"

"Yep. I guess so. I didn't see them, but it seemed an odd thing to have with you in a field with a bunch of damaged statues. But it was also weird that she was there at all. Someone said that the paranormal tour was publicized all over the convention, and that you couldn't help but know that it was happening. Amy's marketing magic worked. And I wasn't the only one in the group who recognized Dr. Echols."

Nick groaned.

"You okay?" she asked.

"Yep. Someone murdered my prime suspect. Things are now more complicated." He let out a long puff of air. "I talked briefly to Chief Harrison in James City County. We plan to meet tomorrow. This may rise to the level of a multijurisdictional task force. Thanks for letting me know."

"My gut tells me the two deaths are related," she said. "It makes perfect sense. She and Ernie had a history. He was her student at one time, and she left a job because of an affair when he was her student. They had epic battles online and in public, and they were super critical of each other. Amy and I witnessed one spat in the hallway at CreatureCon that was heated. But then on the same night, we saw her go into the Xplorer's hotel room."

Everything was quiet on Nick's end. When he didn't say anything, she continued, "Meredith is staying at the Pearl. Amy and I are pretty sure her romantic thing with Ernie was been rekindled."

"Anything else, Miss Marple?"

"I didn't see this, but Amy said earlier in the day Angel Cruz and his team met the East Coast Paranormal guys at the statues for some promo pictures and to record a podcast. He was gone by the time the tour arrived."

"You never know what detail is going to lead to something else," Nick said. "Get some sleep. I'll call you when I can. I'm not sure how long I'll be tied up with this. Love you."

"You get some sleep, too. I love you back. Let me know if you need me to bring you food or caffeine or dessert."

"Will do," he said, disconnecting.

Jade put a bag of popcorn in the microwave, and Chloe staked out a spot underfoot to make sure she got her share.

The microwave beeped, and Jade took the steaming bowl and a Coke to the dining room.

Dr. Meredith Echols was found dead this evening under mysterious circumstances, Jade texted Delia.

Oh my stars. I'll see what I can find. It's a matter of time before word spreads. 2 suspicious celebrity deaths! What's going on? I'll see what I can dig up. Delia ended her message with a string of surprised emojis.

"And what do Pogs have to do with Meredith and her death?" Chloe moved closer and turned on her best puppy eyes in hopes of scoring some popcorn. "Pogs seem too out of the ordinary to be in a field with a dead body. Did she collect them or play some kind of game? Or was this something related to the side hustle that the guy at the con mentioned?" Jade buried herself in a search about the history of the little disks.

"Chloe, for a while, those little cardboard things were everywhere. I remember kids playing with them in school, but I didn't pay that much attention to them. I think I was too wrapped up in Barbie and Beanie Babies. It says here that some rare ones are collectors' items. Aha," she said loud enough to make Chloe turn her head. "So that's what Pog means. A dairy in Hawaii created a passionfruit, orange, and guava juice drink, and the local kids used the bottlecaps as game pieces. It's an acronym for the drink's ingredients. Hmmm. I never knew that." On a whim, she pulled up a couple of online auction sites and searched for the cardboard disks. "You can still buy them."

Still not interested in the bottlecap craze of a bygone era, Chloe toddled off to the den and hopped on the couch.

"Some of the classic ones are kinda expensive. Bingo!" she said loud enough to cause the dog to flip over and raise her head.

"I'm checking out the vendor section for CreatureCon, and some of the dealers have action figures, classic toys, Pogs, and all kinds of trading cards. Interesting. Maybe I need to hang out with these vendors to see if what I can find."

Jade dove into a search of the CreatureCon vendors' websites. She narrowed down her search list to five for her next visit. "Chloe, I'm beat. Two dead bodies, tons of drama, and a whole bunch of random facts. Do we have one killer or two? I mean, if Meredith murdered Ernie, then who killed her and why?"

* * *

Jade woke up from a fitful dream about a dinner party that was invaded by ghosts. She blinked her eyes to get them to adjust to the predawn darkness in her bedroom. Not able to go back to sleep, she hit the shower. Chloe had other ideas. She snuggled under the blanket until Jade headed to the kitchen for breakfast.

Jade slathered a banana nut muffin with butter and warmed it in the microwave. After filling her to-go cup with enough creamer to turn her coffee tan, she said, "Okay, puppy, let's roll."

Outside, Jade helped the pudgy dog into the front seat of the Jeep. "We'll do our morning walk around the store. And then I need you to guard the place for a bit." The dog rested her front paws on the door and stared out the window during the short ride to the store.

Chloe hopped onto the floor, and then she sprang out when Jade opened the Jeep's door. The little dog made the most of her time outside as she explored the flower beds in front of 'Tis the Season and then the empty lot next door. Today's mission was to check out every blade of grass and all the spring flowers poking out of the mulch.

After a couple gentle nudges, Chloe acquiesced and trotted to the back door to wait for her friend to open it. Jade breezed through the showrooms and flipped on all the lights and the office equipment. The copier whirred and hummed in tune with the coffee maker's chugging.

"Chloe, you're in charge of security. I'll be back as soon as I can. I want to talk to some of the vendors before they get rolling with the conference attendees." She slipped the French bulldog a peanut butter treat before heading out to her Wrangler.

It took her longer to find a parking spot in the hotel lot than it did to drive over to Seaport. She had to hike from the overflow parking to the front entrance. On her way inside, she pulled out a sticky note with the names of the vendors that mentioned Pogs among their offerings. She wended her way through the crowded lobby filled with attendees sprawled out like they had taken up residence on the sofas and chairs in the conversation areas.

The rumpled, bleary-eyed ones looked like they had pulled all-nighters, and a couple of them had their heads back in full napping mode.

Jade pulled on the knob of one of the doors to the dealer room, and she almost bumped into it when it didn't budge. Looking around, she spotted a door propped partially open farther down the hallway. She slipped inside and made a beeline for the novelty booths in the back.

Three of the five vendors she wanted to visit had black cloths covering the tables. At the fourth booth, a guy in a kilt and a Dr. Who shirt arranged Funko Pops and bobbleheads on the table. He had racks and racks of collectibles encased in plastic boxes behind him in tall display cases that sported heavy-duty locks.

"Hi, I'm Jade Hicks, and I'm doing an article on collectibles, and I was wondering if you had some time to talk with me."

"Sure. I'm Wade Jeffries, owner of Rock, Paper, Scissors. This your first con?"

"It's nice to meet you. Yes. Is it that obvious?"

He raised one eyebrow. "You look wide awake. Most of the regulars either partied too hard or stayed up all night gaming. We don't usually see crowds in here until after lunch. You came at a good time to chat and browse. What can I help you with?"

"What is the hottest thing that everyone has to have?"

He laughed. "It depends. I buy, sell, and trade, so folks are always asking me the value of stuff they kept their mom from throwing out. I don't do sports memorabilia; that's a whole other market. I focus on pop culture." He waved his arms wide. "Many of my clients are people trying to recapture a bit of their youth with stuff they didn't have the money to buy in the eighties or nineties. Pokémon everything, Star Wars, D&D, action figures…You name it, someone wants it. There's a market for almost anything."

"Do you ever have folks bring in anything super valuable?" she asked.

He rolled his eyes. "They all think they have something worth thousands. It's rare, but it happens. But more often than not, I have to tell them that what they spent money on online isn't worth what they paid. The problem is, people buy on impulse, and they don't do their homework. I break a bunch of hearts on a regular basis. Like the other day, I had some lady in here. She didn't look like my normal customers. For a minute, I thought she was somebody's mom. But she was actually one of the conference speakers. Anyway, she had some stuff she had bought online. I did an appraisal, and she didn't like it when I told her that she had replicas and counterfeits. She said I didn't know what I was talking about, and she'd sell it online anyway."

As he continued, the hair on the back of Jade's neck stood up. "Some people don't understand that real collectibles have provenance. If you're buying something for that kind of money, it needs to be rated or graded by a reputable appraiser. And don't get me started on the crazies with the Beanie Babies. There are only a handful that are truly worth what every owner thinks they have." He let out a heavy sigh.

"It's sad that people get taken so often," Jade said.

"It happens all the time. People don't do their research to ensure what they're buying is real," he said.

"What kind of thing did the conference speaker you talked with have that was counterfeited?" Jade asked.

"She had a couple of autographs, some Pogs, and some autographed original art from a comic book. I showed her that the artwork was really a copy and not worth anything. She wouldn't listen to me. She got mad and huffed off."

Adrenaline coursed through Jade, and the butterflies came alive in her stomach. "I know there are a lot of things for sale online. How do you know outside of having it appraised that you have the real deal?" she asked.

"You don't, and you're taking a chance. Do your research and check stuff out. I read that like eighty percent of the autographs bought online are fakes. You have to do your homework. And if it sounds too good to be true, it probably is. You need to check out the seller and his or her reviews. Copious amounts of raving reviews or sellers with only a couple of comments can be red flags for a buyer."

"So, if someone is starting out, what are your recommendations of must-haves? What would you suggest that they start with that won't break the bank?"

He smiled. "How much time do you have? My biggest piece of advice is to pick something that you're passionate about. I'd start with one thing. You need to know your budget and stick to it. I see people go crazy at auctions. Shop around and don't be afraid to bargain. Don't let your emotions get in the way of your judgment. I've seen some sad people when they realize their trading cards or autographs were mass-produced and not valuable. People always think their investment will make them fast money. It's atypical that someone finds a gem hidden away in an attic or thrift store. But it can happen."

"All excellent advice." Jade picked up one of his business cards. "For my contacts list. I appreciate your time."

"Send me a link when your article's published. What do you collect?" he asked, stacking T-shirts on a side table.

"Christmas ornaments," she said with a slight smile.

"I have some pop culture ones on my online store. Check it out. The link's on the card."

Jade nodded and made a lap around the floor again to check on the other vendors on her list, but the tables were still shrouded. *Not the early bird crowd around here. He had to be talking about Meredith earlier. Did she get burned with some counterfeits, or did someone involved with her side gig murder her?*

Chapter Fourteen

With hardly any foot traffic in the store, Jade multi-tasked between covering the front counter and updating her next newsletter.

The bells jangled, and Chloe buzzed toward the lobby. She wiggled until Nick leaned over and picked her up for cuddles. After tickles and a pat on the head, he put Chloe on the hardwood floor and kissed Jade. "It's good to see you."

"You look tired. Have you slept more than three hours in the last few nights?" He shook his head, and she continued, "Come on back, I have coffee and tea. Maybe that'll help."

Nick followed her to the kitchenette, where she pulled out two mugs from the cabinet and rummaged through the coffee pods for the strongest brew she could find.

"These long days and nights are killing me. We're investigating each case separately, but the teams meet daily to compare notes. In addition, I had to call in some state police resources to support the team."

"So, they are related…" Jade's eyes widened. *I knew it.*

"Probably. We don't want to exclude any possibilities right now. Tell me again what you know about the tour and finding the body. Was Meredith on the tour?"

Jade shook her head, and while the coffee maker gurgled, she recounted what happened the night of Amy and Todd's tour.

When she finished, he stared off into the lobby for what felt like an eternity. Then he said, "Both victims were strangled. Probably with a cord or some kind of garrote." Nick's phone let out a loud alert. "Sorry. I need to take this."

I need to reach out to Randall. He might have some new details about why Meredith was where she was found and her interest in collectibles.

Nick disconnected his call. "I need to head out. Dinner tomorrow or maybe this weekend? I'll call you later." He leaned over the counter and kissed her.

"Bye." She finger-waved as he strode through the doorway. "Chloe, I guess it's you and me tonight. We'll have to find something to binge-watch." The Frenchie yipped in agreement as Jade's phone blared with Amy's ringtone.

"Hey, girl. What's up?"

"It's been crazy busy here, but I snuck in the back for a root beer and a quick call to see how you're doing and if you found out anything? I've had anime presentations in the store all day, and it's been a zoo. But that's a good thing. I'd much rather be busy with customers than twiddling my thumbs."

"Not much is going on here. I'm glad you've got a big crowd for your event," Jade said.

"Before I forget, some of the guys here were talking about Meredith and how shady she was. I couldn't get a lot out of them without looking like I was snooping. Which I totally was. Anyway, they said she stole some of her students' research and claimed it as her own. She got in trouble for getting too friendly with students, and one guy said she even had some shady side gigs that were really get-rich-quick schemes. There was more to ol' Meredith than her stuffy old prof persona, and there were no shortage of her haters. I haven't heard one single person sing her praises. Sounds like she wasn't the great academic that she told everyone she was. When she was in the store last week, she griped about everything. And you're the one who let me know she defaced that beautiful poster of Angel. At least he thought it was funny. But who does that besides a mean girl? Some people."

"Thanks. I'll see what I can find about the hustles. What're you doing tonight?" Jade asked.

"Probably sulking. Todd went home from work early. He thinks he's coming down with a cold, and he doesn't want to go back over to Seaport with me. What're you doing? Spicy date with Sheriff Hottie?"

"I wish. He's knee-deep in alligators with the murder investigation, and he's working with James City County on the other one. I have a phantom boyfriend again. Maybe I'll get to see him this weekend."

"It could be interesting. You and I could go. We'll hunt for clues at CreatureCon."

"Sounds fun. I'd like to learn more about the Xplorer and Meredith. They both had public personas that weren't exactly like their real-life selves."

"We're on the case," Amy said. "See you around seven? That'll give me time to put this place back in order. I'll pick you up."

"See you then." No sooner had Jade hung up the phone than it rang again. "Hello, Randall. How are you doing?"

"About as good as expected. The police keep coming by with questions. I want to believe that they're doing a thorough investigation, but I have this sneaking suspicion that they're trying to trip me up. I think they're focusing on me now," he whispered. "Please tell me they have other leads besides me. This is such a nightmare, and I can't believe that Mer is gone."

"I'm not privy to the police investigation," she said. He let out a grunt, and the phone went silent for what felt like an eternity.

Trying to fill the void in the conversation, she said, "Maybe you could help me with some information that might help us both. You said Meredith started attending shows and conferences because the pay was more than she was making at the university. Did she have any other side businesses or activities? You never know what might be important."

"Yep, she was always looking for new revenue streams. You might be on to something. Meredith had champagne tastes and always had a bad habit of running up the credit cards that her salary couldn't always cover. She found out quickly that academic publishing wasn't always as lucrative as the private sector. For a while, she dabbled with some side stuff. I think most were pyramid schemes. I turned her on to the conference circuit, and she jumped on it. She raked in tons on her speaking gigs, and when that took off, I think that became her focus. She booked a bunch of appearances, and her publicist got her some media spots."

"Did she ever buy or sell collectibles?" Jade asked.

"Maybe. She mentioned some online auctions a while back. Who knows. She was always looking for new ways to make money. And she liked going to auctions to look at antiques. You think this could be something for the police to explore?"

"Maybe. I'll keep digging. If you come across any contacts she may have had, let me know."

"You may be onto something." Randall raised his voice. "What if she angered someone in one of her dealings. That could be a motive for murder. Maybe it had nothing to do with the con at all. Good thinking."

"I'm still doing research and talking to people." A weird little feeling stopped her from sharing anything else. "I'll let you know as soon as I have something. How long do you plan to be in town?"

He let out a heavy sigh and sniffed. "I'm here until the end of the conference. They've already paid me. Plus, I feel like I'm running away if I head home now. I need to stay here and try to help Meredith." He sniffed several more times. "We had epic fights, but we also had wonderful times. I know she was self-centered and snotty. But I still loved her, and I need to find out who did this to her. If she had just listened to me, none of this would have happened."

"I'll call you if I get any leads," she said.

"And make sure you tell your cop friend what you find. I feel like they are ignoring other suspects. Sheesh. I hate to think that people see me as a suspect in my wife's murder." He sucked in a gulp of air and made a hiccupping noise.

"The sheriff and his team are going through hundreds of leads and tips."

"The list of her haters is long. She had a way of rubbing people the wrong way. It's going to take forever to eliminate anyone she had a beef with. This investigation feels like it's going nowhere. The police aren't forthcoming with answers to my questions, and my second biggest fear is that this will go unsolved. Then I'll never know what happened to Mer. And if that happens, there will always be a cloud of suspicion over my head. People will look at me and wonder. I'm already talking to a lawyer."

"I'll do my best," Jade said quietly. "I'll talk to you in a day or two."

"Sounds like a plan," his tone perked up instantly. "Maybe we can meet for drinks or dinner and exchange notes. I look forward to hearing from you. I want all the details." He disconnected, and it was Jade's turn to let out a long puff of air. *What is it about these people? Usually, I get a good read on personalities. I feel like I'm second-guessing myself on who I can trust with this bunch.*

Chapter Fifteen

Jade set her notes on the dining room table and put her dinner plate in the dishwasher. "Chloe, I have no idea who the killer or killers are. This is making me crazy."

Loud bangs on the bungalow's front door sent the little dog into a growl fest. When Jade opened the door, Amy bustled in. She took one look around and said, "What, no murder wall yet?"

"I haven't gotten around to it yet. Nothing is jumping out at me on my spreadsheet, so maybe a giant visual would help. That's next on my list."

"Well, let's go gather some new intel. Secret Agent Amy reporting for duty. Gotta make sure you have new leads to follow." She saluted.

Jade laughed. "Give me two seconds to freshen up. Be back in a jiff."

"No problemo. Chloe and I will brainstorm suspects while you're gone and narrow down the list of possibilities. Maybe we'll have it solved before you get back."

Jade did an outfit change and a touch-up of hair and makeup in record time. "Okey doke," she said, returning to the dining room. She leaned on the door jamb and slipped on her sneakers. "Let's go see what we can find out."

Jade barely had time to close the passenger door of Amy's blue Forrester before her friend zoomed down the driveway backwards at warp speed. "This car rides nicely."

"And it's roomy. I needed something with more space for all my projects and for hauling books around. And Todd didn't want me to use the hearse like a pickup truck. I like it. It's sporty. I can drive it in the snow if I ever go back to Massachusetts, and it's a nice blue. I miss my zippy Mini Cooper, but this one's a workhorse. I like it, and it has oomph when I mash the gas pedal," Amy said, cranking up the radio. "Okay, do we have a plan for tonight?"

Jade shook her head as the bookstore and the pier whizzed by. "No plan. I popped in over there to talk to some of the vendors the other day. When Meredith was found, some of the guys on your tour spotted Pogs under the body when the EMTs moved her."

"Like that school-yard fascination where the winner would take all after they tossed the little disks and watched them land. Why? That sounds weird to me."

Jade held up both hands with her palms up and shrugged. "I have no idea. One of the vendors told me that they're still popular, and some of the classic ones are collectibles. We talked about a few things, and he said that he does appraisals at these conferences. He said he often has to tell people their items are counterfeits. And he mentioned that he told one of the conference panelists that the memorabilia she was trying to sell were fakes. She wasn't happy when he told her they were worthless."

Amy bounced up and down in her seat. "Yep. I bet it was Meredith! I told you one of the guys at my anime thing accused her of some sketchy dealings. Maybe she was cheating people with knockoffs or replicas? Or maybe she got grifted and was out for revenge, and it turned deadly. I bet she was out in that field to do some kind of sneaky deal, and someone turned the tables on her."

Jade pursed her lips and stared out the front window for a few beats. "Her side gigs are on my list, along with five hundred other rando things about her life to look into."

"She seemed to be a stuffy somebody who looked down her nose at anyone without a PhD, you know, a piled-higher-and-deeper degree in what she deemed was an acceptable scientific field. I've been eavesdropping lately. People are still talking about her. Let's say she is not being remembered fondly. I can't tell you the countless stories where her name is mentioned as the one they all loved to hate."

Jade held onto her seatbelt for a few seconds before unclipping it after Amy skidded to a sudden stop in a parking space near the sand dunes. The blow-up Nessie bobbed in the fountain, and the dragon and Big Foot balloons looked like they were dancing in the evening breeze.

Amy gave Jade a side-eye. "Relax. I got you here safe and sound. And Todd tells me all the time that I drive like I'm still in Boston. Hey, up there, you drive to survive. I keep forgetting that it's a little more laid back down here. I'm working on it." Amy hopped out and clicked her key fob. "Let's roll. I have a good feeling that we may uncover something useful tonight."

I hope you're right. So far, we have overheard a lot of gossip.

As they made their way through the crowds of costumed conference goers, Jade spotted Randall talking to a woman in what looked like a pixie outfit, complete with giant wings and a wand. At the moment Jade turned to duck out of his line of sight, Amy grabbed her arm and yelled, "Hey, Professor. Whoo-hooo" and waved with her free hand and pulled Jade toward him. Jade felt the warmth of the blood rising to her cheeks. She pasted on what she hoped was a passable smile. As they got closer, the pixie waved goodbye and scurried toward the conference rooms.

"Well, hello, ladies," Randall said. "I'm glad you're out and about helping me with this dreadful mess. What have you got to share?" Looking over his shoulder, he spotted two tan loveseats. "Let's snag those, and you can fill me in." His blond hair was perfectly coiffed, and he glided over to the seating area in loafers with no socks. His relaxed-fit jeans and long-sleeved burgundy shirt, open at the collar, rounded out his outfit.

Jade eased herself onto the loveseat as Amy plopped down next to her. Ignoring the empty seat next to them, Randall sat on the coffee table, blocking any hope of a quick escape. "So, ladies, what have you found that will help me clear uh, Meredith and me?" He sniffed several times and swiped a finger under one of his eyes.

"We are gathering all kinds of information," Jade said. "It takes a while to sift through all the people who had contact with her and all the leads those conversations uncover."

"You mean all the altercations and fights she had. Meredith was no shrinking violet. She had no problem telling people what she thought. I always liked that about her. There was no passive-aggressive nonsense with her. You knew where you stood." Randall paused and watched someone in the distance.

"Uh," Amy interjected. "We know your wife was a respected professor who did many speaking engagements. Did she have any other hobbies or interests we should look into?"

Jade let out a little breath of relief that Amy didn't do her usual bull-in-the-china-shop approach.

"Hobbies, like knitting? Meredith didn't have too much free time with research, publishing, school, and the tour circuit. I don't ever remember her doing anything crafty or creative. She did like antiquing, and she bought things online and at auctions from time to time. I guess that's a hobby. She sold some of the stuff she didn't need. Sometimes when you buy things at auction, you get the whole lot of items, and she was usually only interested in one or two things, so she sold the rest of the stuff."

"Like what?" Amy leaned forward into Randall's space.

"Uh, like first edition books, autographs of certain famous people, collectibles. Sometimes she bought or traded items at conferences like this. There are always vendors or attendees who want to swap or buy stuff."

"Did she ever talk about having any issues with buyers or sellers?" Amy asked with a gleam in her eye.

Randall shook his head. "I don't know. She complained about scads of people all the time. She had high standards and didn't have patience with anyone she deemed not worthy."

"Do you buy or sell collectibles too?" Jade asked.

"No, why?" Randall asked. His head turned as four guys in Klingon outfits approached.

"I thought it might have been something you all enjoyed doing together," Jade added.

"Not really. I'm too busy with my research to have any outside projects. Speaking engagements and my research keep me busy."

Before he could continue, the Klingons approached with a stack of flyers. "Party tonight in our suite. Make sure you stop by. It'll be epic. The guy in a space suit with the bony forehead makeup handed flyers to each of them.

"Cool," Amy cooed, taking one of the flyers. "Is it costume only?"

"What costume?" one of the guys grunted.

When the Klingons had moved on to a group of X-Men, Randall continued, "Where was I? The auctions. Yep. Spending all day in a musty antique shop or warehouse is not what I consider fun. And auctions are oh so boring. Mer went to those by herself."

Amy folded the invitation and slipped it in her purse. "What else can you tell us about Meredith that will help? Any idea why she was where they found her?"

Randall's head snapped around toward her. "No. Mer was a free spirit. She did what she wanted. Something caught her attention there that she wanted to explore. She would take off at a moment's notice if she was charged about something. She did many spur-of-the-moment things."

"Had she been interested in the paranormal before?" Jade asked.

He made a face like he had drunk pickle juice straight from the jar. "Not hardly. The only reason she would have been there would have been to debunk the so-called science they were using." Glancing down at his phone, he continued, "Hey, it was great chatting with you. How about you let me know before you leave, and we'll meet up at the bar for a round of drinks? Maybe I can think of something else in the meantime to tell you about Meredith by then."

"Sounds like a plan," Amy said, rising. "Jade and I have to hurry if we're going to make the next panel. Toodle loo." She grabbed Jade's arm and pulled her off the couch. Then, without hesitation, Amy led her down the hallway, not pausing until they rounded the corner. Amy shooed her inside a nearby women's restroom. "That was something," Amy said, after checking for feet under the three stalls. "Whatdaya think? He may have provided us with some new leads."

Jade shook her head. "I know we all grieve in our own way, and their relationship was complicated to say the least, but his demeanor seems to change with the wind. Sometimes, he's the grieving, panicked spouse, and other times, he seems to be ultra-focused on his life. But he is willing to talk. He confirmed that she did buy and sell stuff. So, either she got duped and bought fakes, or she was trying to scam others. That detail might be important."

"Based on everything I've heard about her, my guess is the latter." Amy touched up her lipstick and fluffed her dark hair. "I do want to go to the panel on dragons. You wanna go to that one or split up?"

"I think I'll wander around and see if I can strike up any conversations to uncover info on Randall and the murder victims."

"You go, Nancy Drew. How about I meet you in front of the merchant room in about an hour and a half, and then we can decide if we want to let Randall buy us drinks."

"Sounds like a plan. Keep your ears and eyes open. You never know what you'll overhear."

Amy punched her lightly in the arm. "I'm on the job."

Back in the main hallway, the pair headed in opposite directions. Jade slowed her pace and blended in with a crowd in the common area in front of the conference center. She found a seat on a padded bench near several groups of conference goers and checked her phone.

Three large guys in some kind of battle get-up stumbled over and landed in the nearby chairs. One plopped down on the other end of her bench, and the force shook the whole piece of furniture. Four gals in brightly colored robes sank into the chairs and on the floor on Jade's other side. Jade pretended to be engrossed in her phone as they chatted.

After about thirty minutes and only conversations about parties, hidden flasks, and today's panels, Jade moved on around the corner to another seating area.

"Is anyone sitting here?" she asked a group of guys in Tolkien-like costumes.

The shaggy brown-headed guy next to her said, "Help yourself." *I think he's a Hobbit, or he could be an Ewok.*

"Thanks." She sank into the overstuffed side chair and whipped out her phone. She pretended to scroll as another gaggle of costumed Gen-Zers took over the two sofas near the potted plant. *If I don't learn anything soon, I need to figure out a way to ask questions without sounding like a nosy weirdo.*

A purple-haired gal with her legs up over the sofa's arm yawned and said, "And I was looking forward to hearing the Xplorer talk tonight. Too bad and so sad. I'm bummed."

Jade's ears perked up, and she raised her phone and pretended to be reading something.

The Gen-Zer in the long blue wig next to her said, "I heard he was going to reveal some stuff. He kept teasing on TikTok that he had a big announcement that would rock the science world and prove one of his theories. And his reveal would stick it to all his critics."

"That crazy woman that they found murdered was on a tear about debunking the Xplorer, almost to the point of harassment. I was hoping he'd shut her down. But it looks like someone shut them both down," the gal with the purple hair said.

"Well, we can mark him off the suspect list for her murder. But it's too bad that he didn't live long enough to exact his revenge or make his big announcement," the one with the blue hair said.

"I heard that they messed around while he was one of her students, and she had to leave her job," the gal on the floor said. "It was all over the net. Maybe she killed him for ruining her life."

"That's what happens when you vo-de-oh-do with one of your students. She should have known better," the blue-haired girl said.

"I hope someone else publishes the Xplorer's findings posthumously," a guy on the floor said, looking up from his tablet. "The world needs to know what he found."

"He was supersmart. I heard he was working on an epic project. Maybe the findings will still be made public. It would be sad if the world never knew what he discovered. He had a decent presence on the socials. I'll miss his daily posts," the one in the blue wig said.

The guy with the spiked cranberry hair and huge gauges in his ears leaned forward. "I heard it wasn't the kind of find that everyone thinks it was. I heard from a friend who did a podcast interview with him last week that he would be revealing something big that would shake up the so-called scientists. He and Dr. Echols had their colossal battles of science vs. mythical creatures, but my friend said that the Xplorer had a plan to talk about some project that would turn everything upside down. Rumor was that he and Dr. Echols were working together. Who knows if it's true?"

"No way. They were always fighting or trolling each other. I can't believe that he'd cross over to the dark side," the blue-haired gal said.

"Do you think someone killed both of them to keep whatever they found secret? Oooo, this is getting good," a girl with emerald green hair said.

The purple-haired one said. "This morning, I heard that Dr. Echols killed Xplorer to keep him from outing her as a thief and a liar. Then a couple of followers went after her as retribution. That sounds more like it to me."

"Maybe it was some kind of attack or deadly virus. Maybe it didn't have anything to do with her work," the guy with the spiked hair said. "We should turn this into some kind of online story. It could be wild. Some sort of fan fiction thing. Maybe it could go viral."

"We may never know. You guys can stay here and veg if you want, but I want to see Angel Cruz. He promised to show some treasures that he found and the new species of squid. And he's getting credit for discovering it." The young woman in the blue wig pushed several strands away from her face and rose. "Catch youse later."

"That would have ticked off Dr. Echols. A treasure-hunter taking credit for a new species find. I'm sure she would have railed about it, too," the guy on the floor said, studying his tablet screen.

"Wait up. I want to see the treasure hunter too," the girl next to Jade said. The group slowly rose and disappeared into the crowd that was in constant motion. The hotel hallway looked like Grand Central Station at rush hour.

Jade tapped some notes into her phone. The guys on the other side of her continued a heated discussion about alien abductions. *Interesting, but not helpful with either of the murders.*

One of the guys let out a loud whoop and dove over the top of the couch. "It's Kaaaaarl," he yelled and gamboled across the common area to a guy dressed in all black wearing sunglasses.

"What was that?" Jade asked, trying to recover from the start that his banshee yell gave her.

The guy next to her snickered. "That's Karl Monroe. He's a pretty popular cosplayer. He dresses as the Kraken. If you're interested, he's doing signings and photos tomorrow in full costume."

"Check him out on TikTok. He has an amazing getup. He's got a huge following, especially after that woman made the 'release the Kraken' line popular again," the guy said.

Jade nodded. "Cool," she added when the guy and his friends stared at her. Sensing that her eavesdropping prospects were drying up, she checked her list of vendors and headed across the hall to peruse the variety of items for sale.

Jade waved to Wade Jeffries in a vintage Star Trek T-shirt with his kilt at the Rock, Scissors, Paper booth. She window-shopped three other tables, but the guys selling collectibles had long lines, and nobody looked bored enough to carry on a conversation with a fake reporter. *I'm striking out all over the place.*

Checking her phone, she still had some time before her rendezvous with Amy. Letting out a sigh, she wandered through the rest of the vendor booths. Swords, light sabers, and Gothic jewelry seemed to be the most popular items.

A loud whistle rang through the banquet room. She turned to find Amy dragging two giant stuffed dragons toward her. "What's all this?" Jade asked when Amy caught up with her.

"I couldn't resist. I told you one can never have too many dragons." Amy adjusted the purple one on her hip and almost dropped the aqua one.

"Here, I've got this one," Jade said. "What else did you want to see?"

"I'm about done for the night. Pick up any good four-one-one?" Amy whispered.

"Several juicy tidbits, but no ah-ha moments. Lots of gossip."

"Same here. There was way too much time with nothing going on. And when I got bored, I went shopping."

"How was your panel?" Jade asked.

"Most excellent. And I bumped into Angel Cruz in the hallway. He is out of this world, and he talked to me again. I am so inviting him back to the store.

He said he's coming back in the summer to do some filming here. Maybe I can get him to plug Mermaid Books and do some kind of live broadcast from the store."

"A few minutes ago, folks out in the common area were chatting about looking forward to his talk. Did he say anything about a big announcement?" Jade asked, switching the heavy stuffed dragon to her other hip.

Amy's face lit up. "Yes. He talked about that at my store. His treasure finds are so amazing. He's in the process of opening a museum in Florida to show it all off. But the big thing was that he and his crew found a new species of squid on their last excursion. He gets to name it. He was totally psyched that a treasure hunter and diver would have his name in the record books for a big discovery."

"Cool," Jade replied. "Anything else you want to do or see here tonight?"

"What? You don't want to meet Randall for drinks? We could get a table for five and let him buy us and the dragons rounds."

Jade gave her a side-eye. "I'm torn. Randall never seems to provide the whole story. Just little snippets. I get a vibe off of him that I can't quite pinpoint. Maybe we could tag team him and get him to cough up some real info. I guess a little chat wouldn't hurt."

"The dragons will behave, and they'll help us keep the convo going. And they don't drink that much. I could use something to whet my whistle that's good and caffeinated. Text him and tell us to meet us in the bar. If he's a snooze, we'll duck out."

Jade acquiesced and tapped a quick message to Randall.

His reply was almost instantaneous. **Come and join us. I've got a big table near the bar. The more the merrier.**

"That cinches it," Amy said. "And he's a cryptozoologist. He'll love the dragons."

If it weren't for the giant dragon bobbing along in front of her, Jade would have lost Amy in the crowd, and the dragon Jade carried made a soft shield to block elbows and giant backpacks on the trek to the bar.

The dark paneled watering hole was decorated to look like a dungeon or some kind of secret lair. The low lighting and all the rich wood with iron accents created a toned-down mood. The pair spotted Randall holding court at a large round table. "Welcome," he said as they approached. "These are my friends from Mermaid Bay. Jade and uh…"

"Amy. Amy Pemberton. I own Mermaid Books. Stop by and check it out. We have something for everyone."

"And Amy. Jade here owns the Christmas shop in town, but she's got a reputation as an amateur crime solver," Randall said. Turning to Jade and Amy, he continued, "Gals, this is Kari Sanders, she's an author and YouTuber extraordinaire. And this is Jack Iden, a former student who recently finished his dissertation in cryptozoology. I've known him forever, and now he's added doctor to his name and has the newly minted diploma to prove it. Another round over here to celebrate."

"Congratulations," Jade said. "It's nice to meet you all."

"Sit. Sit," Randall said, pointing to the empty seats around the table.

Amy put the dragons in two of the chairs and selected one for herself next to Kari. "Hi, here's my card. I love to have authors at the bookstore. Let me know if you're ever doing a book tour."

"Thanks," Kari slurred. "Right now, I'm getting ready to head out to Australia for a two-year research gig. This is kind of my bon voyage party."

"Kari's doing research on several species' sightings Down Under. I love it when mythological turns real. It drives the zoologists and the biologists mad. Too bad Mer isn't here with us tonight. I'm sure she'd have something to say," Randall said, reaching for the glass that he raised in the air like he was giving a toast.

Kari winked and flipped her long chestnut curls over her shoulder. "Indeed, she would, and I wouldn't listen to half of her snarky blah blah blah. I liked her better when she wasn't on her high horse about everything. No offense, Randy, but she could be over the top and out of line most of the time."

"None taken. She was good at cultivating her public persona. It was her brand. But you all didn't get to know her for what she truly was." The waitress, in a short version of a prison outfit, walked by, and Randall waved a hand. "One more round over here for this rowdy crew. We have to wish safe travels to my friend here and celebrate an advanced degree. Lots of joy here."

"The same for you three?" the waitress said, pointing to Randall's side of the table. Kari nodded, and the server continued, "And for you, ladies?"

"I'll have an iced coffee," Amy said. "Lots of coffee and lots of whipped cream."

"You want it Irish?" the server asked.

Amy shook her head. "Nope. I've got to get up early tomorrow for a book talk."

"And you?" the server asked.

"I'll have a Dr. Pepper," Jade said.

"Y'all are heavily caffeinated type A-gals, aren't you?" Randall said when the server headed toward the bar. "That's good. Keep your wits about you and solve these murders before we all have to head home or get hauled in for questioning again. I can't let Meredith end up in the cold case files. I owe it to her."

"So you really do true crime?" Kari asked. "Do you have a podcast?"

Jade shook her head, and Amy said, "Not yet. But that's a super idea. Jade divides her time between her business and searching for clues to help her hunky boyfriend, our town's sheriff."

Randall's head turned slightly, and his lips formed a straight line across his face.

"Nick and his team do well on their own," Jade added, giving Amy a slight frown. "People around town tell me things, and I've been lucky enough to solve a handful of situations in the past."

Amy patted her arm. "She's being modest. Not only has she solved at least three murders that I know of, she caught the bad guys and gals red-handed. She's kind of a big deal in these parts. And she's even risked life and limb to stop the bad guys."

Jade could feel the heat rising in her cheeks. *Maybe I do need a drink. Time to change the subject.* "Thanks, but it's more of being at the right place at the right time."

"And that's why she's helping me figure out what happened to Meredith," Randall added, raising his glass in Jade's direction. "I have confidence that she'll get to the bottom of this."

"We," Amy said, pointing to Jade and herself. "I'm her sidekick."

Kari laughed and drained the remaining drops in her glass. "That's adorable. Where is that waitress? And Randy, tell the truth. You're only interested in clearing your name, so you get the insurance money. Fess up. You're her beneficiary. No matter how much you pretend. We all know you two were still married. You always carried a torch for Meredith even when the rest of us couldn't figure out why. And I heard she was doing pretty well with her publishing and all those pyramid schemes. So, where will this big party be when you inherit all your wife's ill-gotten loot?"

A dark cloud looked like it landed on Randall. He recovered quickly after the server dropped off the next round. "Now, Kari, don't be catty. Mer always said you were jealous of her."

"Maybe. But I never understood how you could still be in love with that harpy. But that's a topic for another day." She downed a gulp of her new drink and rose. "You guys be good while I'm gone, and if you need a diversion, come see me in the Northern Territory of Australia. It'll be wild." She flipped her curls over her shoulder again and blew kisses at Randall and Jack.

When Kari wobbled off, Amy said, "So, Jack. How do you know Randall and Meredith?"

A wide-eyed look crossed the thin man's face. He cleared his throat, and his glance darted around the table. "I was a student of Randall's, and he became my mentor and friend. I hung around him quite a bit as an undergrad and in grad school, and at the time, Meredith was living there too. Uh, and he's right, in private, she acted different than she does in public. She could be a nice person sometimes. I'm still kinda shocked that she's gone."

"Jack was an excellent student. He was my teaching assistant for a couple of semesters. Mer and I loved having him around." Randall looked around for the waitress.

"Well, this has been fun, but I still have some worky tasks to do before I can call it a night. Thanks for the drinks. And Randall, know that we're on the case." Amy rose and wrestled one of the dragons from its captain's chair.

Jade picked up the other stuffed creature. "Yes, it was nice to meet you,

Jack. And Randall, I'll text you in a day or two."

"I'll call you before that," Randall said with a wink.

"We'll have plenty of updates soon. We plan to bust this investigation wide open." Amy spread her arms and almost dropped the dragon.

Randall winked at Jade again. "I knew I found the right person. Uh, the right people. I like your partner. She's spunky."

Jade picked her way with the giant dragon through the crowded bar. *Why does this murder feel so different from the others? I hope Amy didn't overpromise on this one.*

Chapter Sixteen

Jade and Chloe trotted across Neptune Road to the store, and the dog downshifted into second gear as she catalogued every blade of grass and pebble on the path. Jade's mind wandered as she waited for the chubby dog to explore. Last night on the way home, Amy talked a mile a minute about Angel, Randall, and all the authors she had invited to her store. She was totally enamored with Angel Cruz and his squid find and over the moon that his publicist was including her bookstore on his next book tour. In between all the squeals and excitement, her sleuthing did manage to turn up an interesting tidbit when she mentioned that Angel's publicist, Marcella Hendricks, had also worked with Meredith. *I need to reach out to get her thoughts on her other client.*

Before Jade could ponder the new revelation further, her phone alerted with a series of rapid-fire texts. Jade peeked at the messages from Vivian Turner and tried to will her blood pressure to stay normal, especially when she saw the string of all caps.

CODE RED. CODE RED. EMERGENCY! MB Business Council Meeting at noon today.

A deputy will be present to keep order and talk about ways we can stay safe.

The key discussion point is whether or not to change our Mermaid Day schedule.

"She panics every time there is a problem. Not sure if this rises to the level of a code red emergency." Jade sighed. "Okay, let's pick up the pace a bit. I need to do work stuff before I head over to the library for the emergency meeting. I may swing by the Pearl too. I'd like to see if I can chat up Randall. I'm hoping that if I catch him away from the conference, I can get some more information from him. You know, a change of scenery to shake it up a bit. Oh, and Lorelei and Neville will be here to keep you company today."

At the mention of her arch-enemy's name, the little dog's ears perked up, and she trotted to the store's back door. Jade flew through her opening routine and started the coffee maker. She flipped through her contacts and phoned Ruby Ellis at the Pearl.

"It's a beautiful day in Mermaid Bay," Ruby's daughter Josie said. "How may I make your visit fabulous?"

"Hey, Josie, it's Jade. Is Randall Medlin still around there?"

"Hey, gal. I haven't seen you in ages. I hope you and Nick are well. Yep, he's still a guest here." She blew out a long puff of air. "I know he lost his wife, but he's been overly cranky. Nothing that we do for him meets his standards," she whispered into the phone. "All he does is sit in the library, drink coffee, yell at people on the phone, and mope. And he thinks we're supposed to be at his beck and call twenty-four-seven."

"I'm going to swing by to see if I can catch him before he starts his day."

"Maybe a visit will brighten his day. We can only hope. See you in a bit. Ciao," Josie said.

"Bye," Jade said to dead air. She hustled through the store and built a small gift basket filled with truffles, hot cocoa, a pen, and a mug. By the time she struggled to wrap the basket in cellophane and tie off the bow, her aunt Lorelei breezed in, followed by Neville, who strutted in like he owned the place. Then the black and white cat leaped onto the counter and made a bed on a stack of papers.

"Good morning. Let me help you with that. I'll hold the bottom, and you floof the bow and the top-notch part. Yep. That looks nice," Lorelei said. "What's the occasion?"

"It's good to see you. You, too, Neville. Chloe missed you. This is for Randall Medlin. I'll drop it off at the Pearl and then head to the library for Vivian's emergency meeting."

"Don't tell me Vivian's on a tear again."

"She wants to talk about canceling Mermaid Day in light of the latest happenings."

"Oh, posh. We've had murders and bad things in this town before. And one of the murders didn't even happen here. That's no reason to shut everything down and board up like a hurricane is coming. She is wound up too tightly sometimes." Lorelei stashed her hot pink Kate Spade bag behind the counter. "Say hi to Ruby and Josie for me. Anything you want me to work on while you're gone?"

"I didn't pull the overnight orders yet."

"I'm on it. I'll print the report and get everything bagged and tagged nicely, but coffee first," her aunt said, sashaying to the back.

"I'll be back as soon as I can. Text me if any bus tours show up."

"Of course. Don't worry about us. We'll keep things humming along here, and if it gets too quiet, we'll do Christmas karaoke or something."

Jade smiled and grabbed her purse. "Be back as soon as I can." She hopped in the lime-green Wrangler and wended her way through the neighborhood streets. As she headed inland, the beach bungalows were replaced by larger Victorian homes. Her friend, Ruby Ellis, and her daughter Josie had turned one of the three-story homes that looked like a dollhouse into the Pearl, the town's first bed and breakfast.

She parked on the street and made her way up the oyster shell path to the kitchen door. Ruby's magnificent garden was about to explode with a rainbow of color. Jade glanced at the trellis and cracked a smile. This was the scene of her most embarrassing moment that went viral when she tackled what she thought was an intruder trying to break in by climbing the trellis. It turned out to be one of the wayward actors from the Love Channel's production. The worst part was that the paparazzi caught her wrestling him to the ground. *I guess that was my fifteen minutes of infamy.*

The kitchen door popped open and distracted her from her trip down memory lane. "Well, hello, Jade. What brings you by? Lovely basket." Ruby wiped her hands on her apron.

"Good morning. Sorry to barge in. This is for Randall Medlin. I was hoping to catch him before he got busy."

Ruby made a face like she had licked a lemon. "Doubtful. He's turned the library into his own personal office. He's been in there at all hours. Go on in. I'm sure he's holding court. He wanted coffee and breakfast at the crack of dawn. Hopefully, he'll be in a better mood than he was earlier."

"Thanks. You and Josie doing all right? I haven't seen much of y'all since the filming wrapped."

"We took a long vacation after all that excitement and drama. Josie and I are staying busy, which is good. You going to Vivian's emergency meeting?" Ruby pushed back a strand of silver hair that had slipped out of the tight chignon at the base of her neck.

Jade nodded, and Ruby continued, "I'm swamped here this morning. Let me know if there's anything important. I don't have time for Vivian's fretting. If you ask me, she cries wolf too much."

"Will do," Jade said, making her way to the vast, three-story foyer filled with antiques and homey touches. Across the hall, Randall sat in the buttery-colored loveseat with his boots on Ruby's coffee table. In one hand, he held a full mug of coffee and a pen, and in the other, he balanced his phone between his ear and shoulder.

When he spotted Jade, he held up one finger with his free hand and motioned for her to come in. "Yep. That's what I said. I want this stuff taken care of. I've got to clean out her office and condo when I get back. Yep. Call me as soon as you know something." He mashed the disconnect button and dropped the phone on the couch. "Hey, Jade. It's good to see you. What news do you have for me? Tell me something. I need anything positive." The worry lines had settled around his eyes and mouth, making him look years older than when they first met at her store.

"Yes, it was nice to meet your colleagues."

"Huh?" Randall stared at her.

"At the bar at the hotel. At CreatureCon. Last night," she said, returning his gaze. *Was he too blitzed to remember that Amy and I were there?*

"Oh, yeah. That. Sorry. There were so many people there offering their condolences. It turned into a kinda celebration for Mer. We shut the place down. I'm actually surprised that I'm up and chipper this morning. That reminds me. I gotta find some aspirin. I'll see if that gal has any." He sat up straighter on the couch and took his feet off Ruby's table. He paused, seemingly lost in thought. Jade set the basket in front of him.

"How nice." He ripped open the plastic and rummaged through the contents. Oooooo snacks. Way better than the birdseed and rabbit food they serve around here."

"My team wanted to offer our condolences." Jade glanced at the notebook, pens, candy wrappers, and scraps of paper strewn all over the antique table's surface. "It looks like you've been busy."

"It never lets up. I'm constantly writing, researching, or speaking. I'm trying to get some of Meredith's affairs in order between booking some of my own speaking engagements. My assistant put too many winter ones in colder climates. I have no idea what she was thinking. She knows I hate to travel where it's cold." He tore open the chocolate wrapper and bit off a hunk.

When the silence and his deadpan stare felt smothering, she added, "Again. My condolences on your wife's death."

"As much of a pain in the butt as she was, she cared about her work, and we loved each other. We scrapped like cats and dogs, but we were meant to be together. I need you to figure this out. Every time I talk to the cops, I get the feeling that they're zeroing in on me. I had nothing to do with this. They want me to take a polygraph now. I don't have time for all the interrogations. I'm slammed with work, and now I have to take care of Meredith's stuff. And if that's not enough, I'm fighting with her university. I need to be able to get the police off my back. I need to catch a break. For Pete's sake, she and I were the victims in all this." *What about Ernie Post?*

"But the polygraph may go a long way to get you off law enforcement's radar," Jade said.

Randall made a face. "Or, like my lawyer said, they could use any nervous tick, or stutter against me. They already got my DNA. There are not enough hours in the day to respond to all the questions and do the executor stuff. I'm getting lost in all of this. I need all of this to be over."

"Any ideas on how the Xplorer's murder relates to Meredith's?" she asked.

Randall's countenance darkened, and his mouth twitched. "What have you heard?"

"Just that you all have known each other for a long time. I'm trying to see if there is anything to connect the two murders. You were close friends, right?"

He waved his free hand dismissively. "We go way back. I mean, that's what connects Mer and me to him, but we haven't had much contact recently. I comment on his Facebook posts from time to time and message him when something's interesting. Everyone's so busy with work and life. We haven't had time to get together." His voice drifted off. "Have you looked into that guy named Topher? Topher Taylor. You should check him out. He knew Ernie and Mer too."

His phone's jarring ringtone echoed through Ruby's library. "Gotta take this. Call me as soon as you find out anything. I've got to put all of this to rest."

Jade nodded and quietly made her way to the foyer and out the front door. *What is it about him? Sometimes, he's attentive and concerned, and then he's back to being flip. I need to talk to Marcella, the publicist. Maybe she'll have some insight into Meredith's life. And then I guess I'll see if I can find this Topher person.*

Chapter Seventeen

Jade hustled out of Ruby's B and B and pointed her Jeep toward the town's administrative center. Parking was at a premium at the library, so she made her own space in the grassy area next to the office lot.

Glancing at the time on her dashboard, she hurried down the sidewalk and dodged kids and book carts on her way to the multipurpose room in the back of the building. Vivian stood near the lectern, and most of the audience milled around the table in the back with coffee and three boxes of pastries from the Busy Bean.

Jade found a seat in the front row and tried to get comfortable on the metal chair. A thunk, thunk, thunk, and a squeal poured from all of the speakers in the ceiling, causing the audience to groan and stare at Vivian. "Sorry." Vivian lowered the microphone and continued. "Good morning. Thanks for coming out today. Please find your seats, and we'll get started in a minute." Vivian scanned the room like she was waiting for someone. Her gaze volleyed repeatedly between watching the crowd and checking her watch.

Seconds passed, and Vivian continued, "Okay, people. We need to get started, so everyone can get back to work. I'm Vivian Turner, president of the Mermaid Bay Business Council, and this special meeting is to raise the question of whether or not we think we should hold the planned Mermaid Day festivities this week in light of recent circumstances. Deputy Sanchez will join us a bit later to offer some safety tips and maybe an update on the investigation. I know that he, Sheriff Driscoll, and the state police are consumed by the recent murder." She whispered the last word and puckered her lips like she was about to shush someone.

The crowd of business owners meandered to their seats, and the scuffling and murmurs died down. *Eeks. I hope Vivian doesn't thump her giant ring on the microphone again. That made a rude sound.*

"Thank you again for coming. I'd like to start with an update from the Mermaid Bay committee chairs, Kelly Jamison and Farrah Rogers. The pair, who looked like polar opposites, made their way down the center aisle. Kelly, the owner of the town's antique store, fluttered to the front with her flouncy batwing blouse trailing behind her like a cape, while her partner, Farrah, one of the town's realtors, sashayed in teal stilettos that matched her tailored business suit. Her big helmet-hair and chunky jewelry looked like something from the nineties.

"Thanks, Vivian," Kelly said, raising the microphone. "Our teams have worked hard this season to plan a variety of events to draw all ages to town to celebrate our mermaids. This includes the vendor arts and craft sale with our food truck caravan on Saturday, the massive Mermaid parade, the glass-bottom boat tours, the giant sandcastle contest, and movie night on the beach."

Farrah cleared her throat and leaned over toward the microphone. In a breathy voice that reminded Jade of Marilyn Monroe, she said, "Yes. We're so excited to have a host of activities planned for all ages, and we've gotten such wonderful feedback. Plus, we're partnering with Seaport's CreatureCon in our marketing efforts. So far, we have sold slots to eighty-five artisans and craftspeople and thirty-two food trucks. The parade has twenty floats, four marching bands, and a variety of community groups. Proceeds from all the events have totaled over one-hundred and fifty-two thousand dollars. But that's not the final total. It could go higher. Oh, and we have to deduct expenses and prizes for the sandcastle contest. So..." The svelte realtor turned toward Vivian and pointed her ruby-red lacquered nail. "If we cancel, it will be an endeavor to do the refunds, and we will not recoup sunk costs. Kelly, the team, and I are hoping this body will make the sensible decision and let the festivities continue. This would be a huge blow to morale if we cancel. Thank you."

Vivian glared at Farrah and made her way to the lectern. "Thank you, ladies. We appreciate all the hard work and time you've invested in this. We want to showcase our town in the best light. Ah, there is Deputy Sanchez. Why don't you come up and give us an update on the unfortunate situation? And let us know if the department is too strapped to deal with the crowds this weekend."

The buff deputy eased his way through the people standing at the door and along the wall. He paused at the lectern and adjusted the microphone. "The investigations into the death of Ernie Post, also known professionally as the Xplorer, and Dr. Meredith Echols in nearby James City County are ongoing, so I can't give you any details that will jeopardize those. Lots of investigators are working round the clock on these cases. Sheriff Nick Driscoll is leading a task force that's looking into the death of Mr. Post. We are partnering with the state and other authorities, including our sister county, in its ongoing investigation. We have been working closely with the town administration, and we have emergency services covered for the weekend. Staffing for the special event will not affect the investigation or our normal public safety efforts. We are ready to support the business council's activities for Mermaid Day." Farrah stood and clapped, and most of the room joined her. When the noise died down, Sebastian continued, "We're asking that anyone with information on either of these murders to call Crime Stoppers." He rattled off the hotline number and scanned the crowd. "I have handouts here if anyone is interested in ways you can make your business and family safer." He held up a stack of flyers.

"I'll put those on the back table for our members," Vivian said, taking the papers out of his hand. "Any advice for us as we make our decision on whether or not to cancel our events? It seems sordid to be celebrating and frolicking around the beach during a time of tragedy." Her gaze seemed to linger on Farrah, who watched every move the deputy made.

Sebastian gave Vivian a side-eye and continued, "At this time, we think these were isolated, targeted incidents, and we don't feel that the public is in danger. I know you all will make your decision thoughtfully, but in my opinion, there is no need to cancel what you have put so much effort into and what folks are looking forward to. My vote is to move forward with your plans."

Farrah pursed her lips and beamed a smug look in Vivian's direction.

Nell Jones, the town's society writer for the weekly gazette, scribbled furiously in a notebook. Jade waited for her to question the deputy, but she remained uncharacteristically quiet.

Vivian approached the microphone and forcefully pulled it closer to her. "Well, thank you, Deputy Sanchez, for helping us stay safe and easing some of our fears about recent events. Does anyone else have anything to add before we vote on this matter?" She stiffened her jaw and surveyed the room with military precision.

Sebastian saluted with two fingers and headed out the door. *I'm sure he and Nick will get a phone call from a certain librarian today.*

Eva Swenson's hand flew in the air, and she waved it around like she was swatting bees. "Yes, Eva," Vivian said.

Jade's diminutive across-the-street neighbor hopped to her feet. "We have put a lot of work into planning these events. I am so sorry that the young man was murdered, but we don't even know if he was killed here. I heard he was dumped under Suggs Pier. It has nothing to do with us, and we should celebrate life and continue on with our plans."

"Hear, hear," Martha Vanderbeek yelled as she jumped to her feet. "We can have a ceremony or a moment of silence. That would be a nice memorial, but I agree with those who have spoken. There is no need to cancel. I, for one, am looking forward to the celebration. There's enough evil in this world. We need to celebrate good things." Applause and a standing ovation rang out across the room.

Vivian gave up trying to restore order. She huffed and waited impatiently for the room to settle down. "Well, we've heard many voices in favor of our festival. Does anyone want to offer a differing thought?" She searched the crowd and waited for what felt like an eternity. When no one responded, she said, "Okay, then. I guess we hold a vote. Bernie, Cecil, you help me count hands. All in favor of continuing with Mermaid Day, raise your hand." Every hand in the audience went up. "All opposed." Vivian paused again.

Cecil piped up from the back. "Viv, that was everyone in favor and zero opposed." Snickers rippled through the audience as Vivian took a deep breath.

"There we have it. We will proceed with the festivities, and the planning committee will come up with a fitting way to pay tribute to the young man. Thank you for coming out today on short notice. Don't forget to pick up the safety flyers on your way out. If the committee members would hang back, I'd like to go over some logistics. Adjourned."

Jade hustled outside. Ditching her plan to beat the traffic out of the parking lot, she pulled out her phone and tapped a note to Delia. **Howdy. One of the guys I talked to mentioned a Topher Taylor. Somehow, he's involved with Meredith Echols. Has his name popped up in any of your research?**

When Delia didn't reply immediately, Jade put the Jeep in gear and headed back to the store. She laughed when she saw five cars ahead of her waiting to exit the lot. *As much as the traffic here slows me down, it's nothing like what I slogged through every single day in Northern Virginia.*

Chapter Eighteen

J ade parked in the back of her store and clicked Amy's contact on her phone. "Hey, lady. How're you doing? Are you headed to the con tonight?"

"Yeppers. Right after work. Todd's got a full-blown head cold, probably from surfing before the ocean warmed up, but he won't admit that's the cause. You going? How about you pick me up?"

"Sounds like a plan," Jade said.

"And we'll grab dinner, and you can tell me which new leads you're pursuing. I should write a mystery novel based on our adventures. Hmmm."

Hoping Amy was kidding, Jade changed the subject. "Okay. I'm doing the closing tonight, so how about I pick you up about six-thirty?"

"Perfect. I'll be here with bells on. Ciao."

"Whoo hooo, I'm home," Jade called when she opened the back door to the empty office. Little toenails clicked on the wood floors, and she was greeted by a jubilant Frenchie. Scooping her up for tickles, she said, "It's good to see you, too, baby. What are Neville and Lorelei up to?"

"We're in here. I was reading Nell's latest post online about the heated council meeting where the voice of the people won out over oppressive decorum. Sorry that I missed all the fireworks. Fill me in on the juicy stuff."

"Wow. She may have embellished just a tad." Jade's eyes widened.

"She didn't call out anyone as the dark warlord, but we know who she was referring to. She said it was a great day for democracy and mermaids. She quoted Sebastian, Eva, Farrah, and Mrs. Vanderbeek. Sounded like a rowdy bunch. Rabblerousers."

Jade leaned over Lorelei's shoulder and scanned the online article. "Oh, my. Vivian will not like this. She was in a tizzy about shutting down the festivities because of the murder, and everyone there was against it. The show will go on, but you could tell she wasn't happy about it."

"Of course, it should go on as planned. Vivian's heart is in the right place, but sometimes, she's wound too tight for her own good. Her tombstone is going to read, 'Here lies Vivian. She followed all the rules and made sure everyone else did too.' It makes me want to shake her sometimes and tell her to lighten up."

Jade cracked a smile. "She's very particular, and she wants everyone to rise to her standards."

"Standards are helpful. Sometimes," her aunt said. "I'm just saying it might be time to change the old guard on the board for some new blood. You should think about it the next time they have elections. You have lots of wonderful ideas. A breath of fresh air would do this town good. It tends to get a little stuffy at times."

"I have enough here to keep me busy. Farrah stepped up to be co-chair of the mermaid festivities with Kelly. That's some new blood."

"I'm glad she's getting involved in things now. She was one of the mean girls when her fearless leader, Trish the Dish, was in charge of the Mermaid Bay real estate market. Since Trish ran away to Florida, her underlings have been stepping out of her shadow. I'm glad for Farrah. She needed to shine on her own."

Jade shrugged. "I hope Trish is doing okay after that very public break-up with Jared Carswell. She seemed to take it pretty hard."

"She's a tough girl. A change of scenery was what she needed. I'm sure she's rebounded personally and professionally in her new digs. Let me know if you hear anything about Vivian having apoplexy over this article. Can't wait for the deets. We have some characters around here and our own little mermaid soap opera."

Jade snickered. "It looks like everything is humming along in the store."

"Smooth like glass. Neville, Chloe, and I have it all under control. The delivery guy picked up the pile of online orders, and we've had small groups of shoppers pop in at regular intervals. I'll be out here checking the gossip grapevine on Facebook. I haven't seen anything new on that Mermaid Whispers site. She's missing in action."

Jade headed for her desk and said, "Let me know if you find anything related to the murders."

"I'm doing Love Channel kinds of research and not Lifetime's murdery tales," her aunt replied with a laugh. "But if I see anything, I'll let you know."

Jade opened her browser and found the website for CreatureCon. *Hmmm. No Topher, but there's a Christopher Taylor. He's the only last name match with the guy Randall mentioned. It can't hurt to do some digging. There are so many dead ends and rabbit holes that it's not even funny.*

At four-thirty on the dot, Neville started caterwauling on the front counter, and it sent Chloe into overdrive. Lorelei picked up her purse and the singing cat. "He's started this recently when he's hungry and ready for dinner. He's my new dinner bell. Let's go, kittycat. Time to get you back to the condo for din-din." The black and white furball melted in her arms and started to purr.

"He's got your wrapped around one paw," Jade said with a wink.

"He's my buddy. See you all later this week. Let me know if you uncover anything juicy. You're always in the know. Find something good tonight." She waved with one hand and flounced out the front.

Jade and Chloe whizzed through the store closing and hustled home to get ready for another night full of costumes and mythical monsters. When the Frenchie was fed, and Jade had changed into a long-sleeved top to ward off any night air chillies, she kissed the dog and waved goodbye.

Her Jeep had barely stopped in front of Mermaid Books before Amy yanked open the door. "What a wonderful night to solve a mystery. Sleuth Amy reporting for duty." She hiked one leg up and hopped to get into the vehicle. "How was your day? Are you ready to find some clues?"

Jade made a half-a-doughnut turn and zipped out of the lot toward Seaport. "Foot traffic has been down a bit. I'm hoping the Mermaid Festival will change that this weekend. How about you?"

"What do you feel like for dinner? I was looking through my coupon book for a new place, and I came up with Magic Kebabs and Bunny's BBQ. Have you tried either?" Amy asked.

Jade shook her head, and Amy continued, "Let's try the BBQ. My treat since I have a BOGO coupon. It says it's next to the go-cart track. That place was fun. I think I need to challenge y'all to a rematch."

Jade cruised down Seaport's main drag and turned into the crowded lot in front of the red building with a wooden facade that was made to look like a barn. An outside seating area, decorated with strings of lights and a tiny stage, butted up against the side of the building.

"This looks fun," Amy said. "Sometimes, the places in these coupon books are tourist traps. Todd and I tried a seafood place that we had to climb a fire escape to enter. I'm not sure it was even a real restaurant. But the pie was out of this world."

Jade followed Amy inside. The bright interior was decorated with yellow and white check curtains and matching tablecloths, and the walls were lined with barnwood. Every flat surface was covered with chicken, cow, and pig statues.

"Kitschy cute," Amy said, sliding onto a bench at a table near a juke box. "It reminds me of that country chic that was popular a while back. Wow. There sure are a barnyard full of pigs and chickens in this place. I'd hate to dust all this."

After the waiter took their orders and returned with iced teas in Mason jars, the pair fell silent and took in all of Bunny's decorations.

"Okay," Amy said, breaking the short-lived silence. "Ernie Xplorer ends up murdered. Dr. Meredith is a suspect, and then she is later found dead by the folks on my paranormal tour. Now her husband seems to be suspect number one, and he wants you to clear his name. Doesn't sound that difficult. Any new leads or ideas?"

Jade shook her head. "The Xplorer was one of Meredith's students, and there was a scandal. Ernie was also one of Randall's friends. Ernie and Randall are popular, and Meredith is, well, was not."

"The Cruella Deville of the cryptid world," Amy added.

"All of Meredith's relationships were complicated. It seemed there was always some drama surrounding her," Jade said, taking a sip of tea.

"No limit to the people she ticked off. This one's a tough one. But maybe it's all about her and has nothing to do with the conference."

"She is at the center of most of the action, but I still keep coming back to Ernie. Did he have something she wanted? Was he blackmailing her? Was it revenge for a romance gone bad? Or a rendezvous they were trying to hide. I know there's a connection between the two murders. And if she killed the Xplorer, then who killed her and why? The likelihood of two random killers running around, knocking off conference panelists doesn't seem plausible."

"She could have been two-timing Randall with old Ernie. Or…maybe it was one of his rabid fans out for revenge after she knocked off the Xplorer? Just please tell me it wasn't Angel Cruz. He is so dreamy. I've been binge-watching his series to get ready for the new season. His life is sooooo exciting. I can't wait to have him back at the store. My heart couldn't take it if he turned out to be some kind of marauding killer. I would lose all faith in humanity."

"Speaking of him. I want to talk to his publicist."

Amy whipped out her phone. "There. I sent you Marcella's email and cell phone. Give her a call. We're chatty buds and Facebook friends. She's a doll and so helpful. I don't know how she juggles so many clients and manages to keep all their schedules straight."

"Thanks," Jade said. The lanky waiter returned with their pulled barbecue sandwiches, baked beans, apple sauce, and hush puppies.

"This smells wonderful," Amy said, reaching for the spicy BBQ sauce. "Oooh, look at all the choices. Who knew there were this many sauce flavors?"

When they had eaten as much as they could hold and passed on dessert, Amy paid the bill and said, "I'm stuffed. That was yummy, but I may have to pop open the button on my jeans. I'm liking all the southern dishes down here. There's always something new for me to try. Whatdaya say we head over to the hotel and see if we can find this Topher guy."

They rode in silence to the hotel. Not finding a spot in the front or side lots, Jade pulled into the overflow lot next door. "Sorry about the hike."

"It's a nice evening, and we can enjoy the sounds of the surf, the sand, and all the people running around in crazy costumes out here. How do we want to work this?" Amy asked, hopping out of the Wrangler.

"Divide and conquer? We're looking for Christopher Topher Taylor. The website has him listed as a speaker, but he's not on any panels tonight."

"We're up to the challenge, and I'm confident that we'll find him. This place isn't that big. We're off! Operation Topher is underway." Amy raised a fist in the air. "Text me if you find anything, and I'll do the same."

The pair separated at the door, and Jade jog-walked down the long hallway to the conference center as Amy ducked into the bar.

Jade changed chairs and couches about ten times as she eavesdropped on snippets of conversations. She would ask about Topher when she could work it into random conversations with strangers without coming off as too weird. *I don't know what I'm worried about. Half of these people are wearing alien or monster costumes. They seem friendly enough, and they don't think it's strange that a thirty-something in street clothes is trying to find some guy.*

Tired of not learning anything new, Jade relocated to the seating area outside the ballroom. *Nobody seems to know this Topher guy.*

Around nine o'clock, Jade's phone buzzed. **I'm tired and my feet hurt. Having any luck?** Amy asked.

Nope. Wanna bag it?

We could stop and get doughnuts on the way home. Amy added three doughnut emojis for emphasis.

Deal. Meet me in the lobby, Jade replied.

Minutes later, Amy rushed over and grabbed Jade's arm. Pulling her toward the door, she whispered, "I think I'm being followed."

"By a guy in a furry outfit?"

"No, don't be silly. I'm serious. Every time I turn around, this tall guy with brown shaggy hair is staring at me. I have seen him at least six times tonight. It's weird," Amy said.

Jade turned around and counted at least a half-dozen guys taller than Amy with longish brown hair. "Okay. We'll be vigilant. I think we're safe. Maybe he wants to meet you." She tapped Amy lightly on the arm.

"Doubtful." Amy rolled her eyes. "This absolutely calls for doughnuts. I need sustenance. I'm a little creeped out by this."

The pair hurried to the parking lot while Amy checked over her shoulder every few seconds. The entire ride to the Sugar Shack, Amy fidgeted in the passenger seat and played with the zipper on her purse.

Jade held the door for Amy. All kinds of vanilla and cinnamon scents greeted them from inside the smallish store. Jade and Amy perused the giant glass cases full of every shape and kind of doughnut imaginable. It took several minutes for them to narrow their choices from the standard vanilla and chocolate fare to the bacon maple or the Oreo cookie-covered monstrosity. Jade picked a half dozen for the rest of the week, while Amy bought three boxes for tomorrow's event at the bookstore.

"There," Amy said, settling in the shotgun seat with the boxes on her lap. "These will be perfect for my anime thing tomorrow. I picked some that had gummi worms and another set with candy bar crumbles. The teens will love them. Todd will also love them. I'll have to hide them if he comes over."

"Find any Tophers this evening?" Jade asked, pulling out onto the main road.

"Not a one. You'd think they wouldn't be that rare," Amy said. "Maybe he's like Nessie or Sasquatch. Or the Mothman. He doesn't want to be found. Though I did see the Kraken signing autographs and posing for pictures tonight. That was one righteous outfit."

Minutes later, Jade pulled around back of the building that Amy's bookstore shared with the Busy Bean. "Well, here we are. Thanks for going with me."

"Thanks for stopping for doughnuts. I needed a snack after all that walking. And I must have asked a hundred people if they knew some guy named Topher. Oh, well. We gave it our best try. Sorry that we have no new leads."

When Amy had climbed the wooden stairs and let herself into the apartment over the store, Jade pulled out on Neptune Road. A small SUV zoomed out of the pizza parlor across the street. Its headlights seemed to disappear because it was so close on her bumper. "What is up with you? There's another lane if you want to pass. And there's no other traffic on this road."

The other vehicle slowed down and zipped down a side street when Jade turned into her driveway. Trying to push thoughts of the rude driver from her head, she unlocked the door, and Chloe suddenly became interested in the Sugar Shack bag. "Breakfast tomorrow," Jade said, clicking the leash in place. "Let's go see the progress of the castles."

Forgetting the deliciously sweet smells for a moment, Chloe pranced down the steps and waited for Jade to lock the door.

At the end of the shell path, Jade had to shade her eyes with her hand. Large portable lights on stands lit up the sand like it was the middle of the day. In the roped-off area, the monumental sandcastles looked like they were standing guard for anything approaching from the bay. Jade and Chloe meandered down the row. Chloe looked at the bases, the only part on her level. One had a giant sea turtle and a dolphin. The mermaid and Neptune ones were still under construction.

No longer interested in the sand art, Chloe chased a sand fiddler in the wet sand at the water's edge. Jade stared at the bay. This was her peaceful place. The sea smell, the constant motion of the waves, and the salty tang on her lips always reminded her that she was home. She closed her eyes for a moment and let her thoughts wander. *Okay, so the search for the Topher guy didn't pan out. I don't think Angel has anything to do with any of this, but I'll call Marcella tomorrow to see what she can tell me about Meredith. This is harder than the last couple of murders to solve. Maybe I should let Nick and his team figure it out. Every lead I chase seems to take me down a meandering path that goes nowhere.*

Chloe snorted, and Jade turned to see what she was up to. A movement or a shadow in Jade's peripheral vision caused her to turn her head and stare into the darkness near the beach houses. Nothing moved. *Girl, you're as jumpy as Amy. It was probably someone out for a walk.* "Chloe, it's time to go home."

The path to her beach cottage seemed darker than normal with all those bright lights on the beach behind her. She flipped on her phone's flashlight, and the pair made their way down the path. Her steps crunched on the crushed oyster shells. Every tree and bush seemed to cast a creepy shadow that looked like the Haunted Forest in *The Wizard of Oz.*

Midway down the path, Chloe froze. She let out a guttural growl and started a barking jag at the shadows.

Not seeing anyone or anything, Jade tried to convince the little dog to move along. "We're almost there. Let's not disturb the neighbors. Some of them go to bed early," she whispered.

Chloe let loose with another fierce growl as a man stepped out between the bushes and stomped toward them.

Chapter Nineteen

Jade squealed. Chloe barked. Jade pointed her phone at the man and raised her other hand in a fist. The man shaded his eyes from the sudden glare from her flashlight app and said, "Don't hit me. I didn't mean to scare you. I thought you heard me approach. I said hey."

Jade stared at the curly-haired guy in jeans and high-top tennis shoes who was actually older than she originally thought. The telltale marks around the corners of his eyes gave away his true age. "Who are you?" she asked.

"The guy you've been looking for all night. I'm Topher Taylor, but my CV reads Dr. Christopher Taylor. I had at least ten of my students say that somebody's mom was looking for me. I got curious and wanted to check it out."

"Somebody's mom?" Every muscle in Jade's body tensed. *I'm still in my thirties.*

"They're in their early twenties. Anyone over thirty looks like someone's mom or grandmom. Don't get offended. Word spread like wildfire that two women were looking for me. So I followed you to see who you were. By the way, great choice with the doughnuts. Perfect evening snack. I've had two already." He cracked a smile, and Jade relaxed slightly. She reached down and picked up Chloe and hugged her until the Frenchie grunted.

"A book seller and a what do you do? Rabid cryptozoology fan?"

"I own the town's Christmas shop."

"So not a PI or someone telling me I have a long-lost inheritance or a kid that I don't know about. Or that I was swapped accidentally at birth or I have a long-lost uncle who needs a kidney…"

Jade was sure her face gave away her true feelings. Trying to figure out where this was going, she said, "No, sorry. Just two curious folks who want to know what happened to the Xplorer."

"I heard about that. That was tragic…"

"And?" she pressed.

"I have no idea. It happened before I even got here. I missed my flight in Atlanta and got delayed. And why do you think I would have something to do with him? I do my job and go home. I don't cultivate a fan club or a social media following. My research is on supposed fantastical species that really do exist in the wild. I'm all about the research, and I don't spend my time trying to capture the media's attention. The Xplorer was all about getting as much publicity as possible, good, bad, or otherwise. All smoke and mirrors. The fans loved him, but he didn't do much to advance the cause."

"Where were you when Dr. Echols was killed?

"When was that?" He stared intently at Jade.

"Sometime Monday," Jade said.

"Like I said. My flight was delayed. I didn't get into Norfolk until after midnight on Sunday. Then it took time to get my stuff and a rental car. And then I had to drive here. I checked in some time after two."

"And?" Jade prodded.

"I fell into bed and slept all day. I got up for dinner. I hit the gym, went to a panel, and hung out with friends at the bar. I didn't leave the hotel."

"Do you know Dr. Randall Medlin?" she asked, hoping to find some connection since Randall mentioned him as a possible suspect.

"We run into each other from time to time. I was Meredith's student for a while when he was married to her. That was about a year and a half before I switched majors, and she had a meltdown about it. Actually, on most days, she wasn't happy about much of anything. I haven't talked to Dr. Medlin in years. And I don't plan to. They are both toxic."

"Toxic, how?" she asked.

"I had him for a couple of classes when I changed schools. He was the cool prof who hung out with his students. But he's not as shiny as he wants everyone to think he is. We haven't talked since twenty-thirteen. I avoid him if we happen to be at the same event. No class."

"Why would you say that?" she asked.

"Let's just say I know he borrowed work from some of his students and passed it off on his own. It happened to a couple of my friends. Not cool. I don't need that in my life…I chose to be around positive people," he said, moving a shell around with the toe of his sneaker.

I heard the same about Meredith. Maybe she and Randall are more alike than they appear.

"If you are interested in my research, I'm on a couple of panels this weekend, and I'm interviewing Angel Cruz tomorrow. You should come and see me. Maybe we can catch dinner afterward or something. Sorry if I scared you. It's not every day I get this much attention. I'm usually the king of geeks. I don't think I've ever had two women hunt me down before. I had to find out who you were."

She nodded. "It's getting late. I'll see if I can make the panel discussion. See you around." Jade darted off and didn't stop until she slammed and locked the front door. When her heartbeat stopped thundering in her temples, she wandered into the kitchen for some iced tea and one of the doughnuts. "No, judging Chloe. Almost-stalkers call for a boost of carbs and sugar. And it's breakfast time somewhere in the world."

Jade downed the doughnut in several bites and dusted her hands on her jeans. "Okay. I haven't heard from Nick or Delia in a while. I'll let D know that she can probably mark Topher off the list. Why would Randall mention him if they hadn't had much contact? He wasn't even here when the first murder happened. Okay, is there more to this story than either is telling?"

Changing her mind, she decided not to call Delia off the Topher search. She dashed off a quick hello to Nick. When she didn't get a response, she focused on her notes. The college and his social media backed up what Topher told her. He had posted videos of him drinking with new friends while he was stuck in the airport bar.

Jade hopped up and rummaged through the junk drawer for sticky notes and a black felt-tip marker. She listed all the major players and the random facts she collected.

Hours later, Jade stepped back and admired her dining room wall that was littered with brightly colored sticky notes. *So far, Ernie, Angel, and Meredith have the most colorful squares under their names. But there are a couple of outliers like Topher and Marcella. And how did Karl the Kraken cosplayer end up on the wall?* She shrugged. *Everyone stays on the wall until I can totally prove they weren't involved.*

Jade sat back down at the table and transferred all the names to a sheet of paper. She used different colored Magic markers to connect the relationships, frenemy lists, and romantic trysts. Her page looked like a rainbow bowl of spaghetti with Meredith at the center of everything.

"Well, that's not complicated or anything." Chloe looked up from her comfy spot on the end of the couch. When she didn't see any evidence of more doughnuts, she returned to her nap.

A knock at the door sent Chloe into a barking fit. "Shhhh, puppy. Maybe, it's Nick."

Jade peeked out the window to find Randall standing on her porch. *What is he doing here?*

She picked up Chloe and opened the door a crack.

"Hey, I thought I saw a light on. I was out for my evening walk and thought I'd take a chance to see if you're up."

"It's after midnight. Kinda late for a stroll," she said, eyeing his jeans, button-down dress shirt, and leather hiking boots.

Before she could reply, Randall continued, "I do my best thinking late at night. It helps me come up with new material. I always go on long walks to clear my head. You know to focus. You have a minute to chat? I can't sleep. Meredith's murder is still on my mind, and it drives me bat crazy that the police think I did it." He let out a long stream of air through his nose. "Nice beach cottage. The B and B lady told me you lived out this way. I was kinda hoping we could talk. Have you learned anything new? I'd love to know what your sheriff plans to do. He keeps me hanging, and as long as the investigation is open, I can't get closure on anything. I'm in limbo with Meredith's estate. I can't move forward. There are so many legal things I need to do, but her stuff is frozen until they figure out what happened to her.

And if that's not enough, the university is trying to distance itself from her. So, on top of murder, they're tarnishing her reputation." He let out another heavy breath. His bright blue eyes had lost their sparkle, and he suddenly looked older and more tired.

"The sheriff's been busy with work. We haven't talked all that much lately… uh, can you tell me about your friend Topher Taylor, the one you mentioned the other day at the Pearl? I think I want to talk to him."

"He's not my friend." The cocky smile disappeared, and he pursed his lips and stared inside Jade's house through the small opening in the door. "Sorry. I got distracted. He was my friend at one time, but he got all weird. He hit on Meredith, and I caught him stealing my notes from my office one time. He's sketchy, and he thinks highly of himself. He's the kind who'll do anything to advance his career. Watch out for him. He's always turning on the boyhood charm to get his way." *Hmmm. Sounds familiar to me. Project much, Randall?*

"Has he reached out to you or Meredith lately? I mean, what brought him up the other day?" she asked.

"You asked if there was anyone in Mer's past who might do her harm. Topher was the first one who popped into my head. He wormed his way into our lives. We were all really close for a while, but he took advantage of people and of us. We leant him money, let him sleep on our couch, gave him a job…I could list hundreds of other things, but he turned on us like a snake when we chose not to be used anymore. It's kind of sad. And no, I haven't had any contact with him in years, even though we do see each other from time to time at these things. He might be worth checking into. He was obsessed with Meredith and me. It was kinda like he wanted what I had."

Randall shifted from foot to foot, trying to get a better look inside Jade's house.

When he didn't continue, she said, "It's been nice to see you. I have an early morning tomorrow, so I need to say good night. Let me know if you think of anyone else I should talk to before the conference is over."

He paused and stared at her a little too long. "Sure. Sorry. I know it's late. I'll think about it tonight and get you some names. I feel out of control. Like the walls are closing in on me, and I don't know what to do. It'll ruin everything if the police arrest me. And I'm sick of all the questioning. I feel like they're trying to trip me up or something."

"Talk to your lawyer. Focus on what you can do. I know. It's hard not to worry about what's going on. I'll see you later at the conference." Jade quickly shut and bolted the door. Randall turned and walked slowly down her driveway and disappeared around the corner.

What a night. First Topher and then Randall. I wonder if I'm getting close to something. Why is everyone so interested in what I know?

Chapter Twenty

Jade tossed and turned all night, and every shadow that moved on the wall reminded her of Topher and Randall popping in to surprise her. Not able to relax her mind from the racing thoughts that now included Ernie and Meredith, she hopped in the shower. *It's probably time for me to be more subtle with my investigating. Too many people have taken notice that I've been asking questions.*

After stepping through her morning routine, she ate her oatmeal and stared at her murder wall. Focusing on Randall's stickies, she reached for her phone and sent a message to Ruby.

Her phone dinged before she could set it down. **Hey, Jade. Neither of us talked to Randall about you, and we certainly wouldn't tell anyone where you lived. Why would he tell you that? He's an odd duck.**

It was weird when he knocked on my door last night, Jade replied.

He's been gone a lot lately at all hours. At first, he moped around. Now, he's suddenly busy.

Thanks for the info. See y'all soon, Jade texted.

Her phone buzzed again with a text from Nick. **I'm leaving here on time tonight. Wanna grab dinner?**

Sounds great. Feel like visiting the con afterward? she asked.

You that interested in monsters?

Maybe. I want to talk to some people before they leave town.

How about TexMex? Six-thirty okay? I need a real dinner that doesn't come from a bag.

Perfect. She added a heart and taco emojis.

"Okay, Chloe, we've got work to do, and I still need to reach out to Delia and Marcella."

Chloe waddled to the front door and waited patiently for Jade to catch up.

After buzzing through two cups of coffee, updating her socials, and filling the overnight orders, Jade took a breather to greet a group of seniors who stopped by to see the decorations. After a nice welcome chat, the five ladies disappeared into the showrooms as the bells on the front door jangled again.

"Morning, y'all," Patti said as she breezed in with a shopping tote, her purse, and an oversized lunch bag. "How's life?"

"The orders kept me busy this morning. How are you?"

"Okay, I guess."

"What's up?" Jade frowned slightly. *This isn't Patti's normal bubbly effervescence.*

"I've been so busy with projects and hanging out with Simon." She fluttered her eyelashes at the mention of her beau. "I haven't had time to keep up the Mermaid Whispers blog. I kinda miss it. It was fun sneaking around town and posting nuggets of gossip to keep everyone guessing."

"You could keep it going. Be mysterious and not let anyone know when you're planning to post next. That way, if there's no schedule, you won't feel the pressure to have new copy every day."

"It is an incredible amount of work. I thought about taking on a partner, but I don't know if it would be the same. I kinda like your idea. I was super bummed about giving it up. It's been an interesting little side project. And any time I get to keep Nell and Vivian guessing, it's worth it." The glimmer was back in Patti's eyes.

Jade patted her friend's arm. "You'll figure it out. If it stresses you out, then stop. If it's something that you really want to do, you'll find a way to make it work."

"Speaking of side projects, have you solved the murders yet?" Patti whispered.

Jade shook her head slightly. "I have a big pile of puzzle pieces, and I can't seem to get stuff to fit together."

"You keep at it. I know you'll wade through the noise and junk to find the valuable tidbits. You have figured out so many in the past. You're a master puzzler."

"We'll see. The murders this time don't involve me or my store, so I kinda feel like I'm on the outside looking in—"

"But Randall asked for your help, so you were invited in. Be patient. It'll come to you when you least expect it. I know you. You'll get a brainstorm and tie up all the loose ends."

"I hope you're right. They're all leaving town soon." Changing the subject, Jade added, "Any plans for this weekend?"

"Not too busy. I have yoga class at five, and then Simon and I are doing a couples' painting class later tonight. The book club is meeting for dinner on Friday, and I'll be here all day Saturday. And that night, Simon and I have a date night planned to check out the mermaid festivities. No plans for Sunday yet."

"Whew. I'm glad it's not that busy of a weekend." Jade winked.

"Just normal end of the week plans. Okay, I'm all settled here. What's first on the schedule for today?" Patti twirled her feather duster around and headed for the two trees that bookended the store's entrance.

"I haven't done a serious check on the inventory lately. I think we're running low on some of the animal ornaments."

"I'm on it. A mission to fill those empty peach baskets with amazing ornaments." Patti disappeared in the back with a "la-di-di-di-dah." *Peppermint Patti is back.*

Glancing at the time on her phone, she punched in the publicist's number. Jade hoped Marcella would have some time to talk before her day started.

After the second ring, "Hi, Jade, what's going on in your world?"

"Hi there. Do you have a minute?"

"I always seem to be working, but I have a few minutes to chat before Angel's first panel. What's up?"

"I heard one of your clients passed away recently, and I was curious what happens when someone with a public persona and all that goes with it dies?"

"You mean Meredith? Well, I guess now she's a former client. I reached out to her lawyer. I do her socials, her website, and her conference schedule.

I spent a bunch of time canceling her appearances. The lawyer said to keep the social sites and her website up until they settle the estate. We'll see what happens. Maybe the executor of her estate will want to keep her publications out there. You know, like her legacy. Sometimes the estate wants to keep things going if royalties or residuals are involved. We'll have to see how all this shakes out."

"Oh, it's not just shutting down a website or a Facebook page if you have to unwind all the business aspects," Jade mused.

"It's sad, but it's what I do best. I take care of all my folks' needs. I handle arrangements, gigs, appearances, publicity, you name it. Some of my clients want the complete package. I mean, I basically work full-time for Angel these days. Others, like Meredith, need help with publicity every once in a while. She would send me her ideas once a month, and I did my best to make them happen."

"She has a nice website. You do good work. As a small business owner, I'm always checking out what others do."

"You've got the perfect built-in audience with your store. If I were you, I'd focus on your email list, website, and socials. Make sure you're doing video posts. But I know you didn't call about that. What's up?" Marcella asked.

"I've been talking to some people. The murders of the Xplorer and Dr. Echols were so shocking. Dr. Echols seemed to play up the villain persona in public and every time I talked to her. Was she like that in real life?"

Marcella let out a giggle. "No. Alone and away from her work, she's quiet and kind of shy. She's a geeky scientist who doesn't get to do what she loved to do anymore. She's a little bitter, and she figured out how to make her 'tude make money for her in the real world. I think she battled with herself over whether she wanted to be the staid academic or the well-paid speaker at monster conferences. People in academia sometimes make my job harder. They take things and themselves too seriously. I can get Angel ten gigs without batting an eye. Let's just say some people are easier to work with than others. People talk, and they shy away from difficult personalities. Hey, my phone's buzzing again. I need to see what Angel wants. Text me if you have any other questions. Gotta run."

"Thanks," Jade said to dead air. "Well, that kinda confirms my impression of her."

"Of who?" Bernie asked, striding toward the counter from the back office.

"That professor they found on Amy's paranormal tour."

"Wow. What an ending to a ghost tour. I bet Amy and Todd's new business takes off like a rocket after that explosive inaugural event. She couldn't have planned any bigger excitement."

"Not sure if it's good or bad," Jade said.

Before she should continue, Bernie said, "Hey, I popped over to see if you had any urgent handyman needs? Cecil's been booking glass-bottom boat tours and excursions for Angel Cruz and some of the monster hunters. It seems everyone wants to see the scuttled ships in the York River and a tour of the bay. They think they're going to find some sort of sea creature. This con thing has been great, but I don't want to get too busy that I neglect my other duties." Bernie chuckled.

"You've taken care of all the seasonal stuff for us for now. I will need you to switch out the screens for summer and to check the hurricane shutters, but that can wait another week or so when things calm down."

"Sounds good. I've been helping Cecil with all the phone calls. It's been hopping with the tours. I don't ever remember it being this busy this early in the spring before. Cecil did have to break some hearts when he told him that the Chessie sea monster sightings weren't on this side of the state line. They didn't realize that's a Maryland thing. It's too bad that we don't have our own monster here. I think we need to work on that. But don't tell Vivian. She'll want to poo-poo it. Cecil and I will noodle on it and maybe get that Mermaid Whispers gal to help us stir up the buzz. It would be something to have our own creature. We could make T-shirts and all kinds of merch to sell to the tourists."

Diesel engines rumbled outside, sending Bernie, Jade, and Chloe to the window to see what was going on.

Two large purple and gold buses rolled into the parking lot. Their airbrakes made a "pitchuuuu" sound, and Patti zoomed in from the back. "Ooooooooo tour buses," she squealed. "Yahooo. Let's rock 'n' roll, guys."

"I'm going to get out of your hair unless you need an extra pair of hands," Bernie said.

"We're good until we set up the tables for the Mermaid extravaganza tomorrow. Thanks for checking in on us," Jade said as a tour guide popped her head in the front door. A crowd in red and purple T-shirts milled around on the sidewalk and on the porch outside and chatted loudly.

The tour guide closed the door and said, "Hello, everyone. Hi, Jade. Hi, Patti. We're here from Trips Ahoy to see the sandcastles, and we had to stop in your lovely shop. I've told them all about how much fun it is in Mermaid Bay, and we took a little detour from Williamsburg to hop over before lunch and the outlets."

"Hey, Gail," Patti said, running around the counter to hug the tour guide. "It's so great to see you again. How's Paul and the kitties?"

"We're all fine." The noise level on the porch increased, and Gail continued, "Whoops, let me get a handle on this before chaos breaks out." She held the door open, put two fingers in her mouth, and let out a shrill whistle. "Ladies and gentlemen, make your way inside. Pick up a basket if you want to shop and check out all the pretty decorations. We have thirty minutes before we head over to see the sandcastles." Turning toward Jade and Patti, she added, "Your place is always a must-visit on my list." She winked and blended in with the crowd.

Patti and Jade spent the next twenty minutes greeting guests and fielding questions about the shop and the Love Channel filming that took place here.

"Whew. That was a workout," Patti said when the door closed behind the last group of tourists. "But it's always good when the buses show up. Gail is such a hoot. My tumtum's growling, so it's time to heat up my lunch. Simon and I did an Asian fusion cooking class last night, and I saved the leftovers. Wanna bite?"

"Yum. Sounds perfect. I've been bad about grocery shopping and meal prepping lately. I think I'll trot on over to the Busy Bean. You want me to bring you anything back?"

"Hmmm. A vanilla iced chai would be a nice treat."

"I am on it." Jade opened the door and spotted something behind one of the bushes near the steps. "Who left their trash out here in my flowerbed?" she huffed. Jade leaned over and picked up the puffy white envelope. It was addressed to her at the store, but there was no return address and no signs of a delivery label or stamps.

Jade tore the flap. Inside the oversized envelope was a braided hemp bracelet, several Pogs, a small pocketknife, and a note. "You need to pay attention before it's too late. I took this from Angel. He's keeping souvenirs of his kills. You need to stop him before he does it again. He's already responsible for two."

Jade froze in place, let out a loud gasp, and stared up at the eaves. The cameras were pointing in the opposite direction—more toward the sidewalk and not the flowerbed. *Someone was aware enough to avoid the security cameras.* Still clutching the envelope, she fumbled for her phone and dialed Nick. Trying to keep her voice from quaking, she replied to his voicemail, "It's me. I found a weird package at the store. It's got some things that might belong to Ernie and Meredith and a note about the murders. Can you come by? I'm heading to the Busy Bean, and I'll be back in a couple of minutes."

Jade made a whirlwind trip to the coffee shop for a Caesar salad, Patti's chai, and a caramel mocha latte and hustled back to the store. On the walks to and from the Busy Bean, thoughts of what the note said ping-ponged around in her head. *And why did it focus on Angel? Meredith and Randall had bracelets like this, but they're sold in every surf shop up and down the East Coast. And what's with the pocket knife? It looks to flimsy to be deadly.*

Nick's SUV pulled into the front lot seconds after she climbed the porch steps. "Hey, I was in a meeting when you called. What did you find?" He covered the distance between them in two or three strides.

"Hi. I opened it and touched the note and the bracelet. I thought someone sent me something. It never occurred to me that it might be evidence."

"Not a problem. Let's go in and check it out," he said.

Patti waved to Nick and Jade as they made a beeline to the kitchenette. Jade doubled back a couple of seconds later to hand Patti her drink. "Sorry. Got sidetracked for a minute there."

A puzzled look crossed Patti's face as she waved Jade back to the office.

"I'll get the deets from you later. That looks intense."

By the time Jade had hustled to the office, Nick pulled out a pair of gloves from his utility belt and carefully spread the contents of the envelope on the table. He photographed them and examined each item.

"Where exactly did you find these?" he asked.

"On the side of the porch behind the bushes. And it was out of range of the cameras." She pulled up her security app. "See, nothing. The delivery guys and the mailman always bring deliveries inside. We had two tour buses come through. I have no idea how long it had been out there."

"Somebody wants you to look into Angel Cruz," he said.

"Is he on your radar?"

Nick grunted and shook his head. "Not as a primary suspect. But we haven't technically cleared anyone. I'm headed back to get this logged into evidence and meet with the task force. Make sure you're aware of what's going on around you. No more looking for trouble, okay?" He raised one eyebrow and then cracked a smile when she didn't reply. "Be careful, and I'll pick you up about six-thirty for dinner."

"You still want to go to the thing at the hotel afterward?" Jade got a little tickle of anxiety in her core. *What if he tries to talk me out of it now?*

"Wouldn't miss it. Who knows, maybe we'll get a bead on one of these characters before they leave town. See ya tonight." Nick kissed her lightly and strode out the back door.

Why Angel? He doesn't seem to travel in the same circles as the two victims. What is the connection, and what does he gain from killing them?

Chapter Twenty-One

Nick pulled into the lot next to Tequila Mockingbird. The building, originally an old steakhouse in Seaport, now had a festive vibe. Brightly colored metal parrots and iguanas perched on the brick wall around the outdoor patio, and paper flags fluttered in the evening breeze. The mariachi music caused Jade to perk up.

"Busy day?" Nick asked.

"The flow of people was steady, and when you're in retail, that's what you want. Yay! How are things on your side of town?"

"In my line of work, I'm okay when there are a couple of quiet days. I wish we had some this week." Nick held the glass door, and the hostess smiled. "Two for dinner?"

Nick nodded and followed her to a booth in back on the other side of the bar. "Your server will be right with you," she said, setting two teal-colored menus in front of them.

Nick glanced at the menu and reached for Jade's hands across the table. "Work has been insanely busy with prepping for the festival, answering Vivian's five thousand calls and emails, and the two murders. Plus, the normal stuff that we do every day. It feels like summer has started early this year."

"Any luck with either of the murders?" she asked, hoping he'd offer something new.

Nick gave her a sly smile. "We're ready for Mermaid Day. Vivian never seems to run out of suggestions, questions, or ideas. But enough about work, tonight's supposed to be a nice break from all of that for both of us. And then we wrap up the evening with CreatureCon. There is no telling what we'll encounter there."

"It's been an interesting experience so far. The costumes have been amazing, and I liked how you dodged that question."

He winked and cracked a smile as the server approached. "Hi, I'm Sean, and I'll take care of you tonight. What can I get to start you all off with?"

"I think we know what we want," Nick said, glancing at Jade.

"I'll have the shrimp taco meal with the rice and beans and an unsweetened iced tea," she said.

"I'll have the shrimp fajitas and an order of queso for the chips with an Arnold Palmer," Nick said, handing him the menus.

"Gotcha. That will be right out." Sean headed toward a table across the aisle.

"Where were we?" he asked, taking both of her hands in his again.

"You were saying how much you were going to enjoy a night away from your desk," she said.

"You betcha. I swear, I've eaten burgers and fries and junk out of the vending machine for the last eight or ten meals. It's good to see you. You ready for the Big Mermaid shindig?"

"I think so. Bernie and I'll set up the rest of the tables tomorrow. I've got a full house of artisans inside the multipurpose room and a bunch on the front lawn. I'm hoping we have lots of people through the doors."

"Hey, you're next door to the food trucks, so that should be a big draw. They're always a fan favorite," he said.

Trying to divert the conversation, she asked, "How's everything with the task force?" Jade dipped a chip in the salsa and stared across the table. *I wish he'd share more than the highlights from the press release.*

"As expected. I've got everyone on OT until next week. And the task force is running on adrenaline and caffeine. They're chasing down every lead, and we're working with our partner agencies on both cases. Lots of tips keep pouring in, and they're spending hours chasing them down."

"Any news on the stuff from the package on my porch?" she asked.

"We sent it to the lab. Hopefully, they'll be able to pull some prints or DNA from it. It didn't look like it went through the mail, so someone had to drop it off. Anything show up on your cameras?"

"No. It was far enough out of range for both front cameras."

"Someone knew enough to avoid the cameras." He let out a slight sigh. "We've got a pile of stuff to follow up on, and none of it ties neatly together." Nick dug into his dinner, and the conversation faded.

"Like what?" she asked, taking a bite of her taco.

He finished chewing and said, "There was a note in Meredith's room that she killed the Xplorer because he betrayed her and then tried to extort money from her. Her husband said it was her handwriting, and he thought it was a suicide note. But the handwriting folks we consulted couldn't confirm that with any certainty."

"So, you're suspicious?"

"I'm always suspicious. It's my nature. From what others have told us and what we know about Meredith Echols, that interpretation of the note doesn't seem to fit."

Jade's thoughts zinged around in her head. "That doesn't make sense. We found her miles from her room and the Con, and you said she'd been strangled. Why would someone leave the suicide note in the room and go to another location?"

"You can strangle yourself, but it's rare. Usually, it's accidental. Something is fishy with this case. When we checked her room, her belongings, including her valuables, were there. The only things missing were her laptop and phone. Her husband and Josie verified that she had had them with her when she arrived. The husband did say he couldn't find her favorite earrings and a rope bracelet that matched his. We found the earrings in the Xplorer's room, and somebody probably sent you the bracelet if it's the same one."

Jade's eyes widened. "Maybe she left them in his room. I think she and Ernie were still a thing." Her thoughts flashed to the paradox of Meredith and the Xplorer's argument and then her escape to his hotel room. *Or was she trying to get close to the Xplorer in order to kill him?*

"We're still investigating," Nick replied.

"Do you think the killer could be collecting souvenirs?" she asked, setting her taco on her plate.

Nick shrugged. "Usually, the type that keeps trinkets from his kills or attacks doesn't part with them. The value is having the memento and the reminder of what he did. That's why your package is odd. The team is looking at both notes for any similarities."

"When I read the note in the package, it felt like someone was trying to frame Angel. I don't get the sense that he's mixed up in all the drama that the others are embroiled in. He's confident and successful. He's the consummate professional. He doesn't do the drama," Jade said.

"The guys plan to talk to Angel and his crew again. Like I said before, he's on the list, but not in our top ten."

Sean sidled up to the table and asked, "Everything good here? Anyone want dessert?"

"I'm stuffed. Thanks," Nick said. "What about you?" Jade shook her head, and he continued, "Just the check. Thanks."

When he was out of earshot, Jade said, "I keep hearing stories about other researchers and students that Meredith treated badly. There are tons of people who she had run-ins with. And then there are all the folks she's insulted at the conventions and online. If it's one of those people, then that doesn't explain Ernie's death."

"What did you want to see at CreatureCon tonight?" he asked, changing the subject again.

"A chance for early Christmas shopping. Where else can I find Amy's gifts? She has a thing for dragons."

"Then it sounds like the place," he said, handing his card to the waiter when he walked past. "But I know you and that you have an agenda. Spill it."

"Not always. The last few times, I've picked up a bunch of tidbits by hanging out in the common areas and listening. Maybe that will work again." Jade stared across the table at the guy who was a goofball of a teenager who always made her laugh. She smiled at the guy he had grown into, the town's protector. *He's always been there for me. How did I get so lucky?*

Chapter Twenty-Two

Nick wedged his behemoth truck in a spot at the back of the hotel lot and trotted around to open the door for Jade. "You ready, Mrs. Fletcher?" he asked, taking her elbow. "Lead on."

Jade pulled the lanyards out of her purse and handed him one. "There now, you're official." He pulled out his badge case and flipped it open with his other hand. "Okay, so I guess you're always official, but now you're cooler because you have a VIP pass to CreatureCon."

"Good to know. You do realize that we stand out. There's no way of blending in with this crowd."

"You up for costumes?" He gave her a look, and she snickered. "You do radiate that cop look. No undercover work for you tonight. See, that's why they talk to me. I look sweet and harmless."

Nick scanned the entranceway filled with a sea of costumed attendees. "Sweet, yes. Harmless, I'm not sure about. The outfits are elaborate. I like the Kraken, and Sasquatch is a close second," he said, nodding his head toward a cluster of creatures.

The pair wandered through the lobby and mixed in with the scads of superheroes and monsters. Not finding any seating, Jade took Nick's hand and led him toward the conference rooms.

"I need some coffee. Want some?" he asked, tapping her on the shoulder and pointing toward the bar.

"The perfect drink for stakeouts," she whispered in his ear. "I'll meet you in front of the conference rooms here. Maybe I can find a decent spot for lurking." Jade pointed to the couches midway down the long hallway.

He nodded and ducked into the front door of the Dungeon.

Jade followed the crowd and ended up next to a seating area by the glass doors that overlooked the outdoor patio and the bay. The crowd spilled outside and lounged around the gas fire pit while others walked on the beach. The full moon reflected on the choppy waves and created an eerie look. Jade snapped a picture, but it didn't look as ominous as it did in real life.

A crowd in alien costumes swarmed the seating area and took over the benches near her. Jade leaned in a little closer to eavesdrop as she pretended to stare at the water.

The guy closest to her started speaking gibberish, and the guy next to him answered in whatever alien dialect it was. She pulled out her phone and gave it a voice command to translate as she held it closer to the pair.

"I'm tired. And we still haven't found the items for the quest," her phone said.

The alien closest to Jade stepped out of his character when he laughed and pointed to her phone. "Not from around here?"

Jade shook her head. "I don't think I'm in Kansas anymore. I need a translator sometimes."

The alien laughed and returned to his group's conversation that had nothing to do with the murders.

A tap on her shoulder made Jade let out a slight squeal. "Sorry, I didn't mean to startle you," Nick said, handing her a coffee. "I had him put in vanilla creamer with sugar and a little coffee."

"Perfect. I was lost in thought for a moment."

"Anything interesting besides our alien friends here?" he asked.

She shook her head. "Nope, but the moon looks cool over the water." She blew on her coffee and then took a sip. "What's next? The Topher guy has a presentation at seven-thirty, and then Angel has some kind of demo. I thought we could pop in on those. Even though neither of them seemed like the killer type to me," she whispered.

"Neither did Ted Bundy." Nick took a gulp of his coffee. "Maybe we should divide and conquer. We can meet outside of Angel's room before his thing. Stay out of trouble and text me if you see anything hinky or if you want to leave earlier than we planned."

"Hinky's an official police term?"

He nodded, and she continued, "Okay. Sounds like a plan." He kissed her and vanished into the crowd near the vendor area. *I wonder what caught his attention. I have half a mind to follow him.*

Dismissing her curiosity about where Nick was going, Jade checked the schedule on the con's app and made her way to the room where Topher was supposed to speak about sea monsters that turned out to be real creatures. She plodded through the throngs of conference goers until she located the room down the hall and around the corner.

Finding an aisle seat near the front, Jade got comfortable in the padded chair. Minutes later, a woman with crimson hair tapped the microphone and introduced the panel of two, Topher and a marine biologist. Topher spotted her in the audience and waved. Then she turned around to make sure he was looking at her. He laughed and pointed at her and nodded. Jade could feel the heat rise in her cheeks. She pulled out her phone and tapped in any names that the group mentioned as they showed pictures of mythical sea creatures and marine animals that had been discovered over the past fifty years. *The list was longer than I imagined. I guess the sea keeps her secrets.*

Jade's head jerked up from her screen when Topher mentioned Dr. Echols. She focused her attention like a laser on the conversation on stage, hoping to catch any new detail about the dead woman.

Topher said, "Even though we didn't always see eye to eye, I want to thank Dr. Meredith Echols for her words of wisdom and help with my early research. She also helped me realize that I didn't want to be a marine biologist." When the audience's laughter died down, he continued, "My research is on marine species that have had a presence for centuries in folklore. The team works hard to document and categorize sea life that was often mistaken in years gone by for monsters." Slides of squid, manatees, and a giant octopus flashed on the screen. "And while we're here, I'm heading out to do some research on Mermaid Bay. You never know what we'll find off the coast. Watch my blog for pictures and updates."

When the presentation shifted into question-and-answer mode, Jade slipped out the door. Someone in the back asked the panel if they had any details on the tragedies that befell the Xplorer and Meredith.

Jade froze by the back exit and listened to the replies. Most were the standard thoughts and prayers for the families and friends. And then Topher said, "I'm sure the authorities are zeroing in on the killer or killers. Both victims were outspoken and had many, many detractors, but they did contribute to the cryptid community. I'm sure the police have long lists of suspects to go through, including a couple of people at this conference." He paused for the laughter to die down. "Speaking from experience, Ernie 'the Xplorer' Post may have ruffled some feathers along his journey, but down deep, he was a good guy, and he cared about this community. And he didn't pilfer others' work. I won't comment on anything further because it would be speculation."

A guy in the aisle waved his hand. "I heard you were really, and I mean really close to Dr. Echols at one time. Any truth to the rumors floating around?"

Topher glared at the man in wrinkled khakis and rumpled dress shirt. "I shouldn't have to dignify that, but I will since you raised it in public. I was her teaching assistant when I was an innocent undergrad who thought marine biology was my calling. Meredith and others helped me to see that it wasn't. She was my professor and my advisor, and she tortured me like she did all her teaching and research assistants. That's it. There was no other relationship if that was what you were implying."

"Not what I heard," the guy said to a chorus of boos.

Topher stood up and waved his hands for the crowd to settle down. "Hey, he asked his question, and I answered it. I hadn't seen either of the victims in person in a long time, so there's no way I could have been involved in any way. And I was stuck in the airport in Atlanta when the first murder happened. Hey, don't boo him. I'm grateful he gave me the opportunity to put some rumors to rest. And don't forget, the villains in the movies, like in life, often play a key role as influencers."

Applause rose up from the audience, and Jade slipped out the door after she checked the schedule for Angel's presentation. No updates from Nick. *I hope he's having better luck than me. At least Ernie and Meredith were mentioned a couple of times. Topher is charming and seems sincere. I hope I'm not getting distracted by him.*

Nick waved at her from across the hall. She felt like a salmon swimming upstream as she tried to make her way across the carpeted area to where he stood. When she managed to make it through the throngs, he handed her a bag. Peeking inside, she let out a squeak. "Thank you," she said, hugging him. She slid the dainty gold bracelet with a jade charm on her wrist. "Find anything you can use for either of the cases?"

"Nope. You?"

She shook her head. "Nothing we didn't already know. Angel's thing starts in a minute. Want to get a seat? Maybe we can find one in the back row in case we want to sneak out early. Topher mentioned Meredith, and some guy asked him if he had a thing with her."

"And?" Nick asked.

"He repeated the same answers as before—he was her teaching assistant, and he transferred and changed majors."

Nick nodded and put his hand on her shoulder as she led the way across the vast hallway to the conference center. Finding two seats in the second-to-the-last row, they sat down and waited for the presentation to begin.

The lights dimmed a couple of times, and a guy with a purple mohawk crossed the stage and thumped the microphone. "Hello, everyone. I'm Zac Collins with the Ocean Adventures podcast, and I'm excited to be here tonight to talk to Angel Cruz and Jax Collins. So, find your seats, and we'll begin momentarily."

After Angel and a rail-thin blond woman took their seats behind the speakers' table, Zac said, "Good evening. I'd like to welcome you all to Ocean Adventures with Angel Cruz and Jax Collins." The applause echoed through the room for what felt like an eternity.

Zac spent about ten minutes detailing each speaker's biography, and then he lobbed questions at both of the panelists. The conversation paused only when they showed video clips of some of their adventures.

When Jade caught Nick trying to stifle a yawn, she pointed toward the door, and he rose. The pair slipped out and made their way to the truck.

"Nothing new there either," Jade said as Nick shut his door and started the engine.

"I saw some interesting getups," he said. "I didn't have to arrest anyone, so it was a good night."

Jade laughed. "Don't mention the costumes to Amy. She's already planning her Halloween extravaganza, and she expects everyone to dress up."

"Great. Oh, but I'm sure I'm on duty that night," Nick said with a smirk.

"What, no couple's costume?"

"Hmmm." He rolled his eyes and adjusted the radio. "I talked to some of the dealers. The scuttlebutt tonight seemed to be about the conference and not the murders. I didn't learn anything except that some of those fans are rabid. They spent some serious time and money on their costumes and props. They take all of this very seriously."

The pair rode in silence until he pulled into her driveway. "Thanks for dinner and a fun evening," she said, unlatching the seatbelt.

"It was nice to hang out tonight." He walked her to her front porch and pulled her close under the light for a kiss. Jade was sure she saw the porchlight across the street snap on. *Mrs. Swenson is the unofficial Neighborhood Watch for our block.*

"You want to come in? I might have some Oreos and maybe some Twizzlers. Oh, wait. I have some Thin Mints in the freezer," Jade said, admiring her new bracelet.

"Sounds fun, but I need to swing by the office and check on the night shift. We're working these cases round the clock, and I want to make sure the night crew didn't run into any roadblocks."

"So much for getting a break. Take it easy. I know you guys will find out who did this."

He kissed her again, and a spark of excitement zinged through her like she was zapped by lightning. *Wow. I think that curled my toenails. Mrs. Swenson is getting a show tonight.*

Chapter Twenty-Three

"Chloe, we need to hustle. Today's prep day for the festival, and Bernie and Patti will be there to help us get ready for this weekend's festivities. And there will be food trucks." At the mention of the magic "f" word, the dog's ears shot up, and she trotted down the sidewalk like a boss.

When they were almost in front of the store, Chloe let out a tiny growl at the figure in the vacant lot who was hunched over, pounding stakes in the ground. Jade scooped up her chubby guard dog and walked toward the activity. Vivian took about fifteen steps and pounded another stake in the ground with a handheld sledgehammer.

When she stopped swinging, Jade said, "Morning, Vivian. Do you need help with anything?"

"Nope, it's an awesome stress reliever. I'm staking off the areas for the food trucks. Kellie and Farrah should be here shortly to assist. And for now, I have the pier gang handling the tape." She nodded toward the gaggle of older men who were chatting at the end of the line of stakes. She glanced at her fitness tracker and scowled.

Vivian wiped the perspiration off her brow with a tissue and returned to swinging her hammer. *Maybe that'll burn up some of that excess energy, and she won't call Nick so much today.*

As Jade and Chloe turned to leave, Bernie let out a shrill whistle. "Jade, hey Jade. You might want to see this." He, Cecil Jacobs, and Lester Coggins stood as if frozen, staring at the mulch bed under the oleander hedge at the back of the property.

"What's all the lollygagging?" Vivian asked, when she waddled over to the cluster of men.

"I think Jade may want to take a look at this. And she'll want to give Nick a call too. I think it's a clue," Bernie said.

"What is it?" Vivian demanded.

"It looks like a piece of braided rope and a broken cell phone," Cecil said.

"Don't touch it," Lester commanded. Vivian jerked her hand back like she had touched a hot stove. "It may have prints or DNA on it. We have to preserve the chain of evidence." *Somebody besides me watches true crime shows.*

"It could be important. Let's see what Nick has to say." Jade snapped a picture of their find and texted it to the sheriff. Then she tapped his contact and waited for the call to connect.

"Hey, whatcha up to this early in the morning?" he asked.

"Are you at work already?" she asked.

"Yup."

"Did you even go home last night?"

"About one-thirty. We went through the evidence again. It took a while. Hey, what's that photo of?" he asked.

"Bernie and his crew found some stuff in another one of my flowerbeds. It looks suspicious, so we called."

"Don't touch it. I've got to head over to the Town Manager's office for a meeting, but I'll send Sebastian by to get it. Can you wait there until he can get there to bag it?"

"Not a problem. We'll be here. He can't miss us. Vivian has a sledgehammer."

"I'm not even going to ask," Nick muttered.

Vivian tapped her fitness tracker again and pointed to the stakes. The three septuagenarians shuffled back to their tasks like schoolboys who had been scolded for being naughty. "We have a schedule to keep," Vivian said under her breath. "Jade can watch the stuff until the police get here. We don't have time to waste."

Jade watched Vivian take out her aggression on the wooden stakes while the three men tied ribbon around to mark off the vendor spaces. She pulled out her phone and checked her camera feeds.

Deputy Sebastian Sanchez strode across the grass toward them. "What did you all find so early this morning?" he asked.

Bernie, Cecil, and Lester zipped over, leaving Vivian pounding like she was helping lay track for the continental railroad.

"The guys and I found these this morning, and we alerted Jade," Cecil said, pointing with both hands at the discarded phone. "At first glance, it looked like junk, but with everything that's been going on around here, it could be important. We didn't want to take any chances. We think it might be evidence."

Sebastian leaned over to get a better look at the rope and the phone. After he took pictures from every angle, he placed the items in separate evidence bags. "Thanks. I'm sure Nick will want to take a look at it. Any idea how these got here?"

The three Musketeers shook their heads and stared at Sebastian.

Jade waved her phone. "I checked the outside cameras. The one that sorta points this way didn't catch anyone in the bushes. I had one clip of a cat wandering through, but I don't think he's our culprit," Jade said with a wry smile.

"Can you do that technical forensics magic on it and figure out who the owner is?" Lester asked. "Then maybe you can track all the places where that phone has been. It could lead to the killer, especially if you can match the timeline of the murders, or maybe you could figure out when it was last used."

"And maybe the rope's origin can be traced to a specific store. We could get lucky if there are security cameras at the store," Cecil said.

Sebastian looked at the rope again. He held it up for the men to see.

Lester scrunched his mouth. "It looks like common hemp or natural fibers. That stuff is sold everywhere."

"Dern. I thought we might get a break," Cecil said. "At least the phone might turn out to be an important clue."

"It's weird that it's back here," Bernie added. "Y'all found the body under the pier. It looks like if someone wanted to get rid of something incriminating, they'd throw it in the big wide bay where nobody would ever find it. Why dump it back here?"

Sebastian shrugged. "If you find anything else, give us a call. Keep your eyes peeled."

The three amigos perked up with a new mission.

"We're on it," Lester said.

Sebastian turned and jogged toward his SUV, and Bernie's gang reluctantly trundled off to finish Vivian's tasks.

"We've got work to do, Chloe." The chonky dog yawned and plopped down in the grass.

"Don't tell me you're trying to get out of work too," Jade whispered as she scooped Chloe up for the quick walk to the back door.

"We'll be over in a little while to set up your tents," Bernie yelled. "As soon as Vivian grants us parole from her chain gang." His cronies dissolved into fits of laughter as Vivian swung her sledge a little harder than necessary.

Inside the store, Jade turned on all the equipment and the lights, slid a mug under the coffee maker, and pressed the blue button. "Chloe, normally, I'd say that was a lost phone, but that braided rope looked similar to Meredith and Randall's bracelets. Too much of a coincidence."

Not seeing anything she was interested in, Chloe circled her puffy bed twice and settled down for a morning nap. She added a heavy sigh and a couple of yawns.

"Whoooo hooooo," echoed through the store as Peppermint Patti bustled in with several shopping bags and a platter. "Good morning. What're y'all up to? I can see Miss Chloe is getting her beauty rest."

"It's been a morning. We were outside watching Vivian and Bernie's gang rope off the food truck area, and they found a cracked phone and a piece of rope in the oleander bushes."

"A clue," Patti said in her sing-songy voice. "Back where you and Chloe found the murder weapon that that gal from *My Coastal Valentine* used? Wow. Who knew your back lot was a dumping ground for murder stuff? You'd think they'd toss them off the pier or something. It would have been easier. Nobody said the criminal mind was brilliant. Well, I'm glad to see you're still on the case. And maybe you'll see a reference to the find in Mermaid Whispers."

"Make sure the Mermaid credits Bernie, Cecil, and Lester. It'll make their day. I'm hoping the find helps Nick's guys. They need a break in this case."

Bernie and the guys bustled in the back door with lots of chatter about all the forensics that Nick could do to locate the owner of the damaged phone. After listening to a half dozen of their theories, each one more fantastic than the last, Jade and her team spent the morning setting up tables inside and in the front lot for the craft show.

* * *

After the last chair was in place, Jule said, "This looks ready. Thanks for all of your help."

"Anytime," Cecil replied. "We were already here doing Vivian's stuff."

"But yours is fun. Vivian is kind of persnickety." Lester helped himself to the cookies that Patti offered.

"Jade's team always has tasty snacks," Bernie said.

"Hey, Bernie." Jade waved her hand. "I think you should send a note to the Mermaid on her website about your idea for a town monster. Who knows, maybe she'll answer you and tell your story."

Patti raised an eyebrow and stared at Jade.

"That's an idea. See ya tomorrow." Bernie reached for a handful of cookies on his way out.

When the door shut behind the three pals, Patti asked, "What was all that about?"

"Bernie and his crew want to create a mythical monster for Mermaid Bay, and they were wondering who could help them."

"Maybe the Mermaid could help. But Vivian certainly wouldn't like it. Hmmmm. I'm on it. Any ideas of what kind of creature we want?"

Jade shook her head. "Maryland has its Chessie monster in the Chesapeake Bay. And we all know about Nessie."

"Maybe a sea serpent would be appropriate. I could see it on T-shirts."

Patti pulled out her phone and started scrolling.

"These tent cards are for the tables in the multipurpose room. It'll make it easier for the vendors to find their spots. I'll set the ones for outside here on the counter. Remind me to put them out tomorrow morning."

Patti nodded and offered her the platter. Then she let out a long breath that sounded like a leaky beachball. "I don't know about you, but I'm worn flat out. I need to get some caffeine to keep me upright for the rest of the night and to be revved up for tomorrow's excitement. I'll bring some monster and mermaid snacks tomorrow. We will have a blast."

"You are the Energizer Bunny," Jade said. "And you do way more in a day than anyone I know."

"So much to do and so little time. I gotta make the most of it." Patti fanned herself with one of the flyers on the counter.

The afternoon grew quieter as the hands on the nearby Santa cuckoo clock inched toward closing time. The foot traffic disappeared like a morning mist over the bay, so Jade and Patti busied themselves with packing the online orders.

"That's a wrap," Jade said as the delivery guy took the three bins of orders. "I think we should call it a day and get plenty of rest for tomorrow's main event."

Patti dusted her hands and started to gather her things. "Sounds like a plan. Hot date night for you?"

"Nope. Nick's buried in his investigations. I'll see him after this weekend. I hope. Chloe and I have plans to hang out and catch up on some house projects."

Patti raised one eyebrow. "Laundry and dishes do not a Friday night make. But, if you're scouring the internet for clues on our murder or murderers, then go home and be a crime-fighter."

Jade smiled. "Shhhh. Don't blow my secret Bat Girl identity."

Patti's laugh echoed through the lobby. "You crack me up. See you guys tomorrow bright and early."

"Have fun," Jade called out as the front door closed behind her friend.

"Chloe, let's close this place down and pick up a pizza." The little dog's ears shot toward the ceiling, and she bolted through the lobby to the showrooms. Zoomie time.

The bells on the front door jangled again, and Jade hurried back to the lobby to see if Patti had forgotten something. She tried to hide her surprise when she found Randall leaning on her front counter. His khakis and white dress shirt looked rumpled, and his usually over-styled hair looked like he had rolled out of bed. "Hi. I was closing up. What can I do for you?" she asked.

"Uh, I hadn't heard from you in a while, and I thought I'd stop in to see what you've uncovered. Any new suspects? Please tell me you have some news. Your cop friend hasn't returned my call." Before she could comment, he ran his hands through his hair and continued, "The cops brought me in again last night. I'm sick of all the questions. I want to help, but I need them to focus their energy on other suspects. I. Did. Not. Kill. Meredith." He pounded his fist on the counter and made Jade jump. Chloe zipped in to see what was going on, and Jade picked her up before she could start a barking jag.

He clenched his fists together several times and then released his fingers. "I'm sick of saying it over and over, and nobody's listening. I can see why people lawyer up and don't cooperate. I feel like the cops are trying to wear me down." He closed both eyes and paused for a beat.

"I'm sorry that you feel that way. I'm sure that the police are trying to follow every lead, and any information you can give them helps."

He rolled his eyes. "I want to get back to my life and put this to bed. I need your help. Tell that boyfriend of yours that he needs to focus on Angel Cruz and maybe even his pretty publicist. She could have been in on it. She didn't like Mer. I think she was sabotaging her, and there's always that Topher Taylor and Emory Wilson."

"Who's that?"

"Some guy at the university that Mer was seeing at one time, when we were on a break. It was announced that he was selected to take her faculty spot next summer. Sounds like a motive to me. He benefited from her death with his new cushy tenure."

"Is he here at the conference?" she asked.

"Doubtful, but who knows? But he was jockeying for her job, and that sounds like a reason to kill to me. The police need to check out all possible leads."

Jade hoped she didn't roll her eyes. "Thanks for stopping by. I have an early day tomorrow, so I need to finish closing. I'll call or text you if I hear anything or if any of these leads you mentioned pan out."

He raised his head, and his eyes brightened. "I knew you could help me. I am so scatteredbrained lately. I left my ring, my jewelry, and my phone at the Pearl." He grabbed at his back pocket. "At least I have my wallet."

Jade's thoughts flashed to the phone and the rope bracelet they found. *They probably weren't Randall's, but what if it was Meredith's missing phone? Nick and his team should be able to tell pretty soon who it belonged to.* Swallowing the thoughts of sharing the find with him, she straightened the flyers on the counter.

"Uh, have you had dinner yet? No, of course not. You're still at work. We should grab a bite somewhere, and it will give us a chance to go over all the key players who might have wanted to harm Mer," Randall said.

Against her better judgment, she said, "Why don't you head over to our pizza place on the other side of this field and grab a table on the patio. Chloe and I will be over in fifteen minutes or so."

"Yep. Sounds good." His scowl faded into a smile that looked like the Randall she met earlier this week. "I'll be waiting for you."

As soon as he scooted out the door, she locked it and hurried through the rest of her closing routine.

Jade pulled the door behind her and Chloe, and they hustled over to Pizza D'Action. "Chloe, the weather will be perfect this weekend for the festival. And it's a nice night to eat out on the patio." The chubby dog sniffed the air and followed the delicious scent toward the small strip mall on the other side of the lot, filled with spots awaiting tomorrow's food trucks.

Jade scoped out the patio. No Randall. "We're only five minutes late. I can't believe he didn't wait, especially after he sounded anxious to talk." Jade hoisted Chloe under one arm and opened the glass doors of the pizzeria.

"Hey, Jade," Anthony Rossi yelled from behind the counter. "What brings you out on this fine evening?"

"That wonderful smell wafting over to my store." She glanced around the small seating area. No Randall here either. "Could I get a small sausage and cheese to go?"

"It'll be out in a flash. And Chloe, I'll make sure there's a pepperoni treat for you."

She tapped a text to Randall while she waited. **Where are you? I'm at the pizza place.**

She tried to push thoughts of the cryptozoologist and his strange behavior out of her mind. First, you didn't want to have dinner with him, and now you're mad that he ditched you. He's not thinking clearly. He's grieving and under a lot of pressure. But why is he dropping names for me to check out every time he sees me? It feels kinda like he's pulling at any loose string. She took a deep breath and slowly exhaled.

"Here you go," Anthony said, handing her a warm pizza box after she tapped her card at the register. "I haven't seen your sheriff around here lately. He must be super busy with the festival, and you know…" he whispered.

Jade nodded, indicating she understood his cryptic message. "Thanks. I'm so glad you and Delores moved to town. It's nice having our own pizza place." She set Chloe down and held the door for her fuzzy sidekick. This time, the little dog wasn't interested in dillydallying. She had eyes and a nose only for the garlicky-smelling box.

After checking the mail and dumping her things on the dining room table, Jade grabbed a raspberry iced tea and ate her dinner from the box. "Yum, Chloe. Mr. Rossi made you a pepperoni and a sausage snack. And he left me a cannoli. He's the best." She cut up the pizza treat and put them in the bottom of Chloe's bowl. She covered the snack with kibble, and it took seconds for her to root out and make Mr. Rossi's treat disappear. The pudgy dog smacked her lips and looked around for more.

Jade stared at the stickies on her wall. She added the new names Randall mentioned, with not much hope of them leading to anything. Still no response from Randall. *I guess something else came up.* "Chloe, he still hasn't answered my text about ditching us."

Her phone dinged as if Randall could read her mind. **Forgot I was on a panel tonight. Had to rush to the hotel. Can we reschedule? See you tomorrow.**

Chapter Twenty-Four

After pulling on a long Mermaid T-shirt and teal leggings, Jade rummaged through Chloe's wardrobe and pulled out her teal and purple collar and her tiny mermaid shirt. "There. Now we both look festive. Almost twinsies. We have to be ambassadors for the festival." Chloe gave her a bodacious side-eye and waddled over to check out her food bowl.

"Okay, let's get this show on the road. Patti and Lorelei will be there today, and Bernie's coming by after he does his stint on his special float. Hopefully, we can get a free moment to sneak out and watch some of the parade."

Still not thrilled with all the hubbub, Chloe plopped down in front of the door and waited for Jade to gather her things.

After a brisk walk down the street, they paused on the corner to watch two public utilities guys unload sawhorses to block traffic on Neptune Road. "Let's move it, puppy. We need to get everything ready before the vendors start showing up."

Next door, brightly colored food trucks filled the staked-off areas. They offered a wide variety of food that included street tacos, stuffed cheeseburgers, turkey legs, kebabs, and falafel. Several generators chugged along as whiffs of grilled onions and frying bacon swirled around on the morning breeze.

"This is going to be fun. And you thought the pizza smelled divine. I'm ready for lunch already." Chloe toddled up the steps and sniffed around. "And Neville will be here later."

At the name of her nemesis, Chloe's ears shot skyward. Jade opened the door, and she trotted through the store, looking for the tuxedo cat under all the Christmas trees.

Jade spent the morning printing online orders, getting vendors settled, and chatting with the guests who were starting to line the parade route.

At ten o'clock, her store emptied, and all of the crowds rushed to the sidewalk to get a prime viewing spot. Lorelei and Patti took turns watching the outdoor festivities.

Jade looked up from the computer behind the counter as the bells jangled. Patti bustled in the front door, followed by loud music from the high school marching band. A medley of *Little Mermaid* songs caused Jade to sing along.

"Everything's going swimmingly out there. You should go take a peek. I can handle things here. I'll hang out with Chloe and Neville, and we'll eat mermaid snacks if we get bored." Peppermint Patti shooed Jade toward the front door.

Jade waved to neighbors and walked around the line of spectators to find a spot near the curb. She smiled when she spotted the Ecto-mobile, followed by Todd and Amy in the hearse. Amy had covered the back and sides with banners for their stores. She waved, but she was probably too far back for them to see her. Every block, Todd let loose on the hearse's horn, and Bon Jovi's "Dead or Alive" blasted across Neptune Road.

Jade's phone alerted to a new text as she was snapping photos of the floats. **Hey, I really need to talk.** She let out a heavy sigh. *You ditched me yesterday. Be kind, girl. He's going through a rough time. But, you don't have to answer him immediately.*

Jade took some pictures and looped around by the food trucks. The scents of grilled meats and fried dough caused her stomach to rumble. She breathed in the food truck smells and eyed the choices. *Wow. Way too many awesome lunch options.*

Tailgate-party tents outlined the perimeter of the walkway in front of her store. She strolled by each table and admired the handcrafted ornaments and jewelry. Jade's favorites were the stained-glass sun catchers and the hand-blown glass earrings. As she leaned forward over a table to get a better look at some handcrafted dog collars, someone tapped her on her shoulder, and she jumped.

"I didn't hear back from you, so I thought I'd pop over," Randall said. "Do you have some free time to talk?"

"Today's Mermaid Day, and we are expecting big crowds. I should be free later this evening if you want me to call you."

He glanced around at the cheering crowds. "I really need to show you something across the street." Randall grabbed her forearm and started tugging.

She tried to pull away, and he tightened his grip. "This is important. I'm sorry about last night, but you need to see this." He led her toward the street, and when there was a break in parade participants, he said, "Hurry up. Let's go. If we don't run now, we'll never get across." He pulled her across Neptune Road seconds before the next float made its way in front of 'Tis the Season.

Ignoring stares from the spectators, Jade knew that Vivian would have something to say about people cutting across the street during the grand parade. She followed Randall through the throngs of people lined up on the other side of the street. He led her across the Hot Diggity lot toward Mermaid Books, where Todd was standing in front of the hearse, watching the remainder of the parade. He waved hesitantly when she and Randall didn't stop to talk.

When Jade slowed her pace, Randall nudged her toward the beach by the pier. He said something, and between the wind and the crowd noise, Jade couldn't hear him. "What? Where are we going?" When she paused in the sand, he pointed toward the pier.

Amy jogged out of the bookstore and chased them across the dune. "Jade. Jade. Is everything okay?"

Randall finally stopped, turned around, and glared at Amy, who gulped in several deep breaths. "Sorry. We're in a hurry. I need to show Jade something. We'll be back in a second." Amy frowned as Randall kicked up dry sand in his wake.

As the pair approached the pier, Jade was surprised at how quiet this part of the beach was. The crowd noise from the street was barely audible, and there were only a handful of people on the sand near the sculptures. The breeze picked up and fluttered Jade's bangs.

The quiet lasted only a moment. "Sorry for all the drama, but there is something I have to show you under here. It's important. This way…." He headed under the deck and zigzagged around the giant wooden pylons. Then he dropped to his knees and started digging like a dog after a bone. Jade watched from a few feet away. *What is he doing?*

Randall popped up and ran to another wooden pylon and repeated his digging routine. At about the time Jade's legs started to fidget, he ran to another pylon farther under the pier. She let out a heavy sigh. *I can't wait here all day.*

"Hey, Randall. I've got to get back to the store. I can't leave my team short-staffed for this long. Just text or call me with what you found." She turned and trudged back toward the beach.

Randall scurried over, covered in sand. "This is nuts. I'll find it. I thought I marked the pylon, but maybe somebody messed with it. I gotta find it. It's going to break this case wide open."

When she started walking again, he grabbed both of her wrists to try to slow her retreat, and she grabbed his. He winced and jerked his arm away. He cradled his left wrist for a moment and then shook it.

"What's that?" She pointed to his arm.

He shoved his hand in his pocket. "It's nothing. It was a stupid accident." Looking over his shoulder, he waved her toward the underside of the pier.

Jade planted both feet in the sand and said, "Listen, I have to get back to my store. Just tell me what you found. I've been gone longer than expected. And all this clandestine stuff is too much. I gotta go." *I know he's grieving the loss of Meredith, but his moods are all over the place.*

"Sorry," he said again. "I found something earlier, and I need to show it to you. It will prove that Meredith and I were right all along."

"Right about what?"

Chapter Twenty-Five

"What I found will change everything. It's about her research and her big announcement. It proves that Angel stole her research. And if he's willing to do that, then he's probably capable of something a lot worse. Maybe even killing her," Randall said, lowering his voice.

"But what about the Xplorer. This doesn't make sense. How does he fit into all this? And Meredith wasn't killed here. I need to call the sheriff if it's about his investigation," Jade said.

"He's busy with all the stuff going on today. Come and look at it, and we'll call him afterward. And who said Ernie's murder had anything to do with Meredith's? You'll thank me after you see what I found. Hurry up."

"Enough," she said firmly through gritted teeth. "What is so important that you drag me over here? What? Just tell me."

A pained look crossed his face, and he ran his hands through his already messy hair. His eyes teared up, and he turned his head as Amy and Todd jogged over.

"I'm glad we caught you," Amy said, balling her hand into a fist and landing it on her hip. "Patti's been trying to reach you. Some buses pulled into your store while you were gone."

Jade pulled out her phone and glanced at Patti's 9-1-1 text about the influx of people. "I gotta go. Randall, call the sheriff's office and get them to come and look at what you found."

Randall scowled and muttered something that Jade didn't catch. She waved to Amy and Todd and hurried down the beach, hoping the parade was over, so she wouldn't have to run across the street again. She jogged back to the store, but Randall's odd behavior kept worming its way to the forefront of her thoughts. She shook off the creepy feeling, promising herself to look into later, after she and Patti assisted the crowd of tourists.

Tourists from three buses milled around the vendor tables and stood in line at her front door. Jade's part-timer, Tori, and Lorelei mixed in and chatted with the visitors. Forgetting about Randall and his weird behavior, she jogged around to the back entrance.

She, Patti, Lorelei, and Tori stayed busy for several hours ringing up customers and answering questions that ranged from "what's the weather here like in the winter" to "how do you like having Christmas every day." Then in an instant, the noise level dropped as the tour guides corralled their charges back on the buses.

"Wow," Lorelei said, leaning against the counter. "That was summertime busy. My arms and my face got a workout. I haven't smiled that much in months."

"Awesome for sales. It looks like I'll have to do inventory again next week, but that's a great problem to have," Patti said, waving both hands in the air. "I love chatting with people from all over the place. That second bus was from Tennessee this month."

The front door bells jangled, and Tori blew in. "Here are the name cards that were left and the extra flyers. All of the outside vendors are gone. Do you need me to do anything else?"

"I think we're good. Thanks for all you did today."

"My pleasure." Tori beamed. "I'm headed over to check out the food trucks. See y'all later." The teen waved and pranced out on the porch.

"It's definitely been an interesting day," Jade said, pulling out her phone and tapping a note to Nick. "I need to make sure the toy room is ready for Bernie to hold court later this afternoon."

"Let's get fortified for the second round. First tourists and now the munchkins," Lorelei said, making a beeline to the coffee machine. "Anyone else want coffee?"

"All of my cookies are gone," Patti said, picking up both platters. "Not even any broken ones are left."

"I've got some Christmas candy in the cabinet if we want to put some of that out, and there's a bag of frosted pretzels," Jade said.

"I'm on it. I think the treats always make it festive," Patti said, following Lorelei.

Patti returned and poured white-chocolate-covered pretzels with sprinkles into a large bowl. Then she dumped a tin of colorful hard candy in a festive bowl. "I call this stuff Grandma candy," she said. "It always sticks together, but it looks pretty in the bowl."

"Yum," Bernie said, grabbing a handful of pretzels. "I missed lunch. Thanks, gals. There's a gang of kids behind me. They followed me across the street. I think we're in for a lively afternoon." He hustled toward his throne in the showroom as Jade followed behind him with a water bottle. "Everything okay. You want me to bring you some lunch?"

"Busy morning. Cecil, Lester, and I plan to visit as many of the food trucks as we can for an early dinner. The parade was a hoot. I felt like a rock star."

"Your fan club is waiting outside. I'll send them in when you're ready. We've had quite a busy day here, too," Jade said.

"I'm heading to the North Pole after this for a rest." Bernie chuckled. "And if you don't mind, it's a bit warm in this fur suit. You mind putting the AC on back here?"

"Gotcha covered." Jade detoured to the thermostat.

By four o'clock, a steady line of children and their parents had made their way in to see Santa. When the last group left, Bernie headed to the back for some coffee.

"All the vendors have packed up and left the multipurpose room. I locked the door after putting away all the tables," Patti said, straightening items on the back counter.

"You should have hollered. We could have helped you," Lorelei said.

"I took care of it. My powerlifting class is paying off," Patti said, flexing her muscle.

"Well, ladies, by the register totals, this was a record-breaking sales day," Lorelei beamed. "Great work."

"Hear that?" Patti asked.

Lorelei and Jade said, "What?" in stereo.

"The noise level is back to normal now. We can enjoy the quiet for a moment or two," Patti said with a smile.

"I felt like I was yelling for most of the afternoon," Lorelei said, as Bernie waltzed out in a Hawaiian shirt and cargo pants. His outfit and deck shoes with no socks gave off the perfect beachy vibe.

"Hey, Santa. Is it casual day at work?" Lorelei said.

"Santa is plumb worn out. And I still have to head over to the pier to get ready for the sandcastle contest and movie night on the beach. I'm sleeping in tomorrow. Oh, Jade, Cecil and Lester and I will be by later to put up the tables and tents outside." He picked up his costume bag and grabbed a handful of pretzels for the road.

"Thanks, Bernie. You did great today," Jade said. Her stomach grumbled loud enough that she was sure the others heard. "Hey, anybody want to get a late lunch at the food trucks. I think we've earned an early closing."

"Neville and I are about ready to head home. Steve's picking me up at seven, and I was hoping to catch a little catnap with Neville before my dinner plans. See y'all next week." She and the tuxedo cat sashayed out the front like they were in a dance number in a Disney movie.

Patti gathered her things as Jade shut down the lights and equipment. "I need to head home, too. I've got to get ready for dinner with Simon, and then we have to pick up my sister and her kids for movie night. I need to make sure we're well stocked on the snack front. See you later this week. Congratulations on a banner day."

Jade locked the front door behind Patti and said, "Let's go eat either a late lunch or an early dinner."

While waiting in line outside an Asian fusion truck, Jade checked her phone. Three more texts from Randall.

Can you meet later over at the pier? I found what I was looking for. It may be too late. But I still need to talk to you. Later tonight? Can you make it?

Jade tapped a reply. **Did you take a picture of what it was? I thought** you were going to send me a picture.

I'll send it in a minute. Can you talk later?

Did you call the sheriff? she asked.

Not yet. Need your opinion first. I'll send the pix & U tell me what U think.

Jade took the to-go container the woman at the window of the purple and orange truck handed her. She and Chloe made their way around rows of trucks and through the crowds. *Why is Randall being so evasive? And why won't he call the police?*

After feeding Chloe and settling down to her own dinner, Jade checked her phone. Randall had gone radio silent again. And still no picture of whatever he found. *This makes no sense. He's amped up, and then he ghosts me. He is so fixated on whatever he buried. But, I am a little curious about what he thinks he found. Why is he being so cagey?*

Chapter Twenty-Six

J ade's phone buzzed, distracting her from Randall's unusual behavior.

"Hey, girl," Amy said. "How was Mermaid Day for you?"

"Great sales," Jade replied. "What about for the bookstore?"

"Same here. Everything cryptid-related flew off the shelves. Big win. Yay for me. You going to movie night tonight? The sandcastle announcement is around seven. Then there's the *Under the Sea* costume contest on the pier. Then it's movie night. I reserved a table on Todd's deck. You going?"

"Sounds like fun. You're not doing the costume thing, are you?" *Who knows what kind of costume Amy would try to rope me into?*

"Nah. Not this year. Come on and enjoy the merriment. I'll provide snacks. Any time before seven. Toodles."

"Sounds like a date. See ya," Jade said. "Chloe, movie night always means popcorn."

Chloe rubbed up against the dining room rug and wiggled out of her mermaid shirt. "You done with the costume? It's been a long day. We'll get you settled here, and you can guard the house."

A little before seven, Jade checked the doors and Chloe's water bowl. "I'll be back after the movie. Not sure I'll stay for the double-feature. You're in charge while I'm gone."

Jade pocketed her phone, which had been uncharacteristically silent. Randall must have had something else to do. *I hope he called Nick's office.* She blew out a long puff of air that fluttered her bangs. *I've talked to tons of people, but what I've uncovered is like a huge box of building blocks that don't fit together. I feel like I'm spinning my wheels in the sand. And if Randall really did find something as earth-shattering as he claims, he needs to tell the police. He's acting very weird lately.*

She looped back inside and grabbed a hoodie before she took off for the beach.

Crowds had gathered around the monstrous sand sculptures. The beach was full, but the chilly spring breeze that whipped off the bay reminded Jade that the unofficial start to summer was weeks away. Pulling up her hood, Jade plodded around the people and climbed the weathered steps on the Hot Diggity Dogs deck.

Amy hopped up and down like a bobber in the water. She waved and said, "You're just in time. Vivian and Bernie are getting ready to announce the winners." She took a swig of something from a metal thermos. "Hot chocolate. I brought you some. And I have snacks in that bag if you want anything."

"Thanks," Jade said, taking the other metal drink container Amy offered.

The drumline from the high school marched across the sand, and their music drowned out the sounds of the waves. They encircled a platform where Vivian stood, brandishing her bullhorn.

When the drummers finished, Vivian cleared her throat and said, "Ladies and Gentlemen, the Mermaid Bay Business Council is so glad you all could join us tonight for the inaugural sandcastle contest for Mermaid Day. It is my pleasure to bring you the winners, though by the looks of these artistic pieces, they're all winners. But sadly, we can have only three that can earn the prizes. So without further ado, Team Catamaran is our third-place winner with its version of King Neptune." When the cheers calmed down, she continued," Bobby's Sand Crabs placed second with the giant crab and clam sculpture. And now, the moment you've all been waiting for, The Sea Pirates' mermaid on the back of the sea turtle is our first-place winner this year. Congratulations to everyone for your amazing work. All the entries will be in a special edition of the *Beach Comber* next week, so make sure you get your copy."

"Good choices," Amy said, when the noise drifted off. "The costume contest is up next. I wonder if any of the cosplay folks entered? The Kraken would be a hit if he showed up."

"Vivian would have a stroke if the monsters showed up and crashed her party. Her vision is everything mermaid today."

Amy laughed. "Then I may have to enter next year. I could do goth mermaid or Frankenmermaid. Oh, I could have some fun with this."

"Where's Todd?" Jade scanned the beachfront below the deck.

"He didn't want to leave his team with the crowds that have been flowing through here today. He's in there slinging hot dogs. I saw your beau on the corner with Sebastian. They were keeping law and order in our fair town."

"Usually Vivian does that," Jade added, and they both dissolved in a fit of giggles.

"She was over there too with her clipboard and bullhorn," Amy said.

"That's better than the sledgehammer she had the other day." Jade took the white cheddar popcorn bag that Amy offered.

A row of costumed kids followed by their doting parents paraded down the edge of the pier and waved to the crowd. Vivian, Farrah, Kelly, and Bernie eyed each costume as the contestants passed by.

Vivian introduced the contestants and described each outfit in minute detail like this was the red carpet walk at the Oscars. Amy and Jade finished off the bag of popcorn and broke out a box of Junior Mints before Vivian finally said, "Thank you, everyone. The judges will confer and be right back with the winners." The high school band struck up "Under the Sea," followed by a medley of other cartoon classics.

When the band finished, Vivian took center stage on the wooden pier. She waved one arm. "May I have your attention, please. The judges have reached their decision. We'd like to thank everyone. It was a tough job to narrow it down to a handful of winners."

Farrah reached for the bullhorn, and Vivian reluctantly released it. "Hello, all. I'm Farrah Rogers. On behalf of the judges, we'd like to award third place to K. C. Jenkins." When the applause died down, she continued in her breathy voice, "Our second place goes to Emma Woods, and our first-place winner is Jordan King. Let's give a big round of applause to all our participants. And thank you all for making Mermaid Day such a success."

Vivian reached for the bullhorn. "Participants, please stay by the pier, so that we can take a group photo. Thank you all for coming to our sandcastle and costume contests. We have had so much fun today. As soon as it gets dark, we'll begin our movie double feature. Feel free to find seats right below here for our mermaid cinematic extravaganza." The drumline tapped out a rhythm, and the judges marched down the pier.

"Well, that was a hoot," Amy said. "We are so dressing up next year. Who says it's only for kids? Todd can be Aquaman. Too bad Nick's always working during these things. We could come up with a great costume for him."

Jade made an exaggerated surprised face. "He's tied up with sheriff stuff during these events, but even if he weren't, I'm not sure he'd play along."

"We'll work on him. He'll come around. So, Nancy Drew, speaking of the hunky sheriff, what have you uncovered lately to help him solve these murders? Find anything earth-shattering?"

"A whole bunch of stuff on sticky notes that doesn't seem to go together, where Meredith is at the hub of all the activity. She had so many altercations with way too many people to count. And there are all kinds of rumors about affairs, shady deals, and taking credit for others' work."

Amy's eyebrows shot up under her dark bangs. "And don't forget she loved being the one who stirred up the stink. Going with tonight's movie theme, she's the Ursula of the story. It's hard to feel super sympathetic for her when she caused most of her own problems."

Jade let out an extended sigh. "Randall wants me to find out what I can and keep him updated on the investigation. I have nothing new to share with him. He keeps giving me names of people who held a grudge against his wife. So far, none of them have turned into substantial leads. And now he thinks he found something important, but he won't tell me what it is or call the police." Jade rested her head on her folded arms on one of Todd's picnic tables. "This one is not like the other murders. And even with Delia's help, I still feel like I'm running around in circles."

"Okay, so who's your best suspect? You don't have to have all the facts. Go by your gut feeling. What is that little voice in your head telling you?" Amy asked.

"Initially, I felt like Meredith killed Ernie. But, she didn't strangle herself, so there has to be another person involved. I guess it could have been one of his supporters out for revenge, but that theory feels a little complicated. My gut tells me that both murders are by the same person, and we have to figure out the details."

"Easier said than done. But we like a challenge," Amy said.

"Randall keeps mentioning students and colleagues. And he's brought up Angel Cruz a couple of times."

"Nooooo!" Amy said, lunging forward. "I have spent so much time with him and Marcella. They are focused on his explorations and his tours. It can't be him. Why would he think it's him? That is crazy."

Jade shrugged. "I've heard rumors that he and Meredith had some big, separate announcements, and Randall hinted that they were planning to scoop the other. Meredith didn't announce anything, and Angel mentioned a giant squid, but it didn't seem to be as earth-shattering as Randall made it out to be."

Jade chewed on her bottom lip. She pulled out her phone and tapped a quick text to Marcella. **Was Meredith on the brink of making some big announcement about her research? Just curious.**

"You okay?" Amy asked.

"I'm fine," Jade said, pocketing her phone. "Sorry. I had a question for Marcella. I'm hoping she can help me tie up one of a thousand loose ends."

"I still don't think it can be Angel. He has too much to lose to get involved with what looks like amateur hour or high school antics with these characters," Amy said.

The pair fell silent and watched the crowds mill around in the sand, and the gulls dip in and out of the bay. The evening breeze picked up, and Jade pulled her hoodie closer around her. *I think it's one killer, but how in the world will I prove it?*

Jade's skin felt prickly, and it wasn't from the bay breeze. *I have a weird sense that someone is watching us.* Her thoughts bounced to the paranormal explorers and the presidential heads. *What am I missing? Did I see something that evening that is bubbling up in my subconscious now?* Her thoughts zinged around like a wild pinball game, but nothing came to the forefront. Jade took several deep breaths and focused on the bay. The constant roll of the waves calmed her anxiousness.

A deep "hey" from behind them caused Jade to jump, and the pair whipped their heads around to the screen door to Todd's hot dog stand.

"I thought that was you. Jade, I hope I'm not intruding. I'm checking out the festivities on this side of the pier. When I got up to leave, I thought I saw you out here." Topher stepped outside and scanned the beach. "Nice night."

"Hi," Jade said with a tentative wave. "Amy, this is Dr. Topher Taylor. He's a cryptozoologist."

Amy's head bobbed in place. "Nice to finally meet you in person. I'm Amy Pemberton. I own the bookstore over there." She pointed toward the pier and waved her hand around. "So tell me what is your specialty?"

He paused and snickered.

"I meant your research specialty," Amy snapped.

"Oh, of course. My background is in marine biology, but I blended that with my love of fantasy stories and ended up majoring in cryptozoology. My specialty is researching species that were thought to be mythical but turned out to actually exist."

"Like what?"

"Well, manatees were often mistaken for mermaids in the early days of seafaring. There are plenty of stories about giant squids and whales as sea monsters. Lately, plenty of discoveries in that area have given new life to the Kraken stories. I'm headed to Australia next year for a four-month fellowship. They have all kinds of critters down there that are mythical in their own right. And there's a new theory that Nessie is a giant eel. The jury's out of that one still."

"Be careful. They have loads of deadly stuff down there. No thanks. No camping in Australia for me or diving in those deadly waters," Amy said, scrunching her nose. "Have a seat. The movie's about to start."

"Thanks, but I need to head back. There's a thing at the hotel later this evening that I need to go to. It was nice to bump into you both. See you around." His head pivoted from Jade to Amy.

Topher pulled out his phone and climbed down the sandy steps. When he blended into the crowd near the pier, Amy whispered, "He happened to see you in the twilight from behind. I guess it's possible, but that was kinda weird. Something felt stalkerish. Keep him on your list of suspects until we can figure him out."

"It's rumored that he and Meredith had a thing years ago, but he says he was only her teaching assistant," Jade whispered.

"That's what they all say," Amy said, bobbing her head.

"Did I tell you the other night after CreatureCon, I was walking Chloe near my house, and he stepped out of my driveway and scared me to death. He said he wanted to see who was asking about him."

"I got a weird vibe from him. It seems we've stirred up a hornet's nest. Maybe you're getting closer than you know," Amy said. "And how did he know where you lived?"

"He said he followed us."

"Mark my words. Creepy." Amy waggled a finger.

"And if that's not enough, Randall keeps popping up randomly, too," Jade said, staring off at the pier.

"Did you tell Nick?"

Jade shook her head. "Not yet. Both of them are more odd than menacing. If it happens again, I'll mention it. I think Randall's just overly concerned. But I'm not sure I can help him solve this."

"I have faith in you. You'll solve this. The pieces will fall into place." Amy patted her friend on the shoulder.

Before Jade could reply, the speakers on and under the pier boomed the opening song of *Little Mermaid*, and the crowd settled in to watch the live-action version.

"I usually don't like remakes, but this is cute," Amy whispered. "The cartoon one came out when I was little. I remember being obsessed with Ariel. I bet you were too, especially since you looked like her with all that red hair."

"*Beauty and the Beast* was my favorite," Jade said.

"That library!" They said in unison, getting some looks from the movie-watchers around them on Todd's deck.

* * *

When the credits rolled, Jade stood and stretched. "Want some more popcorn?" Amy asked.

"I'm full. Thanks for all the snacks. I need to get back and check on Chloe."

Amy put on an exaggerated pouty face. "Too bad you can't stay for *Splash*. I've seen it so many times, I can quote most of the lines. I guess I'll pop in and see how Todd is doing. He's probably beat. Call me this week. We'll go out and do something. We are due for some fun."

Jade waved and descended the stairs. The portable lights around the sandcastles illuminated the beach and dulled the starry night. When she rounded the corner near the shell path, the lights disappeared, and shadows danced on the fences and the sand. She blinked to help her eyes adjust.

The wind whistled through the trees, and the shadows made the hair on the back of her neck stand up. *Stop it. You're being jumpy. There's nobody behind you. What is wrong with you tonight?* She flipped on her phone's flashlight app and jog-walked home.

She slammed her front door shut behind her and leaned on it to catch her breath. *You're being paranoid. Your imagination is on one long, cross-country run lately.*

Chapter Twenty-Seven

After the sound of Jade's heart stopped pounding in her ears, she scooped up Chloe and gave her a hug. "Let's do your nightly constitution in the front yard tonight." She flipped on the floodlights and clicked the leash in place. For good measure, she gripped her phone in one hand and slipped the thin container of pepper spray in her pocket.

While Chloe wandered around and sniffed the front yard smells, Jade glanced at her phone.

Hey. Angel had a big announcement that he's using to kick off his next season of shows and his new book tour, but I don't know of anything Meredith had going. She'd been flying under the radar lately. Sorry. I'm no help, Marcella replied to Jade's earlier question.

Thanks, Jade tapped into her phone as Chloe hustled up the cement steps. *Interesting. How can it be a big reveal if your publicist doesn't know anything about it? Something is not adding up, and Meredith is smack dab in the middle of all of this.*

Jade knocked the sand off her shoes and opened the door for Chloe as a dark sedan drove slowly by and turned around in one of her neighbors' driveways. It drove slowly by her house as she watched from the front window. *Stop it. You are being so antsy tonight. Go focus on something productive.* She double checked the locks on the front door – just to be sure.

She handed Chloe a chunky, meaty bite and poured herself a Dr. Pepper. "I need the energy tonight, even if it keeps me up. It's time to do a deeper dive on Dr. Echols and the Xplorer."

Not interested in the marine biology drama or anything other than sleep, Chloe hopped on the couch and snuggled under the lap blanket.

On a whim, Jade started with Ernie the Xplorer. There were connections between him and Meredith that spanned more than ten years. And rumors always seemed to swirl around Ernie, Meredith, and Randall. Some liked him romantically with Meredith, while others depicted them as sworn enemies. And still others pitted him against Randall for Meredith's affections. It doesn't make sense that Meredith would kill Ernie if they really weren't enemies, and there was a secret romance. *Which story is true?*

Switching tactics, Jade scoured hundreds of pictures on his website and Instagram account for any kind of clue. Most of the recent ones were of him on deep-sea dives or on the lecture circuit. In some of the photos, she found Randall posing with Topher. "Interesting. Topher said he hadn't had contact with Randall lately. I wonder when these were taken?" She made a mental note to ask Randall about it.

She paused and rubbed both eyes that felt like sandpaper from so much screentime. "Chloe, I'm not finding anything. Wait, what was that?" Jade scrolled back to group photos at the top of one of his blog posts. Buried in between several shots of Ernie at a lectern and candids of the audience members, there was Meredith and her signature blond braid. Another shot showed her at a long farm table with a group toasting Ernie. Jade enlarged the photo. Ernie's arm was draped around the back of Dr. Echols. "Chloe, these were posted two weeks ago. The blog has a date stamp."

The little dog opened an eye and then rolled over on the couch.

She scanned the rest of the photos, but none of the others featured Meredith. "Chloe, that's interesting. The restaurant picture with Meredith was at the Blue Rooster Brewery. Too bad I couldn't find anything else except their menu. But this could substantiate the rumors of a recent Meredith and Ernie fling. It did look like more than colleagues hanging out in a brewery in Jupiter, Florida." She made copies of the photos for her file on Ernie.

After hours of searching, Jade hadn't found any other photos or clues. She copied what she had found and sent them along with the links to Nick.

"Now for a deeper dive into Angel's life." *I hope I don't break Amy's heart.*

Jade scanned page after page of his photos and videos. All looked like they had been created in a studio with his swash-buckling brand front and center. No spur-of-the-moment or goofy shots. And no family pictures. "That's interesting. There's one little bio on his website and no mention of his private life."

A motorcycle or a big truck outside revved an engine, and Jade sat up straight and groaned. Her neck and back ached from falling asleep on her notes again at the dining room table. "I'm too old for all-nighters, Chloe."

The lap blanket on the couch stirred, and the round dog stuck her nose out to see if breakfast was happening. When she didn't smell anything worth investigating, she snorted and rolled over.

"I thought you were my partner in this. I have about twenty pages of notes on Meredith and Ernie. Everything from bad student reviews to her committee assignments at the university. Nothing jumps out as notable. And everything on Angel radiates his brand and his accomplishments. Marcella does a great job with his publicity. On a hunch, she pulled up Marcella's business site, and her stuff was as shiny as Angel's. But Meredith's Facebook page was out of date, and her posts were bland and too wordy. She could have used Marcella's help.

Jade rubbed her eyes and temples. She picked up the pudgy dog and headed off to brush her teeth and to fall into bed. Maybe she could get in a few more winks before the alarm sounded in a couple of hours.

A truck backed up in the distance, and the beeping alert drug Jade from a fitful dream. The sun peeked through her bedroom curtains. The traffic noise didn't seem to bother Chloe. She snored like a buzz saw from her spot in the middle of the bed.

"It's shower and coffee time. Too bad Nick's busy. A leisurely brunch would have been nice," Jade said to herself.

Thoughts of Meredith, Randall, and Topher bounced around in her head as the warm water pulsated over her. *I don't think the killer is Topher or Angel. No clear motives. Could it be another student? I need to take another look at that Rate-my-Prof site.*

Not divining any ideas from the shower or the fogged bathroom mirror, she toweled off. After some gel and some time with the hair dryer, it was time to start her day. "Coffee, first," she said to her dog, who watched from the bed with one eye open.

Jade zinged around her bungalow and paused only to pack her notes in the messenger bag. "See, I did find a bunch of stuff yesterday, but it's still like looking for a needle in a haystack. We'll take a leisurely walk this morning. It may not be full-on brunch, but we can stop by the Busy Bean to see what James and Sophie have on the menu."

The pair walked down the beach past all the sand sculptures, where the sandpipers and gulls outnumbered the people. A barge and a trawler crawled across the horizon. *No one was in a hurry this morning.*

Stopping outside the town's only coffee place, Jade stomped her feet on the cement stoop to knock off the sand. Inside the cozy shop, smells of strong coffee, cinnamon, vanilla, and bacon tickled her nose and made her stomach rumble.

"Good morning. What can I get for you?" James asked. "Sophie's been busy in the kitchen since the crack of dawn."

Perusing the large chalk menu above and the glass displays filled with delicious-looking muffins and other breakfast goodies, Jade said, "Oh, it's so hard to choose. Let's see. I'll have the Mermaid quiche with a large iced vanilla latte. That should take care of my sweet and savory cravings this morning."

"Sounds like a plan," James said as she tapped her card on the reader. "Chloe, I didn't forget you. There's something for your morning. Bacon," he whispered, pointing to the bag.

"Thanks," Jade said. "Y'all survived Mermaid Day unscathed."

"We ran out of some of the specials, and Sophie had to do some emergency baking, but we're not complaining. We love the crowds." James handed Jade her purchases. "Here you go. Enjoy!"

Jade waved and nudged Chloe toward the door. The chunky dog dawdled in front of the display counter. Finally acquiescing, Chloe followed Jade to the exit.

The street was as quiet as the beach. The pair strolled by the pizza parlor and across the lot that looked vacant without all the food trucks. When Jade unleashed Chloe, the dog dashed through the store with a burst of energy. "Sorry, baby. Neville's not here today. It's just you and me. Hey, do you want the yummy bacon treat James gave you?"

She zipped into the back room and yipped. "I thought so," Jade said, patting the dog's boxy head.

Sunday morning was slow and easy in the quaint beach town when it wasn't the height of the summer tourist season. Jade spent her morning straightening displays and ordering additional inventory. The store felt empty, so she cranked up a pop music station to liven up the mood a bit.

She looked up from her laptop when the front door opened. Topher stuck his rumpled head inside and looked around. "Neat place." He stared at the monster ornaments on the giant trees that stood sentry at the entrance. "These are cool. I'll have to get some for my office."

"If there's something special you want, let me know. I can put in an order and ship it to you if you don't see it here in the store." Jade watched him rummage through the ornaments.

He filled his arms with one of each of the Yeti, Nessie, and Bigfoot ornaments. Hey, the Mothman. You really do have everything. You should be a vendor at the cons."

He set his pile of plastic figures on the counter as his glance darted around the room toward the display areas. "Any more monsters?"

"There's a Halloween tree back there, past the rainbow room. It has some of the classic creatures from pop culture and horror movies, and there's a dinosaur tree in the toy room."

"I'll have to check them out. You have a catalogue?" he asked, handing her a debit card.

"Not a printed one, but you can shop online on my site." She did a Vanna White demo with her business card and dropped it into his bag with his purchases.

"Cool," he said, fidgeting with change in his pocket. He glanced behind him at the door several times.

"Here you go. Is everything okay?" She offered him the bag and his card.

"Just fine." He reached for the bag. "The paparazzi descended on the con this morning. I got ambushed at breakfast. That was kind of a surprise. I wasn't ready for my fifteen minutes of fame before coffee."

"What set them off?" Jade asked.

"News broke on some true crime podcast that I was the guy who caused Meredith to lose her job. And the so-called podcast detective is speculating that I had the biggest motive to kill her because she ruined my life and my chances of being a marine biologist. I had to turn my phone off. My voicemail and socials are jacked up. I normally fly under the radar, so this isn't my thing. Especially when it's not true."

He wiped his nose with the back of his hand and continued, "Now everyone thinks I killed her. I'm doing my panel after lunch and heading out. I hope it's not a total disaster. With my luck, it'll be filled with people who want to ask questions about Meredith and why I killed her."

"What do you know about Ernie Post?"

"The Xplorer?" Jade nodded, and he shrugged. "I told you before. He's a decent guy. We hung out sometimes. I met him through Randall. Pretty popular if rumors are to be believed." He looked over his shoulder and lowered his voice. "He and Meredith were dating on the sly. His room was on the same floor as mine."

"I thought they argued a lot," Jade prodded.

"Con life is like professional wrestling. It's all for the entertainment," he said with a wink. "The fans like it when there's ongoing conflict."

"I saw some photos of an event Ernie did at the Blue Rooster Brewery. You were in the group photos. It thought you all didn't socialize."

"The one in Jupiter? That's from years ago when I was in college." He pinched the bridge of his nose with his two fingers. "All this ancient history coming back to haunt me. I had nothing to do with these murders. And now I'm being harassed by armchair detectives, true crime podcasters, and a bunch of conspiracy theorists. Maybe I'll use my panel time to set the record straight." His voice trailed off.

"Meredith left her university about the time you were her teaching assistant, right?"

"I had already transferred to another school when that happened. I don't know why she left. Maybe she ticked off the administration or some rich alumnus. She didn't schmooze well. I wasn't the guy that caused her romantic scandal. That was Ernie. Everyone back then knew that," Topher said. "I didn't kill either one of them. I didn't have any contact with her unless I happened to run into her at a conference or an event."

"What about Randall Medlin?" she asked, deciding to poke the bear.

"There's not much to tell. He was one of the cool profs. Though I never understood why he and Meredith didn't get a divorce. They obviously went their separate ways years ago." He closed his eyes for a beat and drew a long breath in through his nose. "Though if you talk to him about it, he insists that they're on happy terms and were talking about reconciling. I think he's in denial about Ernie, so she was stringing both of them along. I wouldn't put that past her. She was the master manipulator."

"Was Meredith planning to do some kind of big reveal at this conference?" Jade asked, trying to see what else he would spill.

"Who knows? She was always crowing about her research, which was done mainly by her students. She wasn't that in tune with the science world anymore. It's like her heart wasn't in it. Her focus was on the conferences and all the money she was making. She did one or two a month. I'm surprised the university let her get away with that much travel." He shrugged a shoulder and made a pickle face. "I heard Randall bragging that he was the executor of her estate and her intellectual properties. She authored a couple of textbooks. I'm sure she's still getting royalties off those. She was a decent scientist at one time. She used to care, and then things changed. Money corrupts, I guess."

"How do you plan to respond to all the publicity from the podcaster's claim?" Jade asked.

"I plan to ride it out. Eventually, my name will be cleared. But I'll have to suffer through the lies, false accusations, and harassment. I'm glad my trip to Australia is soon. It'll be a nice break. And hopefully, things will die down by the time I return. Well, bye if I don't see you again. These will be fun additions to my collection." He held up his bag. "My plan is to do my panel and skip town before this story about Meredith and me gets out of hand." He slowly opened the door. Sticking his head outside, he looked up and down the street before he stepped out.

Jade picked up her phone and texted a quick message to Nick about Topher.

Somebody's been sleuthing, he texted moments later.

People talk to me. Just wanted to make sure you know about Ernie and Topher.

Thanks. You never know what clue will break this thing open. You wanna do dinner sometime this week?

Perfect, she replied with a string of heart emojis.

"What caused Meredith to change her focus?" Jade asked the empty lobby. *From what I found yesterday online, her bad student ratings had skyrocketed over the last three years. That correlates with all her conference work.*

Jade spent the rest of the day with her swirling thoughts. "Chloe, something is tickling the back of my brain. It's like I woke up from a dream, and I can't remember parts of it. This is driving me nuts. And I don't think I'm going to get much more work done here, so let's pack it in. I need to touch base with Delia. Maybe she'll have something for me that'll spark an idea or a lead."

Chapter Twenty-Eight

"Hey, whatcha doing?" Amy asked. "It sounds like you're in a wind tunnel."

"Chloe and I are checking out all the sites. And she's keeping our beach safe from joggers, sea gulls, and sand crabs."

"Have you had dinner yet?" her friend asked.

"Nope. That was my next task…to find something in my fridge. It's way past time to get groceries."

"You can go grocery shopping later. I have a better idea. Let's go to Pizza D'Action and have a girls' night. Todd's busy with his gaming buddies, and my pantry is empty too. Whoever gets there first get a table inside."

"See ya in a bit." Jade disconnected the call and said to Chloe, "I'll race you home." The Frenchie gave her a look with attitude and waddled toward the shell path. Speed was not of the essence for the chubby dog.

By the time Jade fluffed her hair and added some mascara, the sun slipped behind the pine trees. The evening breeze hinted that warmer temperatures were on their way, so she bagged the idea of taking the Wrangler and walked to the restaurant.

At the end of her driveway, the hedges moved, and a figure stepped out in front of her. She squealed and clutched her phone.

"Sorry. I didn't mean to scare you. It's me. Randall. I had some thoughts after my last panel, and I tried to reach you a couple of times. You didn't call me back, so I decided to make sure you're okay." *By scaring the living daylights out of me again. I didn't have any missed calls from him. What is he talking about?*

"Maybe you called while I was on the other line. What's up?" She looked up and down the street but didn't see his car.

"I wanted to show you what I found the other day. I buried it when you weren't available. Time's running out. I need to show you before it's too late."

"You buried it? Why would you do that? What is it?" she asked.

"It won't take long. It's over there by the pier, and then you can get on with whatever you were doing."

"I have to meet someone," she said, still clutching her phone.

"I wouldn't bother you if it weren't important. I need your expert opinion on it. Plus, I'm heading out tomorrow, so this might be the last chance I get. It's some stuff I found when I was exploring under the pier. Over here." He pulled her arm in the direction of the beach path. "This way. Please. The light is already fading. I'll be quick. We're wasting time here."

What did he find? Nick's forensic guys combed that area when night we found the body. "Did you call the police about this? They're looking at every lead," Jade said.

"Not yet. I wanted you to look at it first. I don't want to bother them again if it's nothing. I call them all the time, and I don't want them to think that I'm the crazy, neurotic husband." *Which is it? It's super drop-everything important, or it may be no big deal. Why is he fixated with what's under the pier?* Jade reluctantly followed him after she rescued her arm from his excited grip. The pair tramped past the sand sculptures, and Jade had to pick up her pace to keep up with his strides.

"What is it exactly? Did you take a picture of it?" she yelled to his back.

"It was too dark…and I didn't have my phone. I think it's stuff related to Ernie's death. Murder. Whatever. It was kinda in a pile. I buried it and left a marker to remember the spot. I think it will exonerate Mer and me. And I can finally get on with my life."

You couldn't find it last time you dragged me over here. But what if it is something important? It couldn't hurt to see what he found, even if he's being a Secret Squirrel about it. I hope he didn't damage whatever it was by burying it. Nick will have a fit if he destroys evidence.

Their conversation faded as the pair walked in the sand near the edge of Suggs Pier. Jade slowed her pace. "I need to call the sheriff and have him send a deputy over if it's related to the murders."

"No time," he yelled. He tugged on her arm again to get her moving. "Come on before it's too dark. I don't want to wait until tomorrow morning. I have an early flight. And I need to put this whole Meredith thing to rest. I don't have time to deal with it. I've got a lot of paperwork and other junk to take care of when I get back home. I have to get her stuff in order."

She glanced down at her wrist that he clutched. His braided rope bracelet was back. A flash of adrenaline jolted through Jade. She was right. It matched the one in the envelope and the piece of rope that Bernie found in the mulch. Was Randall trying to implicate others and throw suspicion off himself? Her thoughts bounced to Nick, and how he was the exact opposite of this guy. *Nick is a tad overprotective sometimes, but nothing like this. Randall has morphed from caring about his ex to some dark obsession.*

Pieces started clicking into place. She pulled out of his grasp. "I need a minute to catch my breath. I think I'm going to be sick."

"Take a couple of deep breaths. You'll be okay. The light is fading. We need to do this now. I've got other stuff to do tonight."

"Your bracelet is like the one Meredith had," Jade said, pointing at his wrist.

He paused, and his countenance softened momentarily. "Yep, we had them made when we were in Jamaica. I miss her and all the good times we had together. I kept it to remind me of all that was right between us. And I guess what will never be." His voice drifted off as he turned his head. Then his face darkened; he grabbed Jade's arm and squeezed until it pinched. "Enough of this. I'm tired of playing. You need to see this before it's too late."

"Ow. That hurts. Let go of me." Jade dropped her phone in the sand and bile surged in her core. *I can't lose my phone. And I've got to get away from him.*

"I wouldn't be this adamant if it wasn't important. Now come with me, or I'll pick you up and carry you. This is life or death for me. And you've been too busy to look at it. Enough! Why can't you see how important it is? I need for all of this to be over. I have to tie up all loose ends. Now!"

Jade frantically scanned the beach for anyone who could help her. Not a soul in sight. Just a couple of seagulls. Panic welled up inside of her. *Stop it. You've got to keep it together and find a way out of this mess.*

"It's over here. I marked the spot with some rope on the pylon. Just a few more feet," Randall said. He led her deeper and deeper under the dark pier. The acoustics amplified the normal wave sounds to a cacophony of crashes. Jade took several deep breaths to calm herself. *You've got to stay alert and look for a way out. Focus.*

"I thought you'd be the one to help me, but you haven't discovered anything. It's me leading you to clues that I found. What have you uncovered about Meredith's death? I thought from the way folks here talked about you that you'd have this solved in a flash and help me clear my name. I can't have anyone thinking I'd hurt Mer. You're not that good, huh?" His voice dropped an octave and sounded ominous. The lack of light and the sounds under the dark pier distorted her senses and made her feel claustrophobic. *Okay. You need to ditch him and find your phone. You've got to catch him off guard and run.*

Randall yelled, "It's right over here." His voice bounced off the nearby pylons and echoed for a couple of beats. *Now is the time. Run, girl.* But before Jade could put her plan into action, he grabbed her from behind around the neck. "Yep. The rope is mine. You think you're so smart. I saw your interest in that bracelet, and it was a matter of time before you put two and two together. I tried to warn you off, but you can't seem to take a hint. You should have ran with that Topher lead. None of this should have happened like this. Ernie wouldn't leave Meredith alone. He kept interfering with our lives. I tried to talk sense into him. He wouldn't listen. And he had to pay for the trouble he caused." He tightened his grip around Jade, and she gasped.

I've got to keep him talking. "What about Meredith?" she croaked in a voice strained by the pressure he put on her neck.

"She was supposed to come back. Instead, she wigged out and didn't want to talk to me. Everything would have been okay if she had gone along with the plan, but I'm telling you, she freaked about Ernie's death. I couldn't leave loose ends. No matter how much I loved her."

Jade tipped her head forward to try to keep her airway open. Then she dropped to her knees in a squat. Her quick movement caused enough of a diversion for Randall to loosen his grip. *Thank you, Patti, and that self-defense course you made me take.*

Without any further hesitation, Jade bolted toward the beach, screaming a hoarse squeak as loud as she could. It was hard to get traction in the dry sand. She stumbled several times and caught herself before she landed face-first.

Randall didn't seem to have any trouble with the terrain. He gained on her with every second that passed.

Jade looked behind her as he lunged toward her and fell, managing to grab one of her ankles. Jade screamed again and kicked him in the nose. Randall let out a string of obscenities, and another, the well-placed kick bought her enough time to dodge his grip. Glancing back, he tried to staunch the flow of blood from his lip and nose with the sleeve of his sweatshirt.

He rose up from the sand with a primal screech and an alarming sneer that looked like some kind of sand monster. Jade's heart pounded, and her lizard brain emptied of all thoughts except to run.

Randall let out another shriek like a wounded animal, and then a crack that sounded like a homerun streaking out of a ballpark made her stomach flip. Randall jerked toward one of the pylons and hit his head on the cement base. He crashed to his knees and fell forward in the sand.

Jade paused. Randall Medlin didn't move. Before she could stop the battle in her head of whether to run or to check on him, she heard, "Jade. Jade. Come here. Now."

Amy stepped out of the shadows of one of the pylons. She clutched a gardening shovel with both hands. "I saw you two heading over to the pier, and I followed when something didn't look right. I grabbed the first thing I could when I thought you were in trouble. All I could think of was to get over here I didn't even stop to call the police. But I think I clocked him pretty good. He should be out cold for a while." Amy held up a shovel. "Jade, I was scared. He went from normal to crazy in seconds. I didn't know what else to do."

Jade hugged her friend. "Thank you. You so earned your sleuthing cred today. Forget sidekick, you're hero material. Your timing is impeccable."

"He really killed his wife and that other guy?" Amy asked, staring at the prone Randall, who didn't seem as menacing when he was face down in a sand drift.

Jade nodded.

"He had that rope thing in his hands. I knew I had to do something before he choked you. I have never been so scared in my life." Amy paused and leaned forward to catch her breath. When she stood up and stretched, she asked, "Hey, what are you doing?"

Jade swept the nearby sand with her foot. "I dropped my phone somewhere over here. Could you call 9-1-1? From the looks of him, Randall needs an ambulance or a hearse."

"Hey, we have one of those," Amy said with a mischievous grin. She punched in the numbers and quickly gave a rundown to the dispatcher while Jade continued her search.

When Amy disconnected, Jade hollered, "Call my phone, please. All I can see out here is sand, and that's getting difficult as the last rays of daylight fade."

Jade heard her ringtone and darted toward her half-buried phone. "Thanks. I got it. That's a relief."

"Uh, but this isn't," Amy said. She dropped her gardening shovel and landed full-force on the back of Randall, who had started to stir. "Oh, no, you don't. You've caused enough trouble, and you're not getting away. You stay still until the police get here, or I'll hit you in the head again."

Randall let out a whimper and sank deeper into the sand.

"How did you find us? I didn't see anyone on the beach earlier." Jade dusted sand off of her phone and clicked on her favorite apps to make sure everything was still working.

"I was heading out of my apartment, and I saw him grab you. It didn't look friendly, so I dropped everything and seized my trusty shovel here. I'm glad I left it out now. And if I do say so myself, all those years of softball practice paid off." A grin bloomed on Amy's face as she sat atop Randall and waited for the paramedics and the police. "And now that I'm officially your sidekick, we need to have jackets or business cards made up."

Sebastian and Nick were the first two to arrive. "Are you both okay?"

Sebastian asked, scanning the scene.

"We had Randall under surveillance, and he gave our deputy the slip earlier," Nick added. "We've been looking for him."

"And we found him. Jade and I had to teach him some manners."

"I see," Nick said, helping Amy up.

Sebastian cuffed Randall and then checked for a pulse.

"His rope thingy is over there where he dropped it." Amy pointed to the spot near her shovel. "We didn't touch it. Well, Jade did because he was trying to choke her with it."

"Who's shovel?" Sebastian asked.

"Mine. I grabbed the closest thing I had handy when I saw Jade was in trouble." Amy pushed some strands of her dark hair that had escaped from her ponytail out of her eyes. "It's been quite a day, and I have a hunch that it's not over yet."

"You okay?" Nick asked Jade. She nodded. "Randall killed both of them. He was obsessed with her. I realized it when I saw the bracelets. It was the same as the one sent to me, and Bernie found some of the rope with the cell phone that day in the mulch bed."

"It matches the rope on this garrote thing he dropped over here," Nick said. "How did you and Amy end up with him?"

"He kept insisting that he had something to show me that would prove who killed Meredith. He said he buried it the other day when I didn't have time to look at it."

"You think there's something here?" he asked.

She shrugged. "He's not the most truthful person. It's hard to tell. But he was insistent about it."

"Probably a ploy to lure you over here, but I'll have the forensic techs go over the scene just in case," Nick said.

"There were so many false flags and so many theories of stolen work, ambitious projects, and weird alliances, but it all came down to love and betrayal," Jade said.

"Sounds like a soap opera," Amy said, fanning her face with her hand. "Love and hate are two sides of the same coin."

"Details, please," Nick said.

"Randall wanted Meredith back, and she was hinting like they would reunite, but she was sneaking around with her old fling, Ernie. I'm guessing there was some kind of altercation, and Randall killed him. He was angry that Meredith freaked out and didn't come running back into his arms for comfort when the Xplorer died. He said he had to eliminate her, too, to tie up loose ends. And his elaborate plan was to cover up both murders, collect the insurance money, and deflect the blame onto others. He gave me a list of people to look into to throw off suspicions from him, but none of them had anything to do with either murder."

"Like the amazingly fabulous Angel Cruz," Amy added. "I told you it wasn't him."

Before they could continue, four EMTs hiked over the sand dune and swarmed around the prone Randall. Sebastain cordoned off the area with police tape as other deputies arrived with portable lights. The scene under the pier lit up almost like daylight had arrived again.

"Before you take off, could one of you check them out?" Nick pointed to Amy and Jade.

"I'm totally fine," Amy said. "I might have gotten a blister from white-knuckling that shovel handle, but otherwise, no biggie. Please check out Jade. That idiot grabbed her and tried to strangle her." Amy made a face and clutched her neck with both hands.

After a thorough prodding that seemed to last forever, the EMT said, "You're okay. If you feel dizzy later, go and get it checked out. Make sure you stay hydrated, and your neck and throat may be a little sore, but that should fade in a couple of days."

"Thanks. I may have a bruise or two, but that's way better than the concussion that Amy gave Randall," Jade said.

Amy and Jade plopped down in the sand and watched the emergency workers continue to tend to Randall. Eventually, they carried him out on a backboard, and forensic technicians photographed the area and searched the sand for hours with rakes and shovels.

Jade pointed and yelled to Nick. "Randall said he marked the pylon next to where he buried whatever it was he found." Nick nodded and said something to the technicians and pointed at the pylons.

"I'm getting cold," Amy said as the police searched every inch under Suggs Pier. "Hey, Sheriff, you need us anymore? Your forensic stuff isn't as fast as it is on TV."

Nick shook his head and stepped closer to the pair. "I'll need to get a formal statement from both of you, but it can wait until tomorrow. The deputy who went with Dr. Medlin to the hospital said he hasn't used his right to remain silent since they revived him. He's blaming everyone and his brother for the murders. And claiming this was all a big misunderstanding, and that Amy attacked him for no reason."

"Not buying it," Amy said, dusting the sand off her jeans. "Not in a million years. He admitted killing those people in front of Jade and me. No takebacks. He can't change his story now. I mean, he can, but he needs to be held accountable for what he did."

"It sounds like you have a busy night ahead of y'all. Try to get home before it's tomorrow," Jade said, patting Nick's arm.

"Not likely, but I'm due some days off next week. I need for things to go back to stolen bikes, lost dogs, and parking issues at least for a couple of days."

"I'm still hungry. What about you?" Amy asked, hopping up and dusting sand off her jeans. "Wanna get a pizza? I think we've earned it."

Jade glanced at her Fitbit. "Pizza D'Action is still open. But I need to check on Chloe."

"I'll freshen up, grab a pie, ditch my shovel, and head over to your place with a giant cheese pizza. Sheriff, can we bring y'all anything?"

Nick shook his head and trekked toward one of the forensic techs who was busy bagging something where Randall had been lying in the sand.

"Sounds like a plan," Jade said, slightly curious about what was found in the sand. *So far, no one has found Randall's buried secrets. Another of his many lies?*

"Sorry, you'll be without the shovel for a while," Sebastian added with a sly grin. "It's evidence."

Amy's eyes widened. "I guess the rest of my gardening will have to wait. Okay, Jade, I'll see ya when I see ya." She tromped through the dry sand toward Mermaid Books.

Jade waved to Nick and Sebastian and trudged home with her thoughts and a sense of relief. How can one man spew so many falsities and send me on so many goose chases? *He was charming, and no one ever suspected the guy with the boy-next-door looks. I guess his sincerity was an act, too. All the while, he was a cold-blooded killer who murdered his wife and friend.*

Jade climbed her front steps and greeted Chloe with a hug. She had enough time to pick up the clutter in the living room and stash the dirty dishes in the dishwasher before Amy rang the doorbell and sent the little dog into attack mode.

"Pizza's still hot," Amy said, bustling in with the box and a bottle of wine. "It's a rosé. It's all I had at home, but we're not snobby about our pizza wine. We deserve it after tonight's scare. That guy turned from the hunky prof into a crazed lunatic in less than two seconds. What did you say to him to set him off?"

Jade shrugged. "I don't remember. He kept on and on with this ridiculous story of burying a clue that I had to see because it would exonerate him and his wife. I mean, really, wouldn't a normal person have called the cops the minute they thought it was valuable information to help him clear his name?"

"He was a strange duck. And I knew that there was no way Angel was involved with any of this," she said with a wide grin. "I told you that early on. Woman's intuition." She tapped her temple with her index finger.

"The pizza smells wonderful. I'm starving." Jade pulled out plates and goblets, and the pair settled in at the table.

"So grouchy Meredith was the hub of all of this. The evil professor was a flirty player, a plagiarist, and an opportunist. Oh, and I forgot a cheat. Sounds like the one everyone loved to hate." Amy waved her free hand around the stickies under Dr. Echols's name. "And not to mention that her sexy husband was a double murderer and a freaky psycho." Amy did a full-body shudder and hugged herself.

"And he was going to try for three if you hadn't intervened." Jade touched her neck lightly, and thoughts of what Randall might have done sent a shiver arcing through her.

"You would have done the same for me." Amy rose and hugged her friend. "We did it. We're a great team," she whispered.

"Somehow, Dr. Echols had a hold on Randall that he couldn't shake," Jade said, wiping her eyes with the back of her hand.

"Wow. Passion so strong that it was worth killing for. I guess he'll have lots of time to think about what he did. Just wait until word spreads of his arrest. It'll be the buzz of the con and the creature world. Not to mention Mermaid Bay. I wonder if Vivian will call another emergency meeting to give us our medals."

The pair dissolved in a fit of giggles. When they had stopped to catch their breath, Jade said, "This event will be remembered for all the wrong reasons." She reached for another slice of pizza and twirled a stray strand of mozzarella until it finally snapped. "Well, Topher and all those other people that Randall accused should be relieved that this is all over."

"I'm sure, and this CreatureCon will be legendary. It'll go down in the lore as the one where the real monsters were the humans. We may want to think about getting vendor booths when they return next year. Maybe they'll put us on panels, and we can sign autographs."

"You just want to add to your dragon collection," Jade said as Amy topped off her glass.

"I told you. One cannot have too many dragons. Oh, guess what? On my way back, a crowd had gathered around the crime scene. Bernie said the press wants to interview us. We have hero status for capturing a crazed murderer. We'll be in the spotlight again. Maybe we'll be on TV this time. We do need to have business cards made up. I wonder what it takes to get a PI license?" Amy tapped her lips with her index finger.

Jade rolled her eyes and reached for her glass. "Just a couple of beach girls trying to protect what we love. How 'bout we finish this and dismantle the murder wall? It'll be nice to have my dining room back. I think we need to fly under the radar for a while. We don't need to be professional investigators.

We have enough to do with the bookstore and the Christmas shop."

Amy's eyes twinkled. "Like Batman. I get it. I kinda like that better. Real-life superheroes." She paused and stared off into space. Then after another sip of wine, she said, "But hurricane season is coming, and you never know what'll blow in or wash ashore next." They clinked their glasses together. "This could be the start of something interesting."

Chapter Twenty-Nine

"Chloe. Why did you let me sleep that long?" The little dog raised one eyebrow and waddled down the porch steps. "It was the first good night's sleep I've had in a while." Jade stretched until her shoulder and back popped. When she stood, she felt stiff from her fight with Randall. "Time for a hot shower, aspirin, and lots of coffee."

The pulsating shower relaxed her aching muscles, and she felt almost normal. After pulling on jeans and a green logoed golf shirt, she hurried Chloe toward the kitchen to start their day.

Somehow, the morning felt extra peaceful with the warm rays of the sun prodding the spring flowers out of their dormant beds and the hedges and trees sporting new green leaves. "It's time to get back to normal and enjoy the nice weather before our crazy summer starts. CreatureCon is over, and Randall is sitting in jail where he belongs."

Not interested in the seasons or Randall's legal woes, Chloe toddled down the street to the store. As they rounded the corner to Neptune Road, Jade noticed the crowd. "What is going on? It's Monday morning." She scooped up the dog like a football and hustled to the back door.

Peeking out the store's front window, she spotted Nosy Nell near the porch steps. She stood with a couple of TV reporters and their cameramen. Nell was talking a mile a minute and waving her arms around like she was swatting bees. The other reporters stood by and watched her gyrations. Jade quickly skimmed Facebook and the *Beach Comber* website for any news. "Word must have leaked out. But why are they here instead of at the pier where most of the crimes happened?" Chloe, bored with the whole thing, moseyed toward the back and her bed.

A loud rapping on the front door caused the Frenchie to change her mind and bolt in with a low growl. "Shhh. It's Lorelei. Get back for a second." Jade nudged the dog away and opened the door wide enough for her aunt to slip in. She set Neville the Devil cat down, and he pounced at Chloe, and the chase through the showrooms was on.

"Holy cannoli," Lorelei said, smoothing down her pale pink cashmere sweater and cream-colored slacks. "They are like rabid wolves out there. Rumor around the Busy Bean is that you and Amy took down the killer at the pier and solved two murders."

"Sort of. I figured out it was Randall, and when he attacked, Amy clobbered him with a shovel."

"You go, girls. End of problem. I'm sure Nick was appreciative of all the help."

"Amy sat on Randall until the police arrived," Jade added.

A slight smile crept across her aunt's face. "I wouldn't expect any less. You ladies are fierce. So, it was the handsome husband after all. He wasn't at the top of my list, but things make more sense in hindsight."

Before Jade could comment, her phone sounded with several text alerts. **Get out here now. We have an audience. We need to strike while the iron is hot. Hurry up. You'll never know what I'll do if I'm unsupervised.** Jade reread Amy's texts and tried not to roll her eyes.

"What is Nell so riled up about?" Lorelei asked, reading over her niece's shoulder.

"It's not her. It's from Amy. And it seems she's out there in the middle of all this."

"Holding court in front of half the town and a gaggle of reporters. You better get out there." Her aunt pushed her toward the door.

Jade stepped out on the porch, and the noise level surged. Amy waved both arms like a giant crazy bird to calm the scene.

Nell rested one of her yellow Crocs on the bottom step. She spoke into her phone, "Nell Jones from the *Beach Comber*. I'm here with Jade Hicks and Amy Pemberton, residents and business owners in Mermaid Bay. We're in front of 'Tis the Season. Is it true that you captured Dr. Randall Medlin, the CreatureCon Killer?" Nell's mouth formed a straight line, and she scooted forward to secure her place in front of the TV crews.

"Go ahead," Amy whispered. "And make sure you mention our stores. We need to take advantage of all this free publicity."

Jade focused on Nell. Ignoring the gaggle of people and the flip-flop that her stomach did whenever she had to do any public speaking. "Yes. Amy Pemberton, owner of Mermaid Books, and I detained Dr. Medlin until the police arrived to arrest him."

"Is it true that he tried to kill you, too? What made him attack you?" Nell asked as reporters screamed a barrage of questions at her.

"I'm sure the sheriff's office will have a statement about the arrest and the murders. You should check with Sheriff Nicholas Driscoll. Yes, Dr. Medlin was arrested for the two recent murders. One here and the other happened in nearby Croaker."

"During my paranormal tour," Amy added.

"So did either of them have anything to do with the conference in Seaport?" someone yelled.

"Of course they did," Nell yelled. "That's why I dubbed him the Creature-Con Killer. You can quote me on that. Eleanor 'Nell' Jones, feature writer. The victims were researchers and panelists at the conference."

Nick made his way through the crowd and hovered near the steps. Everyone except Nell stepped back to clear a path for the sheriff, who towered over the group gathered around the sidewalk. Nick nodded, and Jade waved him onto the porch.

"Thanks, everyone, for coming out. I need to talk to the sheriff here. Make sure you swing by later and check out Mermaid Books." Amy pointed with both arms like she was a flight attendant giving safety instructions. "And 'Tis the Season."

Several reporters stepped forward, vying for Nick's attention. Ignoring the catcalls, he followed Jade and Amy into the store. Before Jade could close the door, Patti burst in. "Oh, my stars, you all are famous again. You did it. Truth, justice, and all that." She leaned over to catch her breath. Her cheeks were as rosy as her fuzzy sweater.

"And now we're all going to get a break from the craziness," Nick said. "How about dinner? I'm leaving on time tonight." He leaned over and kissed Jade as the door popped open and a flash lit up the lobby.

"What?" Nell asked. "A gal's gotta do what a gal's gotta do. Gotta keep up with that whispering Mermaid before she steals my audience." The reporter slammed the door and scurried off the porch.

A panicked look flashed across Patti's face. She opened her mouth and a squeak popped out. She quickly covered her mouth with both hands while everyone stared. "I didn't say or admit anything. And no one knows a thing about the sea monster." She scurried off toward the office.

Nick raised an eyebrow. "Nell left too early. It looks like she might have missed some sea monster scoop. Whatever that is. See you around six for dinner?"

"I wouldn't miss it," Jade said. "Even if we end up on the front page of next week's *Beach Comber. And who knows what the mermaid will post next.*

A Note from the Author

For this mystery, I had so much fun delving into research into the world of cryptids ("an animal whose reported existence is unproved" – Dictionary.com) and cryptozoology ("the study or search for animals and especially legendary animals usually in order to evaluate the possibility of their existence" – Merriam-Webster). Many thanks to Misty Simon. My Yeti is a great muse. And thanks to John Iden for all his insights on cryptids.

Pogs are tiny, colorful discs with photos and logos on them. It's a game where players throw them, and depending how they land, the winner collects the spoils. The game has been around for a while, and it gained popularity in the nineties in Hawaii and spread worldwide. Some of the little discs became collectibles like trading cards and comic books that can sell for hundreds of dollars.

The Presidents' Park, inspired by Mt. Rushmore, opened in Williamsburg, Virginia in 2004 and closed in 2010. It contained eighteen- to twenty-foot busts of forty-two of our Presidents (from George Washington to George W. Bush). The statues, which weighed thousands of pounds, were moved to a field in nearby Croaker, Virginia, when the park closed. Many of the busts were damaged during the move, and one was struck by lightning. For more about the history and to check out the statues, go to Abandoned America: https://www.abandonedamerica.us/the-president-heads.

Patti's Mermaid Blondies

Ingredients:

- 1 box of white cake mix
- ¼ cup vegetable oil
- 1 large egg, beaten
- ¼ cup milk
- ½ cup white chocolate chips
- Food coloring or gel (teal and purple)
- 1 container of vanilla frosting
- Pastel-colored sprinkles
- 1 8x8 greased baking dish

Directions:

1. Preheat your oven to 350 degrees F.
2. In a large bowl, the cake mix, vegetable oil, and beaten egg. Add the milk until the batter is thick.
3. Add the white chocolate chips.
4. Put about a cup of the batter in another bowl. Slowly add the purple food coloring until the batter is the desired color of purple.
5. In the large bowl, add the teal food coloring and mix until you have the desired color.
6. Put the teal mixture in the greased baking dish.
7. Spoon the purple batter on top of the batter in the baking dish. Use a knife to create swirls and whirls.
8. Bake for 40 minutes. Remove from the oven and allow the dessert to

cool completely.

9. Ice the cooled blondies and then add the sprinkles.

Googlie-eyed Monster Truffles

Ingredients:

- 12 ounces of milk chocolate baking bars (divided)
- ½ cup of heavy whipping cream
- 2 tablespoons of canned pumpkin
- ¼ teaspoon of ground cinnamon
- ¼ teaspoon of ground ginger
- ¼ teaspoon of ground nutmeg
- Dash of ground cloves
- Baking cocoa
- Candied googlie eyes

Directions:

1. Preheat your oven to 350 degrees F.
2. Chop 10 ounces of the chocolate baking bars. Move the chopped chocolate to a small bowl.
3. In a heavy saucepan, combine the cream, pumpkin, and all the spices. Heat to a boil. Pour over the chocolate and let it stand for 5 minutes.
4. Whisk the chocolate until smooth. Cool the mixture to room temperature. Refrigerate for 4 hours.
5. Grate the remaining chocolate very finely and put it in a microwave-safe bowl. Dust your hands with the baking cocoa and roll the chocolate mixture into 1-inch balls. Roll each one in the grated chocolate.
6. Melt the unused grated chocolate in the microwave and use it to attach the eyes on each truffle.

7. Refrigerate when finished.

Bigfoot Bacon Burgers

Ingredients:

- Large hamburger buns
- 2 pounds of ground beef
- Salt and pepper (to taste)
- 2 cups of prepared pulled pork
- 1 cup pickle relish
- 8 slices of bacon
- 4 slices of Monterrey Jack cheese
- Crispy fried onions

Directions:

1. Prepare the bacon and set it aside to cool.
2. Preheat your grill or stove to medium-high.
3. In a bowl, season the ground beef with salt and pepper. Form 8 quarter-pound patties.
4. Grill the burgers to the desired level.
5. Place a slice of cheese on the bottom bun. Add the pickle relish, burger, pulled pork, and second burger.
6. Add the fried onion topping.

Kraken (Rum) Bananas Foster

Ingredients:

- ¼ cup butter
- ⅔ cup dark brown sugar
- 3 ½ tablespoons of Kraken rum (or any other brand)
- 1 ½ teaspoons vanilla extract
- ½ teaspoon ground cinnamon
- 3 peeled bananas
- ¼ cup coarsely chopped walnuts
- 1 pint of vanilla ice cream

Directions:

1. Melt the butter in a large skillet over medium heat. Add the brown sugar, rum, vanilla, and cinnamon. Bring the mixture to a low boil.
2. Cut the bananas lengthwise and then across the middle.
3. Put the bananas and the walnuts in the pan.
4. Cook until the bananas are softened (about 2 minutes).
5. Serve hot over vanilla ice cream.

A Nessie Float

Ingredients:

- Lime (or Lime and Orange) Sherbet
- Green food coloring
- 3 cups clear soft drink like Sprite or ginger ale

Directions:

1. Add the soft drink and several drops of the food coloring in a pitcher and stir. Stir until the liquid is the color green you desire.
2. Pour the mixture in glasses until each is about 2/3 full. (This recipe makes about four glasses.)
3. Add 2 to 3 scoops of the sherbet to each glass.
4. Fill the remainder of the glass with the soft drink and stir. The soft drink will make the sherbet frothy. You'll need a straw and a spoon.

Patti's Shimmery Mermaid Bark

Ingredients:

- 12 ounces of white candy melts
- 12 ounces of purple candy melts
- 12 ounces of aqua candy melts
- 1 package of round shimmer candies (any size)
- Silver sprinkles
- Edible gold dust
- Baking sheet with waxed paper

Directions:

1. Pour each color of candy melts in a different, microwave-safe bowl.
2. Microwave each bowl for 30 seconds. Stir and microwave for another 30 seconds. Stir.
3. The candy melts should be smooth. If they are not fully melted, microwave for another 30 seconds and stir.
4. Line a baking sheet with waxed paper.
5. Use a spoon and make dollops of each candy melt all over the banking sheet.
6. Use a spatula to swirl the colors together. Spread the candy to the edges of the baking sheet. Try to swirl the colors for the best effect.
7. Sprinkle on the shimmer beads, silver sprinkles, and the gold dust.
8. Refrigerate the baking sheet until the candy sets (about 15 minutes).
9. Peel the candy off of the waxed paper. Use your hands to break the candy into pieces.

10. Refrigerate the candy until you're ready to serve.

Jade's Mermaid Popcorn Treats

Ingredients:

- 2 bags of plain microwave popcorn (3.2 ounce bags)
- 1 cup mini marshmallows
- ¾ cup light corn syrup
- 4 tablespoons of margarine
- 2 teaspoons of cold water
- Teal or purple food coloring
- Edible glitter

Directions:

1. Pop the popcorn and pour it into a large bowl. Make sure to take out any unpopped kernels.
2. In a medium pot on medium-high heat, combine the powdered sugar, marshmallows, corn syrup, margarine, water, and one color of food coloring. Stir until the mixture comes to a boil.
3. Carefully pour the hot liquid over the popcorn. Make sure to coat everything.
4. Let the popcorn cool. It needs to be cool enough for you to handle safely.
5. Cover your fingers in margarine and shape the popcorn into 4-inch balls.
6. Lightly sprinkle on the edible glitter.
7. Let them cool.
8. Wrap the popcorn balls in plastic and store at room temperature.

Squid Pops

Ingredients:

- 100 g green candy melts
- 100 g orange candy melts
- 100 g. yellow candy melts
- Large candy eyes
- Small candy eyes
- Cakepop sticks or bamboo skewers
- Parchment paper
- 3 Piping bags or large plastic baggies

Directions:

1. Line two baking trays with parchment paper. Spread out six skewers on each baking tray.
2. In a microwave safe bowl, melt the candy in separate bowls. Make sure the candy doesn't burn. Follow the package instructions.
3. Spoon one color of the melted candy into a piping bag or a large plastic baggie.
4. Snip the corner off the bag of candy and pipe the candy over one of the skewers. Use random, squiggly moves. The candy should look like spaghetti on the skewer/cakepop stick. Repeat on three more skewers.
5. Repeat steps 3 and 4 for each of the colors.
6. Then push a random assortment of candy eyeballs in the candy.
7. Place the trays in the refrigerator to set (about 15-20 minutes).
8. Remove and store in a cool, dry place.

Sasquatch Chocolate Tree Bark

Ingredients:

- 12 ounces of chocolate chips or chopped chocolate
- ¾ cup raw nuts or seeds
- ¼ cup dried cranberries (or dried cherries)
- ½ teaspoon of sea salt
- Parchment paper

Directions:

1. Preheat your oven to 350 degrees F. Lightly toast the nuts on a baking sheet until they are golden on the edges (about 8 minutes).
2. Transfer the nuts to a cutting board and finely chop them.
3. Melt the chocolate in a microwave-safe bowl in 30-second increments. Stir the mixture between each interval.
4. Cover a baking sheet with parchment paper. Spread the chocolate with a spatula until it is about a ¼ inch thickness.
5. Sprinkle the chopped nuts evenly over the chocolate. Then add the dried fruit.
6. Sprinkle the sea salt lightly over the mix.
7. Lightly press the toppings into the chocolate.
8. Place the pan in the refrigerator for about 15 minutes.
9. Once the candy has hardened, use your hands to break it into smaller pieces.

Peanut Butter Sea Monster Eggs

Ingredients:

- 6 tablespoons of softened butter
- ½ cup creamy peanut butter
- ¼ cup marshmallow cream
- ½ teaspoon vanilla
- Pinch of salt
- 2 cups powdered sugar
- 1 bag of green candy melts
- Purple or teal sprinkles
- Parchment paper

Directions:

1. In a large bowl, beat together the butter, peanut butter, marshmallow cream, vanilla, and salt until the mixture is creamy.
2. Slowly mix in the powdered sugar.
3. Roll the mixture into 30 small oval-shaped balls.
4. Put the balls in the refrigerator for an hour.
5. Melt the candy melts according to the package directions.
6. When the peanut butter balls are hardened, use a toothpick to dip them in the candy.
7. Place the candy on a piece of parchment paper and remove toothpicks.
8. Cover the candy in sprinkles.

Sea Monster Pizza Loaf

Ingredients:

- 1 medium sweet red pepper
- ½ pound fresh chorizo without the casing (You can substitute any spicy pork sausage.)
- ½ pound ground beef
- 1 small onion, chopped
- 2 garlic cloves, minced
- 1 pound (1 loaf) of frozen pizza dough, thawed
- 2 cups shredded Monterey Jack cheese
- 1 large egg, beaten
- Green food coloring
- 2 tablespoons sesame seeds
- 2 slices of a ripe olive
- Parchment paper

Directions:

1. Preheat your oven to 350 degrees F. Cut one small strip of red pepper and save it for the decorating.
2. Chop the remaining pepper. In a large skillet cook the sausage, beef, pepper, onion, and garlic over medium heat until the meat is no longer pink. Drain the mixture well.
3. Roll the dough into a 14 x 12 rectangle. Spread the meat mixture in the middle of the dough. Sprinkle with the cheese.
4. Wrap the dough around the meat and cheese. Pinch the seam to seal,

and tuck the ends under.

5. Put the seam-side down on a baking sheet lined with parchment paper. Form the dough into a snake or sea monster shape.
6. In a small bowl, whisk the egg and food coloring. Paint the serpent with the green egg wash.
7. Sprinkle on the sesame seeds.
8. Use the olive slices for eyes, and the pepper slice for a tongue.
9. Bake until the dough is golden brown for 30-3t minutes.
10. Let your sea monster cool before slicing.

Sea Monster Sandwich

Ingredients:

- 1 can of refrigerated French bread (Pillsbury)
- 2 lettuce leaves
- 4 ounces thinly sliced cooked ham
- 3 slices of mozzarella cheese (cut in half)
- 2 small olives with pimientos
- 1 small jar of roasted bell peppers

Directions:

1. Preheat oven to 350 degrees F.
2. Grease a large cookie sheet.
3. Place the dough (seam side down) on the sheet and shape it into an "S."
4. Cut 1-inch V-shaped notches to cover the entire surface for scales.
5. At one end, cut a deep cut at least 2 inches for the mouth.
6. Ball up a small piece of tin foil and grease the outside. Use this to hold the mouth open while baking.
7. Bake for 30 minutes or until golden brown. Cool at least 15 minutes.
8. Cut the bread in half horizontally. Cover the sides with mayonnaise.
9. Layer the lettuce, ham, and cheese.
10. Add the olives for the eyes. You can secure these with toothpicks.
11. Cut a roasted pepper to resemble flames. Remove the tin foil and place the peppers in the mouth.
12. To serve, cut the sandwich crosswise into about 6 pieces.

Acknowledgments

Writing is often a solitary endeavor, but it takes a lot of support from family and friends (Stan, Mom and Dad, Cortney and Bill, Meagan, Jocelyn, the gang at work, and my Bethia UMC family) for which I am eternally grateful!

A huge thank you to Shawn Reilly Simmons and everyone at Level Best Books for letting me share all the fun of life in Mermaid Bay.

My talented Sisters in Crime, Guppy, Writers Who Kill, and James River Writer friends are amazing. Paula Charles, Sue Minix, and Jackie Layton, I treasure all of the support!

And most of all to all the readers, podcasters, bloggers, and reviewers. Thank you for letting me share Jade, Nick, Patti, Bernie, Lorelei, Chloe, and Neville the Devil Cat with you all.

See you at the beach!

About the Author

Through the years, Heather Weidner has been a cop's kid, technical writer, editor, college professor, software tester, and IT manager. She writes the Jules Keene Glamping Mysteries, The Mermaid Bay Christmas Shoppe Mysteries, the Pearly Girls Mysteries, and the Delanie Fitzgerald Mysteries.

Her short stories appear in the *Virginia is for Mysteries* series, *50 Shades of Cabernet*, *Deadly Southern Charm, Murder by the* Glass, *First Comes Love, Then Comes Murder*, and *Crime in the Old Dominion,* and she has non-fiction pieces in *Promophobia* and *The Secret Ingredient: A Mystery Writers' Cookbook*.

She is a member of Sisters in Crime: National, Central Virginia, Chessie, Guppies, and Grand Canyon Writers, International Thriller Writers, and James River Writers, and she blogs regularly with the Writers Who Kill.

Originally from Virginia Beach, Heather has been a mystery fan since Scooby-Doo and Nancy Drew. She lives in Central Virginia with her husband and a crazy Mini Aussie Shepherd.

AUTHOR WEBSITE:

SOCIAL MEDIA HANDLES:
  Website and Blog: http://www.heatherweidner.com
  Facebook: https://www.facebook.com/HeatherWeidnerAuthor
  Threads: https://www.threads.net/@heather_mystery_writer
  BlueSky: Heather Weidner (@heatherweidner.bsky.social) — Bluesky
  TikTok: https://www.tiktok.com/@heather_weidner_author
  Instagram: https://www.instagram.com/heather_mystery_writer/
  Goodreads: https://www.goodreads.com/author/show/8121854.Heath
er_Weidner
  Amazon Authors: http://www.amazon.com/-/e/B00HOYR0MQ
  Pinterest: https://www.pinterest.com/HeatherBWeidner/
  BookBub: https://www.bookbub.com/authors/heather-weidner-d6430
278-c5c9-4b10-b911-340828fc7003
  Twitter/X: https://twitter.com/HeatherWeidner1

Also by Heather Weidner

The Mermaid Bay Christmas Shoppe Mysteries
Sticks and Stones and a Bag of Bones
Twinkle Twinkle Au Revoir
A Tisket A Tasket Not Another Casket
Life is But a Scream

The Jules Keene Glamping Mysteries
Vintage Trailers and Blackmailers
Film Crews and Rendezvous
Christmas Lights and Cat Fights
Deadlines and Valentines
Teddy Bears and Ghostly Lairs

The Pearly Girls Mysteries
Murder Strikes a Chord
Murder Plays Second Fiddle

The Delanie Fitzgerald Mysteries
Secret Lives and Private Eyes
The Tulip Shirt Murders
Glitter, Glam, and Contraband
Male Revues and Subterfuge

Nonfiction Work
Promophobia
The Secret Ingredient: The Mystery Writers' Cookbook

ABSOLUTE
JUSTICE